A PRETTY FOLLY

Inspector James Given
Book Two

Charlie Garratt

SAPERE
BOOKS

A PRETTY FOLLY

Published by Sapere Books.

20 Windermere Drive, Leeds, England, LS17 7UZ,
United Kingdom

saperebooks.com

ISBN: 978-1-913335-21-2

But love is blind, and lovers cannot see
The pretty follies that themselves commit,
— William Shakespeare, *The Merchant of Venice*

ONE

6th March 1939

Light is dying in Derby Lane, deepening the ever-present shadow under the crooked medieval shops. Most of the warped structures are empty, where the proprietors have cut their losses and left. Above my head, an army of hinges creaks in the breeze, crying for want of love and attention. One building, a watchmaker's shop, stands out. There's a uniformed policeman outside and, in yellow paint, the word 'Jew' desecrates its window.

The glass reflects an unflattering picture. PC Greenley stands six foot one, several inches taller than the man in the brown suit beside him, whose waistcoat swells just a little too much above his belt. A casual observer would take me, James Given, for a middle-aged bank employee. Not a police inspector barely midway through his thirties.

I turn away.

'Another one, constable?'

'Afraid so, sir, second this week round here. The old boy's inside. Roughed him up they did — he's not hurt but he's pretty upset.'

Greenley had been on his beat by the cathedral when he'd heard a commotion down this side street. Although several pairs of boots retreated along Pepper Lane in the direction of High Street, discretion proved the better part of valour and he'd called the station from the blue box on the corner of Broadgate. The message came as I'd been getting ready to return home to Kenilworth for the night and they passed it to me. Some weeks earlier, my boss had asked me to take the lead investigating these attacks on Jewish businesses in Coventry and I found myself enjoying the challenge. That's not to say I wasn't glad to go back to my home patch each evening when it was through.

The city fathers tell us the city streets no longer have space for both horse-carts and our growing mass of motor cars, so Derby Lane is being cleared for demolition. Five years ago it was packed with people walking home from work at this time, though now the general decay keeps them away. I can't say I blame them; this city can be a worrisome place.

Feeling my way down the dark hallway to a back room, I found the shop owner, who looked to be in his sixties, hunched in an armchair beside a dying fire. Around his shoulders was his prayer shawl, and he reminded me of my father as he fingered the knots and whispered his invocations. Out of respect I waited until he finished. When he had, he beckoned me to take a seat.

'Good evening, Mr Dembowitz, I'm Inspector Given. Do you feel up to answering a few questions?'

The fear crackled in his throat. 'Why would they do this thing? I hurt no-one. I go about my business and try to help my customers. Coming to England, here, to Coventry, I wanted to get away from such things. And now...'

'Did you recognise the men who attacked you?'

'One of them may have been here before but I am not sure. There was an angry man came into my shop one day and left a clock which wasn't working. He returned a week later and started shouting when I told him how much it might cost to repair. The man called me ... names.'

'What sort of names?'

Dembowitz looked embarrassed as though it was he who'd done something wrong.

'The man called me a robbing Jew and he said to go back where I came from. The cost couldn't be helped — there were parts I would need to make and the time it would take would be considerable. It was a quality piece and wasn't worth doing unless it was done well. He swore at me again when I told him this so I asked him to leave my shop.'

'And would you have any idea of this man's name?'

'It will be in my book. There's always a note when someone leaves an item asking for a price. I'm not certain it was this man who attacked me but I will fetch his name for you.'

The walk back to the police station had taken less than five minutes — only a little longer than it took me to wheeze my way up the stairs to my office on the third floor. Flopping onto the chair I dropped my notebook on the desk, ready to write one more episode in a file that had been growing since Oswald Mosley spoke at a Fascist rally in the city four months earlier. None of the incidents were serious in themselves; broken windows, minor assaults, name-calling, and so on, but I understood more than most that this kind of hatred would escalate if not nipped in the bud.

The image of my bulging waistline in the watchmaker's shop window came back to mind and I resolved, again, that I needed to change it. I'd been going downhill since taking this assignment in Coventry. Driving to work, long days at my desk and canteen dinners were taking a hefty toll and it depressed me.

The phone rang and I cursed.

'Yes?'

It was the duty sergeant in Kenilworth. After he'd spoken for a couple of minutes, I realised there'd be no chance of me getting to my bed early this night. I had a murder to investigate.

I live less than a quarter of a mile from Hannah Robinson's Charity School but I'd never been inside and a solitary boy stood shivering at its gates when I arrived, waiting to escort me to his headmaster's house. The poor lad scuttled off to the warmth of his lodgings the minute he'd delivered me on the doorstep.

The headmaster's wife introduced herself as Emily Perelle, then led me through to the kitchen. At the table sat a man about my age, shaking despite the steaming tea he clutched in both hands. Mrs Perelle sat down opposite him, offering me the remaining seat between them.

'Poor Mr Smith, he's had the most awful shock and he's only been with us at the school for five minutes. There are no words, Inspector — how is it possible for something so terrible happen here?'

'These things are always a mystery, Mrs Perelle. Is your husband at home?'

'Laurence has stayed at the chapel with the constable to keep an eye on things.'

Benjamin Smith's muscles showed beneath his tweed jacket and I assumed his chosen subjects at the school would be sport and physical education, quite at odds with the nervous wreck beside me. I asked him what had happened.

'I ... I only arrived here in Kenilworth on Thursday — yesterday, wasn't it?' Smith looked across at Mrs Perelle as if to seek reassurance. 'And I thought I'd explore my surroundings. Guidebooks say the chapel here dates back to the twelfth century, with original timbers and interesting dedications, so I wandered round to take a look. I should have stayed in my rooms.'

If he'd an interest in church architecture was the new man more of an academic than I'd first imagined?

The teacher looked up at Mrs Perelle again and she laid her hand on his to stop his trembling, leaving me to turn away with mild embarrassment. The woman was attractive; not in a way I imagined the wife of a country town school headmaster would be. A floral-print dress tailored to a slim waist ensured her figure would attract attention from the older boys and, with no doubt, all of the teachers with a pulse. Elegant, manicured fingers brushed a strand of jet-black hair from her forehead.

'He'll be all right here with me, Inspector, if you want to join Laurence. We'll just sit a while longer until Mr Smith feels up to going back to his house. You might interview him more easily over there when you're finished.'

It took a minute on the headmaster's step to get my bearings in the cold night air. The solid limestone buildings on three sides formed a shield, the fourth opening onto grass punctuated by white goal posts standing out in the darkness. Beyond there were the Abbey Fields, the last remnants of the monastic site which once dominated this part of the town. In the centre of the school grounds stood the chapel, its half-timbered walls and shingle roof showing it to be centuries older than the surroundings.

The courtyard was deserted and it was obvious that Perelle ran a tight ship. One or two pairs of young eyes might have been expected to be peeking from dormitory windows but there was nothing. Laurence Perelle and PC Blakemore were at the entrance, round the side of the building, the constable hunched inside the porch, smoking. Blakemore stood to attention and stubbed his cigarette out as soon as he saw me. The headmaster was several inches taller than both Blakemore and me, though quite a few pounds lighter than either of us, and peered at me through spectacles halfway down his nose. I'd have guessed he'd be at least ten years older than his wife, and he was no oil painting, so I wondered what she saw in him. In contrast to her, he looked like he belonged in the confines of this small, archaic, school.

'Have you been inside, Mr Perelle?'

'Do you take me for some kind of imbecile, Inspector? Of course I have, to make sure no pupils sneaked inside after Mr Smith fled. Naturally I didn't go downstairs, but I put on the gas lamps so you'll see where you are going. The crypt is on your right, beside the vestry.'

I told him to wait outside a little longer whilst the constable and I investigated. Perelle's look said he wasn't used to taking orders.

The creak from the opening door echoed around the chapel and a weak light came from two mantles above the entrance, as far as Perelle ventured. The building seemed bigger inside and had lots more seating than I'd imagined, although I should have known there'd be enough to accommodate the whole school on Sundays and for special services. The synagogue has been my traditional place of worship and I've always experienced Christian churches as an alien environment. The age and darkness of this one made me feel doubly so and I was pleased to have Blakemore by my side when we edged into a murkier corner. His torch cast a dim enough light, but we soon discovered the door where Perelle said it would be and found it unlocked.

We groped our way down spiral stone steps in semi-darkness with me in the lead. I'd thought it would be damp but the air was dry and somehow brittle, with an odour of something I couldn't quite put my finger on. Blakemore gasped when we turned the final bend and his lamp illuminated a body on top of a stone slab, then laughed at his own stupidity. It was a sculpted stone knight laid to rest five or six hundred years earlier. There were four in that chamber; with a further six piles of rubble left from desecration of other sarcophagi in times gone by.

An arch led off this room, taking us into a corridor with half a dozen vaults, three on either side. The first ones contained nothing other than smashed coffins, with no sign of their long-departed occupants. Someone had swept the fourth vault and cleared everything except for a mattress in one corner.

On top of which lay the body of a girl, with a gold crucifix and chain binding her hands as if in prayer, mocking the pose of the knight which had frightened the life out of my companion.

TWO

Benjamin Smith was calmer by the time I'd finished in the chapel. The pathologist, Walter Naismith, had taken just under two hours to travel over, examine the dead girl and then remove her for a post-mortem. He'd said there was little chance of finding precisely when she'd died due to the state of the body but he hoped its mummification might make it possible for him to, at least, find the cause of death. We need to be thankful for small mercies.

While he'd been doing his work I'd dusted for fingerprints in the crypt but there were dozens of different ones, laid down over years. There'd be little possibility of working out who they all belonged to and even less of finding one to stand up in court. An old claw hammer lay on the floor next to the mattress but it held no clues; no prints, no blood, nothing. Later I discovered a wooden toolbox in the vestry cupboard and I guessed that's where it came from.

Smith dragged the bolt across his door and turned the key in the lock before opening it slightly. He swung the door further to let me in and peeked outside before locking it again. His ordeal had shaken him up so much he was now jumping at shadows. He must have arrived full of hope in a new job, in a new town, and on his second day he'd come upon a dead body.

The teacher's room had a threadbare sofa, a small table and a single dining chair. The wireless sitting on top of an apple box offered the merest hint of luxury. Despite its sparseness the room was cosy with a fire burning in the grate which crackled and spat as we talked. Generations of teachers had polished the oak floors to a deep dark shine over the years, except for the areas where furniture and rugs had been removed to leave a series of lighter shapes, like sunlight shining through windows of different sizes. There was none of the damp smell found in empty houses so it hadn't been vacant for too long. Smith saw me looking around and he seemed to feel the need to apologise.

'I'm still waiting for more furniture to arrive, Inspector. Mr Perelle said he wanted to hear my preferences before placing an order and I think he pulled these few bits together so it wouldn't feel too much like a cell. It seems my predecessor, Mr Neilson, had been in the house a donkey's age so most of the stuff in it was his and he took it when he left.'

The name Neilson clawed at the edge my memory but I couldn't tie down where I'd heard it.

'Do you know where he's gone?'

'He retired but I don't know where. The headmaster might be able to help.'

'Tell me again how you found the body.'

'I picked up an interest in old churches from my father, who was a vicar, and, as I said earlier, the chapel here is old, so I took a look. A blessing it wasn't pulled down when they built the school.'

'What time did you go?'

'Well, I started at about four o'clock, only trying to fill the gap before dinner. They eat here at seven, so it occurred to me that a couple of hours might pass more quickly than sitting around in a half empty room.'

'You didn't find your way downstairs straight away?'

'No, it was closer to six o'clock when I went down there.' Smith shivered. 'I'd spent a good time reading all of the inscriptions on the walls — there are dozens of them in there, recounting benefactors and church worthies going back to the seventeen hundreds. There are even some ancient gravestones laid into the chapel floor, the earliest from the sixteenth century. The headmaster had said I was free to go where I pleased so I poked in all the dark corners and even up into the organ loft. Then I found the door to the crypt. I'd been told it would be the only one locked.'

'So you'd picked up the key from Mr Perelle?'

'Actually, no. The headmaster was still finishing a chemistry lesson when I decided to explore the church. His wife told me where it was hanging in the school office so I collected it before I started.'

'The key was hanging there? On its own?'

'There were several others, but that was by far the biggest and oldest so I'd guessed it must be right.'

This meant anyone might have taken it at any time. With a long-dead body and a freely available key this was going to be a difficult one to pin down.

Smith described his slow progress down the steps and through the chambers. I suspected he ran up again a damn sight faster than he'd ambled down. He'd dashed straight over to Perelle's house — the headmaster had taken him inside before calling the police.

I asked if he'd taught in another local school before coming to Hannah Robinson's. The teacher picked at his fingernails and didn't reply for a moment.

'Nowhere permanently, I'm afraid, at least not in a school.'

'This is your first teaching job? You don't look to be newly out of university, Mr Smith.'

'No, no, Inspector, I graduated five years ago, but I couldn't find a job near home.'

'Home?'

'Winchester. My father became seriously ill so I moved in with him, working in a library down there.' Smith's head dropped. 'But then he died.'

'I'm sorry to hear that, sir.'

'Thank you, Inspector, but it was back in 1936. His loss affected me deeply at the time and so I became unsure what to do with my life. Dad left me a little money which allowed me to travel for a while. Ended up in the French Alps, where my passion for skiing developed. Spent the last two winters there as an instructor.'

So that's where his physique came from.

'And how did you find yourself in Kenilworth?' I asked.

'The skiing season only lasts a few months so I moved south to the Riviera for the summers, picking up the odd job here and there but mainly lying on the beach or sitting around pavement cafés. By the end of last August I'd had enough and I needed to decide where I was going. An acquaintance told me she'd heard a cousin was retiring so I wrote to Mr Perelle when she passed on the address.'

'Which subjects do you teach?'

'Well, we're supposed to turn a hand to almost anything here but my degree is in mathematics. I did rather well at Latin in school so the headmaster has roped me in for that as well — I'm just hoping to remember enough to keep ahead of the children.'

This must be how it is a lot of the time in schools. At mine, in Birmingham, we were expected to believe everything the teachers told us, as if they were expert in every topic. It seemed that they, if Smith's experience was common, were just managing by virtue of age and authority. His revelation made me feel cheated.

My questioning continued for a while but there was nothing further he could recall. He'd panicked when he saw the body and blotted out anything that might prove useful. Smith had no recollection of seeing the hammer and was even unsure about what he'd done with the key so I gave him the station number and said to ring if he remembered anything else. The bolt and the lock clunked comfortably secure seconds after he let me out.

It was well after nine when I'd left Smith. Both the body and the trail to how it arrived under the chapel had been cold for weeks so there seemed little point in interviewing the headmaster at such a late hour. However, I saw a light still on in his window and I gave him a knock. His greeting suggested I should have left it until the morning.

'If it's absolutely necessary at this time of night then you'd best come through to my study.' He led me down the hallway to an austere room at the back of the house. 'Mrs Perelle has taken to her bed, Inspector, we'll be less likely to disturb her in here.'

The headmaster cleared a pile of books from a seat in the corner and gestured for me to sit, taking a place at his desk. Perelle saw that my eyes were drawn to the shelf above his head.

'You like my display, Inspector?'

Secretly, I shuddered. Behind the glass of a polished mahogany case was a splayed rat, pinned to a board and skinned, showing every detail of its internal structure. It wasn't the only dead animal in the room. Bird and mammal skeletons, preserved fish, and jars containing pale creatures floating in viscous liquids, littered every surface.

'I teach all of the sciences, Inspector, but it is biology which is my true vocation. Do you have an interest yourself?'

'I'm afraid not, though it looks fascinating, if a little gruesome. Is that how we all look underneath?'

'More or less, apart from the veins. They're injected with blue dye to make them stand out so well. Now, you have a question for me?'

'Have you any idea who the girl we found might be, Headmaster?'

'A girl? Mr Smith didn't say. Poor chap saw a body then turned on his heels and ran. How old was she?'

'Thirteen or fourteen at a guess. We won't be clearer until the doctor's done his job.'

'We have a lot of pupils here who come and go at that age — occasionally I wonder why they bother at all. The father needs an extra pair of hands and pulls the child into service, or there's another baby in the family and the eldest daughter needs to play mother to the rest for a week or two.' Perelle shook his head and pointed to a framed document hanging on the back of the door. 'That charter tells us we're here to educate the children of our poorer families, Inspector, so I'm not surprised when they're kept at home for a while. Sometimes they come back and sometimes they don't.'

'But you must keep records?'

He looked at me as if I was stupid.

'Of course we keep records, though I don't carry them round in my head. I've more important things to think about.'

I wondered what he might consider more important than the welfare of the children in his care but another look at the specimens lining his study gave me a clue.

'Could I ask you when you were last in the chapel, Mr Perelle?'

'Last Sunday, like every Sunday, Inspector. Why?'

'What about the crypt?'

'I haven't been in the crypt for six months. I've no reason to go down there.'

'You seem pretty clear about the time, Headmaster — why did you last go?'

Now he gave me his naughty pupil act, lifting his glasses from the bridge of his nose down to the tip and peering at me over the rim.

'Really, Inspector, is there nothing you won't take literally? Six months was simply a turn of phrase. I'm a busy man and can't really remember when, or why, I was last in the crypt. It's possible Mr Sprigg, the caretaker, asked me to take a look at something.'

'Surely you'd have noticed a young girl's dead body lying on a mattress though, wouldn't you? Unless you were too busy of course.'

'There's no need to take that tone — I'm merely explaining that I wouldn't go below the chapel often.'

'That's understood, sir, but you must see how important it is for us to work out how long the girl has been dead. And who might have dumped her there.' I let these last few words hang for a moment. 'You've made it clear you need a good reason to venture into the crypt, so please stop evading my question and tell me why you needed to go down there last.'

Perelle leaned back in his chair and rubbed his forehead, lowering his voice almost to a whisper when he answered.

'Fine, have it your own way. It would have been in the summer; late June I believe. A friend of my wife came to visit and I showed her round the chapel. There was nothing out of place then as far as I remember.'

'So why the big secret?'

'Because there was ... how do I put it ... an incident with Ruth, my wife's friend, and I didn't want you digging it up. It didn't seem relevant.'

'An "incident"?'

He hung his head.

'Yes. It was nothing. Ruth and I courted for a short while before I met Emily and she seems to think I still have feelings for her.'

'Finally. I've half a mind to drag you down to the station for the night for wasting my time. Instead, what you'll do, for the morning, is go through all of your records and identify every child, regardless of age, who has been absent since the last time you were in the crypt doing God knows what with your lady friend. You'll then find which ones haven't yet come back and send the list round to the police station.'

I doubted anyone had spoken to Perelle in that way since he had become headmaster and I thought he would explode. Most of my teachers had been decent, caring men but sometimes there would be one who would act the bully like him. I'd had to accept it as a child but no longer. Recognising this, he glared across the desk, then nodded he'd do as I'd instructed.

THREE

Next morning the luminaries on Superintendent Dyer's oak-panelled walls in Warwick smiled down, at odds with our grim conversation.

'A teacher discovered the body around six o'clock last evening, sir. He'd been exploring the crypt in the chapel of Hannah Robinson's Charity School.'

Dyer listened while I explained about the mattress, the posing, the stone knights and the crucifix. That crucifix, a glittering contrast to the dust and death all around it, had looked brand new. Bought for that specific purpose? I shook its image away.

'She'd been there a few weeks, though pretty well preserved considering. As a result, we're still trying to make a proper identification. I'd think she would be thirteen or fourteen years of age judging by her height. The headmaster, an arrogant man, name of Perelle, telephoned the station about quarter past six and I got the message in Coventry shortly afterwards so chased straight back.'

'And you say the body hadn't decomposed?'

'No, sir. It's too cold down there for the flies and maggots to do much damage. I've seen this kind of thing before in a church in Dublin and it seems something seeping into the air from the bedrock keep the corpses from rotting. All that happens is that they shrink through evaporation and the skin dries up.'

'So she was like those mummies in the pyramids then?'

'More or less. From what I've read, they're embalmed, and ours is naturally preserved but it's basically the same.'

'Should we be assuming she's a pupil?'

'It does seem most likely, don't you think? It's an odd place to dump the victim if she isn't from the school. We've no reports of a body being carried through the streets of the town as far as I'm aware, sir.'

The boss ignored my sarcasm and asked if we'd got any leads.

'None at all, yet. Perhaps when we find out who the girl is we'll have some luck. There's a gash on the side of her head so the hammer we found could be the murder weapon. We'll know better when she's been cleaned up and the autopsy's finished.'

'You seem certain it was murder, James. Couldn't it be natural causes?'

'I'm not saying it wasn't but it seems an odd way to die naturally. Even if she wasn't killed, I can't see how she'd be lying the way she was unless someone did it after she was dead.'

The boss wasn't convinced but he changed tack.

'Doesn't the headmaster have any notion who she might be? Surely they keep records of pupils.'

'Well, according to Mr Perelle, they maintain very good files but the school was set up originally —' I consulted my notebook — 'to "educate the children of the working poor of the parish" and he tells me that's who the pupils are. As a result the children are sometimes required at home and might disappear for a month or more at a time. Apparently it's a real challenge trying to keep their schooling up to scratch.'

'If you're coming down on the side of the girl being a pupil, does that mean you also think someone from the school killed her?'

'Not yet, sir. That's a different proposition altogether, though there's a good chance the murderer must have a connection with the place, even if he doesn't actually work there.'

'He?'

'Sorry, it could be a man or a woman, I suppose. Someone would need to carry the body down the steps then lay her on the mattress or lift her from the floor if they killed her down there. The girl wouldn't have been heavy so a strong woman might have lifted her, though my money would still be on it being a man.'

'Well, let's keep an open mind for now, James. Best not go jumping to conclusions.'

Sometimes I think Dyer imagines he can see the obvious where others can't and I'm often bewildered where I am with him. He can be the most supportive boss imaginable at times, at others he's the bumbling bureaucrat, kowtowing to pressure from the press or those upstairs. At first he was different but now he's settled into his job, happy to spend his days at a desk or in meetings, ticking the calendar until his retirement. A shudder ran through me as I remembered his recent suggestion that I should think about going for promotion when a Chief Inspector vacancy comes along.

Dyer struggled for his next words.

'Why, James? Why would anyone do such a thing? As if the killing itself isn't enough, the monster then feels it necessary to put the lass on display.'

There were two telephone calls to make before I left Warwick. The first was to Laurence Perelle.

'I need to ask you about your ex-colleague — Mr Neilson.' His name had been bothering me since Benjamin Smith mentioned him as the previous occupant of his house. 'Had he been with you long?'

'Oliver Neilson was at the school an absolute age, Inspector, even before I arrived. Excellent teacher. Taught Latin and mathematics, like Mr Smith, but also helped me to cover R.I.'

'That would be religious instruction?'

'Yes, yes, of course religious instruction, much easier to abbreviate it.' His patronising voice again. If he kept it up I'd need to have words. 'My wife is trying to take his place in her own little way until I can find a more suitable replacement. The new man can't do it but teachers with good maths are few and far between so we couldn't miss out on Mr Smith when he got in touch.'

'He told me his predecessor had recently retired. Do you have an address for him?'

'Oh, he's only nearby, just down the hill, in fact. By the castle.'

That's where I'd heard his name. Neilson had moved into a cottage two doors away from mine some months earlier and he'd called round one evening when he was introducing himself to his neighbours. I'd been on my way out so we took a minute to exchange names and a few words but he seemed like a nice chap. I'd not seen him more than once or twice from my window since and our paths hadn't crossed in the street. At least I'd not have to go far to interview him.

As I put down the receiver it struck me as odd that the headmaster hadn't asked me how the investigation was going. At the very least I'd have expected him to enquire if he should take any precautions to protect the children still in his charge.

My second call was to John Sawyer's sergeant, Tim Bryant.

'Nice to hear from you, Inspector — we haven't seen you for a while.'

'Much as I'd have liked the drive out there, Tim, it's not been possible. Always plenty of work to be done, which is why I'm ringing you.'

'Oh?'

'I need Sawyer to lend me a hand. Hopefully it won't be for too long.'

'I'm not sure I can spare him; I've already got one man in that area off sick. Can't you find someone else?'

'I probably could, but none I'd trust like Sawyer. He's a good copper, with a brain on him. And keen. Not many around like him.'

Bryant carried on his protest until I pulled rank.

'Listen, there's no point going on about this — you don't want me to have to go back to the boss now, do you? He's already agreed so won't take kindly to you questioning his orders. Send Sawyer down to Kenilworth tomorrow and I should have some lodgings organised for him by then.'

Although it was an end to the argument, I'd need to ask Sawyer about his sergeant's favourite tipple and then get a bottle to him to thaw the frost still lingering when he put down the telephone.

Until Sawyer's arrival tomorrow, I decided to investigate Mr Dembowitz's beating. He had provided the name of Karl Mueller as the man who had shouted at him. I had found out Mueller lived on the first floor of a boarding house off the Holyhead Road and that's where I headed next.

What would once have been a smart entrance hall, with its beautifully tiled floor and mahogany bannister, now housed two bicycles and smelled of stale cabbage. A pinch-faced woman I assumed to be Mueller's landlady accosted me as soon as I pushed open the unlocked front door. Almost certainly she kept watch from a window seat in the substantial ground floor bay.

'Can I help you, love?'

'Does Mr Karl Mueller live here?'

'Oh, the nazzy.' She pronounced it like Mr Churchill. 'He's one flight up. Room 6. Friend of his, are you, love?'

I told her I was, not wanting to admit to being a policeman. There was no need to complicate Mueller's life more than necessary, particularly as I had no proof he'd been involved in the attack on Mr Dembowitz.

The bulb wasn't working on the first-floor landing but I could just make out the numbers on the four doors leading off it. The strains of Fred Astaire singing "They can't take that away from me" were coming from the floor above, almost drowned out by a drunken argument from the room next to Mueller's.

A tall, well-built, man in his late forties, wearing a brown jacket over blue overalls, answered his door quickly when I knocked.

'Yes?'

'Mr Mueller, is it? Karl Mueller?'

'It is. What do you want? I am just going out.'

He spoke with a Coventry accent, distorted by a very slight German clipping. I explained who I was and that I needed to speak to him. The man insisted on seeing my warrant card before he let me in. The current relations with Germany made this a wise precaution, especially when people like his landlady were making assumptions about his political loyalties.

'You recently left a clock for repair at a shop in Derby Lane. Is that right?'

'What if I did?'

'Then you dropped by and had a row with the shop owner. Called him "a robbing Jew". That was you, was it?'

Mueller grimaced.

'He was trying to rob me. He could see the clock was a good one and assumed I was well off.' The man smiled with set teeth and gestured around the room. 'You can see I am not. The clock was all I have left from my parents. They inherited it from my grandfather, from when the family had money. Before we came to England.'

'So you were angry with the clock repairer? And took your friends along to teach him a lesson?'

'Who says I did? I argued with him in the shop then left with my clock, still not repaired. I never went back there. Why would I?'

'Can you tell me where you were on Friday afternoon, between half past four and half past five?'

'Where I am every day at that time — at work.'

He had a job sweeping up at the Morris factory in Courthouse Green. Mueller had worked there for five years and could provide witnesses for him being at his job when the attack occurred. There was no doubt he was shocked when I explained what had happened to Mr Dembowitz and I was regretting having wasted the trip.

His voice shook as he opened the door to let me out.

'It is sad, though understandable, Inspector — these are difficult days. Someone is attacked and you have to follow any leads you can. If that someone is a Jew and you have a suspect who is German, it all seems to add up very easily. That is not me, I can assure you. My parents moved to England when I was a boy and my father was interned here during the War. We returned to Germany for a while but I couldn't stand what Hitler was doing so came back. It was wrong to lose my temper with the shopkeeper and to use those words. If you could tell him I'm sorry I'd be grateful. If you are looking for those who hurt Mr Dembowitz, perhaps you should look for the men who are recruiting Fascist supporters around the pubs.'

'Go on.'

'There are two, not English I think, and they came into the Ragged Staff a couple of nights. A few misguided men drinking in there think Hitler is correct, so the troublemakers spoke with them for a while. Now, as I said, I must be getting to work — I will be docked pay if I am late.'

I made my way downstairs and out into the street. About a hundred yards to my left a swinging pub sign showed a bear chained to a wooden post — the Warwickshire crest. At least I now knew where to look.

FOUR

Sawyer had joined me at the school just before lunch the next day and I noticed he'd put on a little weight since I last saw him — perhaps the result of an overindulgent Christmas. Despite this, he was several years younger and half a foot taller than me, still fit and imposing in his uniform as we stood outside the headmaster's house. I wished he'd taken up the chance to move into Kenilworth as a detective constable when I'd been able to offer it, but he'd stuck with being a village copper for a while longer. His local connections and family were important to him so I'd not tried too hard, and there'd be other opportunities in the future. With luck this case would whet his appetite for a less sedentary career.

Mrs Perelle led us into the front parlour, a room furnished to proclaim respectability and permanence. Nothing was of the highest quality but it was solid and you knew you were in the domain of someone in authority. A slight mustiness showed it wasn't used often; merely when it's necessary to reassure potential benefactors or to overawe parents of children attending the school.

Sawyer and I settled into two substantial leather armchairs and I briefed him while she looked for her husband. Perelle joined us after about ten minutes, flustered because he'd left a class, his chalk-dusted black gown flowing behind him when he came through the door.

'This isn't very satisfactory you know, Inspector. I've needed to leave my wife in charge over there; 3C can be a handful sometimes and not fit to be left on their own without causing a disturbance. You might have given me some warning what time you'd be here. Now, give me just a minute and I'll pull out those things you asked for.'

I was about to tear him off a strip for not sending the names up to the station as I'd asked but he shot out of the door and disappeared, soon returning with a manila folder in his hand.

'I've been through the files and listed the children who have had time off since July; you said that would be long enough, didn't you? These were then cross-checked against those who've now come back to school. There are two boys and two girls still missing.'

On the list I could see the girls, Vera Channing and Edith Caldwell, had been away for more than two months.

'Are you sure there are no more, Mr Perelle?'

The headmaster bristled.

'Without any doubt, Inspector. We take a register in every lesson and I've been through every page most carefully. It took me half the night but you're welcome to check them yourself if you're not happy. I can bring them through if you wish.'

'No, thank you, sir, I imagine you've been very meticulous. I was simply checking you were confident with what you'd found.'

At this stage I couldn't be sure he wasn't involved in the girl's death himself and might have falsified the records, but that would be a question for another day.

'Did you bring the other item I asked for?'

Perelle passed me another sheet of paper. It listed the school staff and was surprisingly short.

'And this is everyone?'

'It is. This isn't a wealthy establishment, Mr Given — we survive on an original endowment and occasional donations from past pupils or well-wishers. Most of our teachers double up on subjects and we keep the maintenance staff to an absolute minimum.'

There were ten names on the page: four teachers, Perelle himself, a part-time school secretary, a cook, a caretaker, a groundsman and a cleaner.

'I see Mrs Perelle isn't on here, though you said she is teaching Religious Instruction.'

'Well, technically, it's me teaching it, but she's helping out at present — she's not actually a member of staff. It goes with the territory, I'm afraid. The lot of a headmaster's wife.'

'Have they all been with you for a while?'

'Mr Smith has just joined us, as you know. Everyone else has been here for at least two years, apart from Mr Jenkins who joined us last autumn. We received a rather generous donation from an ex-pupil who's done rather well for himself in business and it has enabled us to take on another teacher.'

I queried two names on the list, the groundsman and the cleaner, Alan Johnston and Stella Johnston.

'Related?'

'Husband and wife. Nice young couple. As with the teachers, we try to get as much benefit as we can from everybody we take on. There's a house in the town goes with the groundsman's job so it's become a minor tradition that his wife also acts as cleaner. It has always seemed to suit them through the years, and it certainly helps us.'

I thanked Perelle for his assistance and asked if Sawyer and I could continue to use his parlour for a little while. He left us to it, his gown again flowing behind as he headed off to do battle with 3C once more.

The man struck me as officious, condescending and something of a bully, and I couldn't help pitying his pupils.

There was a chance he might be completely different in the classroom, though I doubted it.

'Do you think he could be involved, John?' I asked Sawyer.

'I wouldn't think so, sir — why would he bump off a child from the school and then leave her body so close to his own front door? If it was me I'd dispose of the evidence as far away as I could.'

'But we're not necessarily dealing with someone who thinks logically, are we? Few killers do in my experience. We have a posed body with a shiny gold crucifix wrapped round her hands. Any murderer who did that would be yearning for her body to be found.'

I sent Sawyer to talk to the families of the absent girls to see if he could find anything, though I suspected it might be fruitless. If Vera or Elsie had been missing for as long as the body had been underneath the chapel, it was more than likely that it would have been reported, unless the parents had been involved in their disappearance. If the dried remains in the crypt didn't belong to either of the girls then the investigation would become even more difficult.

I called on the school secretary to ask her to make arrangements for me to speak to all of the staff after school finished for the day, and then there was nothing else to be done in Kenilworth for the afternoon, so I drove into Coventry to follow up the information Mueller had given me.

The Bear and Ragged Staff had been built since the Great War, squeezed into a space between two rows of terraced houses. A mishmash of architectural styles, its red brick walls set off with grey stone mullion windows and half-timbered gables — everything new and at odds with all other properties in the street. The public bar was still busy with lunchtime drinkers and I gagged at the stench of cigarettes and beer when I pushed open the door. Several older men were playing dominoes in one corner and another was occupied by lecturers from the nearby technical college. Most of the clientele were workers in the small factories scattered around the area, grabbing a pie and a few pints for their midday refreshment, with overalls and khaki warehouse coats distinguishing labourers from foremen.

Pushing into a space at the bar I asked the thin man serving for a Vimto. Even when I used to be a drinker I was never keen on doing it in the afternoon. I found it fogged me too much, without providing any of the lift I was looking for. I passed over a few pence and asked if he was Andrew Weatherall, the licensee's name over the front door. The publican guessed straight away that I was a copper.

'It's Andy. Only my mam calls me Andrew. What is it — can't you see I'm busy?'

'Sorry, Mr Weatherall, it should only take a few minutes and —' I looked around the room, then at my watch — 'I really don't want to come back again after closing time.'

It was certain if I did return when the law said he should be closed; he'd still be obliging a few customers who had nothing better to do with the afternoon. He cottoned on quickly, so waved me behind the bar and through to the snug, locked and deserted at this point in the day. In here the smell of the polish liberally applied to the red leather bench seats did little to mask Weatherall's unfortunate halitosis. I told him I'd heard two foreigners had been in, talking to some of his regulars.

'Listen, Inspector, I don't want no trouble. We get all sorts in here.' He glanced over his shoulder. 'You've seen 'em, and I mind my own business when it comes to what they're talking about. Obviously you're not a drinking man yourself but if you knew what some of these fellers say when they've had a few you'd understand why I don't pay much attention.'

His assumption that I never drank made me cringe. I'd been in enough pubs and been drunk enough times in my younger days to appreciate exactly what he meant.

'I don't believe for a second that you miss much,' I replied, 'and I don't want to have to ask the local bobby to keep looking in on you. Be surprised at what he might find. Now, I know for a fact that these men have been in here at least twice, peddling Hitler's filth. So what can you tell me about them?'

'As I've said, I don't listen to what they were saying. One of the regulars told me what they were up to. Now, I don't hold with politics of any kind being put about in my pub so I'd already decided that if they came in again I'd tell them to sling their hook.'

'Can you describe them?'

'Not really. Dark-haired, tanned, one older and heavier than the other, but I'd have guessed they were brothers, they were so alike.'

'Names?'

'They called one of them Benito. Thought it might be a nickname because he was Italian — you know, like Mussolini.'

All the way back to the Charity School I was stunned by the news that the Sicilian brothers, Benito and Paúlu Demma, were active here, in Coventry. They were names from my past — brutal gangsters who had taken revenge on me after I exposed them as cheats in a high-stakes poker game by murdering my friend, Heather — and I was desperate to get them behind bars. Months ago I'd had them in my grasp and refused the opportunity to put them inside on minor charges. They'd sunk away — only to resurface now like the scum they are.

It was a little after five o'clock when I found my way to the classroom which Perelle made available for my interviews. In the corridor outside, three teachers were already waiting on a long wooden bench. They each wore a gown and a nervous expression, and none of them appeared to be over thirty years of age. I'd already spoken to the new man, Smith, and to the headmaster, so had not asked for them to come in to see me again. The first in the queue introduced himself as Robert Bennett and unlocked the classroom door for me.

'The caretaker, Mr Sprigg, asked if I'd open the room for you, Inspector — he's tied up with a small problem in the kitchens which needs to be fixed or else none of us gets to eat tonight. Said he'll be along as soon as he can. There's also a message from Mrs Spelding, the cook, that she can't come just now, because she's the one preparing the evening meal, but she's happy to talk to you later or in the daytime.'

In each of the interviews all I could ask any of them was if they knew Vera or Edith and if they'd seen anything suspicious around the time the girls stopped attending school, or since. Two of the teachers, Bennett and Rosebury, had taught them but didn't appear to know much about either. They didn't recall seeing anything unusual, nor seeing any strangers around the school in the last couple of months. So I asked them to think back further, just in case, but still they had nothing to add. The third teacher was Dominic Jenkins who ran the school choir in which Vera sang. He shifted constantly in his seat and never once looked me in the eye, claiming not to have witnessed anything odd over recent weeks.

'You're fairly new here, Mr Jenkins?'

More squirming.

'I came in the autumn.'

'Might I ask where from?'

'Is it relevant, Inspector?'

'Perhaps.'

'Oh, no matter, I was teaching in Cheltenham.'

'So why did you leave?'

'Can't a man change jobs nowadays without having to answer for it to the police?'

'Of course he can, sir, though it would be extremely helpful for you to explain without me needing to take you into the police station whilst I follow it up with your old employer.'

The fidgeting stopped and the colour drained from his cheeks.

'No need for that, Inspector. There was something came up in my private life over which the headmaster and I agreed we should part company.'

'Oh?'

'An affair. Someone much younger than me and the school didn't approve.'

'Are you saying you had an affair with a pupil, Mr Jenkins?'

'God. No! Nothing like that. It was a young woman who lived nearby. Her boss was a school governor and he found out.'

Jenkins's responses didn't ring true but, despite pushing him further, I'd have nothing concrete until reports were back from the pathologist so had to leave it. As I was seeing Jenkins out of the room, a young couple, who I assumed were the Johnstons, scurried along the corridor towards us. The man spoke first.

'Sorry we're a bit late, sir, Stella, here, took ages to get ready. I said she needn't bother but she insisted.'

Alan Johnston hadn't taken quite as much trouble. He was still in his working clothes, his shock of black hair not combed and a smudge of dried mud lay under his right ear. Despite this he was a good-looking young man, with a face which wore an ingrained smile.

Unlike Johnston, his wife, Stella, was dressed to the nines and it was obvious she'd made an effort. Her pleated gabardine coat was of much better quality than might have been expected on a school cleaner, and its belt hugging her waist helped make the most of her figure. With her Jean Harlow hair, crimson lipstick and rouged cheeks, Stella Johnston would have turned heads wherever she went. She nudged her husband in the ribs.

'Why, Alan, what a thing to say. Always try to look nice when we go out together, don't I?'

The groundsman looked skywards and, still smiling, shook his head and asked who I wanted to talk to first. I suggested it might be his wife, so with a sweeping gesture of his arm he encouraged her into the classroom then took a place on the bench.

Stella sat at the side of a desk until I'd finished sorting out my paperwork from Jenkins's interview. My questioning kicked off, as I with all the others, by asking what her responsibilities were at the school.

'Cleaning, Mr Given, that's all, sweeping the classrooms, the main hall and the headmaster's room every day, then giving them a mop every other day. I'd also wipe over the teachers' desks, empty the wastepaper baskets and so on.'

'Are those the only places you clean, Mrs Johnston?'

'Well, the boys and girls share the cleaning of the dormitories and common room and the teachers look after themselves. Mrs Perelle does theirs as well. If there's something special on in the chapel, the headmaster might ask me to help out there, but that wouldn't be often. Oh, and the kitchen. Cook asks me to give her a hand sometimes when she fancies a good tidy.'

'Do you have another job besides this one?'

She seemed taken aback by my question.

'No, Mr Given, why?'

'It's just that you look ... how might I put this ... a little well dressed for a cleaner. I don't imagine Mr Johnston earns a great deal either, does he?'

Stella sniggered.

'No, he doesn't, despite all my nagging for him to get a better job.' She pulled herself up short when she realised she'd said more than she should. 'I just mean he's a bright feller and might get work in a shop, or even an office, but no, he's for the outdoor life. Says it's worth more than extra cash. We have a few pounds put by in the bank but I try to cut corners where I can by making my own clothes. The patterns you get these days are great, right up to date, and I keep my eyes open for bargains at the jumble sales. It's important a woman looks her best, don't you think?'

She raised an eyebrow ever so slightly and shifted position to ensure she certainly did look her best.

'You've done well, Mrs Johnston — I'd have guessed you were dressed from one of the best shops in Coventry or Leamington. Now, could we move on to what you might have seen over the last month or so? Have you noticed anything unusual, anyone hanging around the school?'

She hadn't, just like all the others. Finally, I asked her about the crypt.

'You've said you help out with cleaning in the chapel now and again, have you ever been down the crypt?'

'Never, Inspector, there's not been any reason. I've heard tell it's full of dead bodies so I wouldn't want to go down there, it would be creepy.'

I let her go, asking her to contact me if she remembered anything. She took her husband's place on the bench and sent him in. He plonked down on the chair, almost before I'd invited him to do so, and leaned back with his hands clasped behind his head. There was an arrogance about him often seen in tall, good-looking young men. His job kept him in good physical condition and he'd acquired a healthy tan from long days spent outside. Despite the differences in dress sense, the Johnstons made a very handsome couple.

The groundsman could offer no more than any of the interviewees so far; he'd not noticed anything unusual in the previous three weeks and claimed not to have known either of the missing girls, at least not by name. He'd see nearly all of the pupils at some time or another on the playing fields but he'd know few of their names.

'I find that hard to believe, Mr Johnston.'

'Why?'

'Well, you're a good-looking bloke, surely some of these girls would have a crush on you?'

He puffed up like a peacock, which was the desired effect. Johnston was too conscious of his effect on women not to respond by boasting.

'One or two. You know how it is, Inspector, what can I do?'

'And were Vera or Edith amongst them?'

'Possibly, I don't really know. As I said, I wouldn't remember many names.'

I paused and made a note. He gritted his teeth when he realised he'd made a mistake.

'So what happened, Alan? You take one of the girls into the church, it all goes too far and she threatens to tell the headmaster?'

'What? No. Nothing ever happened with them. I wouldn't. It was a crush, schoolgirl daftness. They'd hang around me when I was working, trying to act all grown up but they weren't. They were just children. I'd pretend to chat them up, make them blush, that kind of thing, but that's as far as it would go.'

At this point I'd no reason to think he was involved, I was just poking around under stones to see what crawled out, so I sent him on his way, less sure of himself than when he arrived.

The interviews had provided nothing except a brick wall. How could someone murder a child in such a closed environment and no-one see or hear anything?

The caretaker showed up ten minutes after the Johnstons left. Arthur Sprigg was a rounded 5'8" and wearing spectacles repaired with sticking plaster. When I asked the same questions as I had with everyone else; there was the same result, nothing. Then a move forward.

'Might you have lost a hammer recently, Mr Sprigg?'

'Actually I did, just after Christmas.'

'Any chance you could be more specific?'

Sprigg scratched his balding head. 'It must have been around 4th January because I know I was using it to fix a screen in the boys' dormitory on that day. It was my wife's birthday and I'd promised to take her out to the pub after I'd finished but it took longer than I expected. She didn't half bend my ear when I got home. The next time I needed it was the following week and I couldn't find it so had to walk up into town to buy another.'

'Do you know which day you discovered you'd lost it?'

'I'm not sure — Tuesday or Wednesday, I'd have said, but I gave the bill to Mr Perelle so that might have the date on it.'

'And you wouldn't have dropped the hammer in the crypt yourself?'

'Unlikely; I can't remember using it in there for a good while. I was down there the afternoon after Peggy's birthday. There'd been a problem with a light in the chapel and the cable comes into the building at the bottom of the steps. It runs along the ceiling for a stretch then up into the main chapel just by the door and I went down to see if that's where the trouble was. Wouldn't have needed a hammer though, so can't imagine I dropped it then.'

'And you saw nothing unusual that morning?'

'It took no more than a minute or two but the funny thing, now I remember, was that the door wasn't locked. I tried it without thinking and it opened. Thought someone had just been careless and forgot so went over for the key when I'd finished and made sure it was secure.'

'And the key was there?'

'It was — hanging where it always does in the secretary's office.'

I asked if he kept his toolbox locked.

'There's no need, Inspector, the kids who come to the school might be poor but I've known none of them steal anything. When I found my hammer had disappeared I imagined someone took it for a little job and forgot to bring it back. It seemed easier to buy a new one than chase round all over the place to find it.'

The caretaker had been employed at the school for almost twenty years so he knew a lot of the pupils by sight. His own niece had attended "Hannah's" a decade earlier, and he'd known a few of her friends more than most, but he said that in each year there'd be one or two who'd latch on to him, offer to help with jobs, or just chat, looking for some adult contact. Neither of the missing girls fell into this category and he didn't remember them in particular.

Sprigg locked the classroom door when we left and he walked me to the gate. Just before I stepped into the street he gave me his thoughts on the murder.

'Hannah's is like a family, Inspector. There're arguments and disagreements from time to time, but the teachers are kind and Mrs Perelle, she's one in a million. No-one here's going to kill a child, not in a thousand years.'

A light still shone in Oliver Neilson's parlour window when I approached my house so I walked the extra few yards and knocked at the ex-teacher's door. The cottage was much like mine on the outside with white walls, black timbers and a shingle tiled roof, although his had a bay window on the front whilst mine was flush. A thin man, sleeves rolled up and a book in hand, opened up after a moment and I introduced myself.

'Apologies for disturbing you at this time in the evening, Mr Neilson — you called round when you moved in but I was just leaving the house and couldn't speak to you. You must have thought me very rude.'

'Not at all — well, not for long anyway. Once I'd heard from your neighbour you're a policeman, I understood completely; you must be very busy. Are you involved in this dreadful affair up at the school?'

I explained it was the reason I was calling on him at the late hour.

'Well, come inside, Inspector, we'll go through to the kitchen and put the kettle on.'

The arrangement of the rooms in his cottage seemed to be similar to my own, with a staircase rising from the hallway, the parlour on the left and kitchen at the back. Several tea-chests under the stairs, containing items wrapped in newspaper, testified to his recent arrival.

'I really should get those put away, shouldn't I, instead of sitting around reading but, you know, after a lifetime of work, I've now become used to the idea that there's always tomorrow. The hallway is bad enough but I'm afraid my kitchen's not much better.'

I whistled in appreciation when he showed me into the room. It was so modern. Despite the untidiness of the paint-pots and brushes stacked in the corner and waiting to be used, it was clear Neilson hadn't stinted on equipping his new home. The whole of one wall was lined with metal cupboards, the latest enamel sink, a brand-new stove and even a gas hot water geyser, from which Neilson filled the kettle.

'This is all my nephew's fault,' he said. 'He told me if I'd had someone else feeding me for all these years I should get myself a new kitchen to learn to cook in. My savings, though not huge, were healthy enough, so I made the investment, though I find it a little overwhelming and haven't gone beyond making sandwiches and porridge so far. They're still giving me the occasional meal up at the school — cook's so very kind — and I'm taking lunch in café's most days, so I'm not starving quite yet.'

We sat at the table whilst the kettle boiled and I asked if he'd answer a few questions.

'That's no problem, Inspector, I'm happy to help in any way I can.'

He paused when he noticed I was looking at the book he'd put on the table when we came in — *A Death on Main Street*.

'My guilty pleasure, I'm ashamed to say, detective novels. This is Terence Spelling's latest in the library. I've read all of his so far and this has been my favourite. Mac Spielberg, his hero, is so tough, and clever with it; solves the crime every time and kills the murderer or makes sure they go to the electric chair.'

I smiled and said I wished it was always so easy, admitting I was a little surprised because it seemed lighter reading than I'd have expected from a Latin teacher.

'You're right, Inspector, but doesn't the Bible say "To every thing there is a season, and a time to every purpose under the heaven"?' This time it was his turn to grin. 'At least, that's how I justify it to myself. If I hadn't taken up teaching I might have become a detective; I almost joined the police when I was old enough but my mother pressed me down a different path. Would have made a good one, too. Think I must have an analytical bent because I always guess the culprits in these novels before the end.'

Something in Neilson's tone suggested he was trying to ingratiate himself but also that he thought he'd have made a much more intelligent policeman than me. I wondered if, even after all these years, he resented the career his mother had forced him to follow. He poured the tea and I asked him about the missing girls. His cup rattled in his hand when I mentioned their names.

'Oh my Lord, Inspector, I knew them both well — do you think it's one of them?'

'Well, they've been absent from school for a while, so it's the line we're following at present. Did you teach them both?'

'I did, in each of their three years. Vera was also in my Christian Union group. She came to Bible studies every week right up to me leaving at the end of term. A lovely girl.'

'That must have been about the last time the two girls attended.'

Neilson looked flustered.

'I'm sure I don't know, Inspector — they were both in school a couple of days before because I took them for maths. Edith was having trouble with a simple problem I set in class — the girl was bright enough in some areas but algebra wasn't a strong point.'

The disdain in the teacher's voice was typical of those who've always found learning mathematics to be easy, lacking any understanding of those who struggle to master the basic concepts. What he might see as clear and logical, even beautiful, might appear as a mere jumble of letters and numbers to half his pupils, despite his repeated attempts to drum it into them. I'm able to calculate the score in a hand of cribbage in the blink of an eye but I still remember the ridicule I'd faced from teachers when I battled to comprehend the mysteries of Pythagoras.

'Did you see either of the girls afterwards, Mr Neilson?'

Not a second's pause.

'No, I retired from the school on the Friday and moved down here next day. Mrs Perelle and the headmaster invited me to their house for tea that Sunday afternoon and I've popped into the kitchen a few times, as I said, but I've had no contact with the pupils.'

Whilst he had noticed nothing strange in the behaviour of the girls, he admitted to having a good knowledge of the chapel, and the crypt where Smith discovered the body, although he claimed not to have been down there since he left.

'Any idea of the last date?'

'I'm afraid not, Inspector — I was so tied up with packing and finishing everything up that December is quite a blur. I went down one day when I had a chance because I didn't know if I'd ever be lucky enough to go again. It's fascinating, you know, I've spent lots of time in that crypt over the years, researching the characters buried there. A great shame the sarcophagi have fallen into such disrepair, hundreds of years they've been there, a testament to the piety of the souls buried under them.'

'Were they really pious, though? They were brutal times when those men lived, with religious persecution on a grand scale.'

'That's the point, isn't it, Inspector? The family burying them had to demonstrate it was of the faith in favour to ensure their survival. The way they laid out the body aimed to display the piety of the deceased, regardless of how much the person might have done wrong in their lifetime.'

On that note, I finished my tea, thanked Neilson for his time, and retired for the night.

FIVE

'Anything from the school, sir?'

My office in Kenilworth station was already small but made to feel even more so with Sawyer filling the chair and the space opposite me the next morning.

'Nothing particularly useful. All but two of the staff have been there for ages and everyone is shocked a thing like this could happen so close to home. We can't check for alibis because we don't even know when the girl died. We'll question them all again when the pathologist gives us something to work with. One teacher in particular, Jenkins, looked like he was hiding something. Gave me a story about an affair at his last school but I'm not sure I believed him. I also think the headmaster's not all he pretends to be. Condescending as hell and a weird hobby — preserving bits of dead animals in jars. Gave me the creeps.'

'So, we haven't identified the victim yet, we don't know how she died, and she could have been killed any time in the last few months. On top of that, no-one saw anything suspicious. Have I got that right, sir?'

'That's about it, John. Any idea on who might have done it?'

Sawyer laughed, admitted he hadn't a clue and I was pleased he was relaxing a little. He'd been annoyed at me for bringing him up to town from his cosy beat in the country, but I sensed he was now relishing the chase.

Six months earlier he'd enjoyed assisting me on the Grovestock House murders and proved a good man to have at my side, when his height alone was enough to put off most people from trying anything physical. Already, he'd been thorough in searching for the absent schoolgirls. The first, Edith, had been easy enough, having been found at home with her family, where the mother had recently given birth to a sixth child and needed Edith to help with younger brothers and sisters. Neither the girl nor her mother had thought it important to let the school know because, as Perelle had suggested, there were more pressing problems in these families' lives than missing a few days of education.

The second child had proved more difficult.

'I'm concerned for her, sir. The house was a real mess when I called round. No sign of a woman's hand there, and no sign of Vera either. Henry Channing, her dad, looked like he was fonder of a drink than of soap and water, and he hadn't seen the sharp edge of a razor for a few days. All he'd say about Vera was she was "away" and wouldn't be going back to school.'

Channing's wife had died of consumption in October and she'd been the one insisting on Vera attending Hannah's when their child was offered the opportunity. The father seemed to believe Vera would be of more use if she was out working and bringing in a few extra shillings for him to spend on booze.

'Did you find out where the girl is staying?'

'Channing wouldn't tell me. Said it was none of my business and I should just believe him that she was safe and well. Should I bring him in for questioning, sir?'

'Not just yet. If the doc can give us anything to show the victim is Vera then we'll have her father in.'

We returned to Arthur Sprigg's estimation of when he'd lost his hammer and agreed Sawyer should go through the school staff again with those dates in mind. There were still too many days to pin anyone down, but at least he might be able to exclude a couple of names.

My phone rang and I answered it.

'Yes, this is Given.'

Sawyer stood to leave and I gestured to him to sit until I'd finished the call. I listened to the Foleshill desk sergeant and scribbled down an address. There had been another attack on a Jewish business — arson this time.

'All right, I'll be over in about an hour.'

Putting the handset back on its cradle, I pondered before speaking to Sawyer.

'I've to go to Coventry again, John, but I've had news of some old friends.' He was as surprised as I'd been to hear the Demma brothers were back in circulation. 'I'd assumed they'd gone back to London, rather than waiting up here for me to come after them.'

'So what will you do, sir?'

'I suppose I'll need to let Inspector Gleeson know, in case they pop up in Birmingham, but I'd suggest we do nothing else for now. You know how slippery they are; go in too fast and they'll disappear into the woodwork. I'm certain they are behind these attacks on Jewish businesses, which are becoming more frequent, and they'll slip up at some point. When they do, we'll be waiting.'

When I arrived at the scene there was water dripping from every girder. The firemen's hoses had drenched them and piles of damp, blackened cloth lay everywhere — some of it still steaming where the fire had taken hold. The acrid smell of burning fabric tore at my nostrils and I wondered how the three warehousemen in overalls picking through the remnants of the blaze could stand it. The workers were turning the bolts of material, one after the other, checking that no sparks were still smouldering beneath.

The fire appeared to have been concentrated in one corner and the broken window above it showed where the source of the conflagration had been thrown through. One fireman told me he suspected a petrol-filled bottle had been used to set the place alight. The fire brigade had received a call at around seven o'clock that morning from someone in a neighbouring factory who'd spotted smoke pouring out of the building.

In the corner, two men dressed in black watched over the devastation through a large office window. One of them, who looked the elder, beckoned me to join them. He introduced himself as Levi Goodman and the other man as his brother, Bernard, joint owners of the business, which they'd run for twenty years. Both shared the same dazed expression. Levi Goodman asked the same question as the watch jeweller, Dembowitz, had a few days earlier. A question I suspected they'd also been asking each other for several hours.

'Why would someone create this carnage?'

I asked if he knew of anyone who might have a grudge against them. He didn't.

'We employ local people and try to give our customers a fair deal. We've been in this area since we set up together and never any trouble before.'

He trailed off, shaking his head. The younger brother spoke for the first time.

'Could I say something, Inspector?'

I told him to go ahead. From the inside pocket of his jacket he pulled four sheets of paper, unfolded them and laid them on the table.

'We've been receiving these for the last three weeks.' He turned to his brother. 'I'm sorry, Levi, I didn't want to worry you. In the beginning I thought it was just some schoolboy prank; that nothing would come of it. I wish I'd gone to the police after the first one instead of hoping it would go away.'

The letters were on the type of cheap paper which can be bought in any corner shop and written in pencil with every word in capitals. The spelling was poor and the sentences clipped, as if the writer had a limited command of English. It was easy to see how Bernard Goodman might think a child had sent them. The message in each was clear, screaming that the Goodmans were 'dirty Jew thieves' and should 'go back to your own country'. There'd been others like them over the past few months in both Birmingham and Coventry, and I'd even come to recognise the handwriting, but each time I picked one up it made my blood boil. I'd told my father that if he or any of his friends received one, they should get in touch straight away rather than contact the local police. Terry Gleeson was handling the investigation in Birmingham but I didn't trust him to do anything. He was as anti-Semitic as they come.

Gleeson had been handed the reins for a while by Superintendent Dyer when the boss put me on the Grovestock House case, one which proved much more traumatic than Dyer had foreseen. I suppose it seemed natural to him to pass the Birmingham end over to Gleeson again when he asked me to help with an outbreak in Coventry. What Dyer didn't believe was that Gleeson disliked Jews almost as much as the thugs who were attacking them in Birmingham. He also had his snout into every bit of corruption in the city he could manage.

Levi Goodman took each letter from me after I'd read it and continued with the same questions.

'Why? Why us? Why now?'

'It's the times we're in, Mr Goodman. Some deluded people seem to think what's happening in Germany should be copied here. There are always plenty of fools who want to blame others for their misfortunes and, sadly, a small number also think it's acceptable to exact their revenge on whoever they see as responsible.'

Six months earlier I'd had to witness the hanging of one such cretin, a follower of Mosley and a mindless thug, so stupid he couldn't keep his mouth shut about what he'd done. He'd kicked and wriggled at the end of the rope; an image that has stayed with me a long time and not one I want to see again in a hurry.

Neither of the brothers could come up with any ideas about who might have sent the letters so all I could do was take their formal statements, ask the senior fireman to send a copy of his report to me, and promise the Goodmans I'd be back in touch if anything came to light.

A short and to-the-point message from the pathologist was waiting on my desk when I arrived back in Kenilworth. *Ring Dr Naismith — URGENT.*

'Afternoon, James, thanks for calling me back. I've finished my initial examinations and there's something you need to know. Our victim wasn't a schoolgirl, she was an adult in her early twenties.'

'You're joking.'

'I know, I could hardly believe it myself. Tiny woman, around five foot two, and painfully thin.'

'Cause of death?'

'Sorry, I have nothing yet. Out in the open the bugs and beasties would have caused carnage, but as you saw, she was well preserved. She's still been dead quite a long time though, so it's hard to pull out anything specific. I have to say I've never seen anything like this up close before — have you?'

'Only once, when I was visiting a friend's family in Dublin which, for him, spiralled into a weekend of unrestrained drinking and left me at a loose end in the city. Gerry's sister, Rosanna, took pity and suggested a few sights I might like. Amongst them was St Michan's Church, a dour, grey, stone building only a short walk from where we were staying in Gerry's family home south of the Liffey.'

I explained to Walter how heavy wooden trapdoors had covered the access to steep steps descending eight or ten feet into dark crypts which tourists have visited for many years. A passageway, perhaps thirty feet long, was punctuated on each side by a series of small chambers sealed with iron gates, the plaques on every gate invoked a litany of the great and the good of Ireland's history. A peek through the ironwork revealed the strange and gruesome sight of coffins piled one on top of the other, all preserved in original states, the only mark of their ages being the layer of dust on each, half an inch thicker at the bottom than the top. They were burial vaults.

The guide had explained how the dryness, low constant temperatures, and gases seeping from the surrounding rock, combined to preserve everything deposited below St Michan's in pristine condition, even the bodies within the coffins, some for centuries. One vault contained the remains of a man, purported to be a crusader, his casket broken open by some accident in the distant past to reveal his mummified body, skin brown and leathery, stretched over bones which refused to rot. It had made me shiver and I'd remembered the smell when I went down the steps to our young woman's last resting place.

'Any idea how long since she died?'

'Almost impossible to say, James. Once a body reaches that state of mummification it doesn't change much even over hundreds of years. I'd have to do some research but I'd guess the minimum would be six to eight weeks. You said you found a hammer at the scene?'

'Could it have been the murder weapon?'

'I shouldn't think so — it may have been used to knock her out but I couldn't find any serious fractures in her skull. The gash on her head is more likely to have been caused when she fell. There's not much chance of seeing any bruising in her brain this late in the day so I can't be a hundred per cent certain. I've still more tests to do so I might be able to give you more in a day or two, though I wouldn't be too hopeful. You know I can't put it down to murder yet, don't you?'

'Of course it's a murder, Walter, how else would you explain her dying down there? Hardly the best place she could choose to end it all, is it? This young lady was killed and laid on that mattress; I'd stake my house on it.'

'It's fine for you to have theories, James, but I need solid evidence before I can give a cause of death. Unofficially I might agree with you, though that wouldn't be enough if it ever came to court. All we can both do is keep digging to see if anything turns up.'

I was grateful for this concession from Walter because I'd need his support if, and when, Dyer wanted to know why I was looking for a killer when we weren't certain a murder had actually been committed.

'I appreciate that. Anything that might give us a clue who she is?'

'Not really, but I can tell you she might not be local.'

I asked him to elaborate.

'The skirt and blouse she was wearing were in a mess but they both had maker's labels. French. Made in Marseilles to be exact, not Paris, so unlikely she'd pick up anything like that around here, even in the cities. I'd expect she actually bought them in France.'

'So you're saying she's French?'

'Not necessarily, only that she could be.'

So why would a young French woman be murdered here in Kenilworth? And why wasn't I aware she was here? It's only a small town and anyone even remotely exotic would be the topic of conversation in no time.

'Anything else?'

'She was wearing a bracelet engraved with the name "Josephine", possibly her mother or grandmother; it doesn't seem to be something a younger woman might wear unless she was given it as a memento. Sounds French as well, don't you think? As for the crucifix she had wrapped round her hands, there's not much to say. It was gold and I'd say it was fairly new, going by the brightness and lack of wear. It was wrapped round in a way would suggest it hadn't been put on by the wearer.'

'Are you sure?'

'Well, as sure as I can be. It was looped round her little finger, then around her hands and finally hung between her palms, almost as if it was tying her hands together. Quite a difficult thing to do yourself. Sorry I haven't anything more concrete, James, but the labels and bracelet might help narrow her down a bit.'

I asked him to cut out the labels and send them to me along with the bracelet and the crucifix as soon as possible. He said he'd be in touch when he discovered anything else which might be useful.

This case was turning on its head. Firstly we're investigating the death of a pupil from the Charity School, where staff are the obvious first suspects, and now we're looking at a young woman, possibly French, where the net might need to be cast much, much wider. We don't even know with any accuracy when she died, who she was, where she was from or even if she was murdered or not. What hope had we of finding out what happened to her?

SIX

Sawyer knocked on my door a minute or two after I'd finished the conversation with the pathologist. He told me he'd found the missing Vera Channing.

'She's living with her mum's sister in Warwick. Seems the aunt wasn't happy for the girl to be left with her father. Said he was regularly drunk and violent with it. She'd had to rescue Vera's mum from his fists more than once. Not surprising Henry Channing didn't want us asking questions. A neighbour told me where she was.'

'You go round and see him again. Find some reason to do him if you can. Nothing too serious, just enough to put the frighteners on him. Then tell Channing we'd like his daughter to be able to continue her education and we'll be watching him. Say that if we even get a whiff that he's touched her we'll be round to visit. The aunt might still not want Vera to go back to her dad but at least we'll have tried.'

I filled him in on what Naismith had told me and asked him to go round all the jewellers in Kenilworth when we received the crucifix, just on the off-chance one of them might recognise it.

'I'll get on to it right away, sir, there can't be many. I'll also go through the missing persons' files again in detail now we know a bit more about the victim, particularly the angle of her possibly being French.'

'You'd best make enquiries around the other county stations as well, John, just in case anyone else is looking for a young woman who's gone missing.'

I spent the next hour or so bringing files up to date, then decided to call to see Laurence Perelle on my way home. Taking an empty mug back to the canteen on my way out I glimpsed Oliver Neilson standing across the road. He seemed to be watching the front entrance of the police station so I waved, trying to attract his attention, but he turned away and walked into a teashop. When I left the building I could see him clearly at a table still looking out of the window. I don't know if he saw me or not, he made no indication that he had, though it was dark in the street and the café lights would be reflecting back from the glass, obscuring everything outside.

Mrs Perelle was overjoyed to hear we'd traced both Edith and Vera. Her husband showed little interest, as if it was simply another minor problem that had now been solved. I wondered again how he could have such scant concern for children attending the school. I told them about the new information I'd been given and asked if it sounded like any past staff or anyone else associated with the school.

'Certainly none of the teachers,' Perelle said. 'The only female teacher we've had in my time was Mrs Leggett and she was near retirement when I joined the school. As for the others, they've all been with us for a while and the only women would be Stella Johnston, you've met her, and the school secretary and the cook, both of whom were very much alive and well this morning. We've never had any French staff in the school to my knowledge.'

'What about past pupils, Mr Perelle?'

'I couldn't make a guess at that, Inspector. Again, I wouldn't know of any children from France in my time and, as for their height, they only stay with us until they're fourteen or fifteen and they haven't finished growing by then. I've seen youngsters shoot up after they've left the school.'

'You keep in touch with them then?'

'With some —' he looked at his wife — 'but that's more Mrs Perelle's interest than mine. She has more time on her hands than I do, don't you, dear?'

Emily Perelle didn't respond other than turning her back on her husband and asking if I'd excuse her for a moment. The headmaster commented on the weather then sat in aloof silence until she returned carrying two albums and a box.

'A lot of the children, particularly the boarders, need a woman in their lives, Inspector,' Emily Perelle told me. 'They're away from their mother or, some, like poor Vera, have no mother, and I fulfil that role as best I can. As a result, a number keep in contact when they leave. Some visit from time to time but most just send a postcard or Christmas card when they can. I'm afraid your description doesn't fit any of those I've seen in the last year or so. For a while I tried to keep their messages in some kind of order but there just isn't always time, so I keep many of them in this box.'

The headmaster looked at his watch.

'I imagine my wife can deal with this now, Inspector — it can't be too difficult. I'll leave you in her hands whilst I get on with something more important.'

Perelle didn't wait for my reply and walked out, his footsteps fading down the hall towards his horror show at the back of the house. His wife's embarrassment was obvious.

'He doesn't mean anything by it, Inspector — he has a lot on his mind.'

I told her it didn't matter, though inwardly I was seething, and suggested we look at the items she'd brought through. Again I couldn't help wondering how she found herself stuck with such a cold fish. I could easily see how he would find her desirable but the reverse could hardly be true.

As she'd said, the cards in the albums were in some semblance of order, dating from her early days at Hannah's. The remainder, by far the majority, were haphazard, stuffed into a mahogany box with brass corners. I looked through them for a few moments but couldn't pull anything useful from them so handed them back to the headmaster's wife.

'I think I may have to come back to look at these again, Mrs Perelle, when I have a better idea what I'm looking for. I trust that will be no problem.'

'None at all, Inspector, it will be a pleasure to see you again. You must pop in for tea sometime when you're passing, I — we — have so few visitors, other than the teachers and the occasional parent.'

I thanked her and asked if she'd pass a message to her husband for him to arrange for both the cook and the school secretary to make themselves available to talk to me next morning. As she let me out I found myself contemplating that it would be very pleasant to call on them socially, especially if Perelle decided to stay in his room and pickle small creatures.

The street outside the school was damp from a shower which had blown through and passers-by scurried homeward with collars turned up against the north-easterly. I heard my name shouted from across the road and looked up to see a sodden Oliver Neilson waving. I crossed over to join him.

'Good evening, Inspector, I didn't expect to see you down here this evening. The weather's taken a turn for the worse, don't you think? Are you following up something over at the school?'

I agreed with him about the weather, ignoring his second question, and asked if he was on his way home, which he was, so we set off down the hill together, heads bent against the wind. It was less than half a mile from the school to the castle and on a good day one of the most pleasant walks imaginable. But this was not a good day. Closer to the town the narrow street funnelled the bitter blast into a veritable gale, which abated when the houses thinned out, only to be replaced by rain blowing horizontally across the fields.

Neilson raised his voice above the squall.

'You didn't say what you were doing at the school, Mr Given. You know, I've been thinking a lot about that poor girl and wondering who could have done it. I've remembered that one of Mac Spielberg's cases involved a murder in a school and he discovered it was one of the teachers, though that was a boy rather than a girl. He was killed because he'd witnessed the teacher stealing money from the headmaster's office. The murderer tried to escape but Spielberg chased him over a frozen lake then shot him to avoid his suffering when he fell through the ice and the detective couldn't reach his hand. Very dramatic. I take it you've interviewed all the teachers by now, but that's where I'd start.'

Once again, I had the impression Neilson was trying to display a superior intellect, despite quoting the penny dreadful detective he was trying to emulate, and I was surprised by how easily he'd betray his former colleagues just to show how clever he was. It was odd how he'd bumped into me. Perhaps not entirely coincidental? We'd only met a few days before and now he seemed everywhere. Had he been watching for me outside the station then from the café and followed me to the school, waiting until I came out? Or was it simply the fact that we'd been introduced and so now I'd notice him, when in the past I'd have walked by without giving him a second look? Like last year, when I'd bought a new hat and suddenly it seemed like every other man in town had the same one. Was this thing with Neilson the same effect? We were, after all, neighbours and shared the same route into town, hence bound to bump into each other now and again, nothing strange or suspicious in that.

'Actually, Mr Neilson, I can't really talk about the investigation, but I can tell you we now know the body we found was that of a young adult woman, not a schoolgirl, after all.'

'Oh my, that changes everything, doesn't it? Have you any idea who she is?'

I gave him such description as I had from the pathologist, leaving out the bracelet and crucifix, and admitted it was not much to go on. He said he couldn't think of anyone but there was something about his denial which made me think twice. Perhaps the catch in his voice was due to the wind and rain still battering us, but I wasn't so sure. When I left him at my front door I was left wondering why he might lie about such a thing.

SEVEN

Martha Clements would have been an attractive woman if she'd let herself be. She was tall and slim with fine features and deep brown eyes behind the bottle-glass spectacles which dominated her face. Perhaps she was teased about these as a child, convincing her she was plain. I guessed she was in her early thirties but she could just as easily have been five years younger or five years older and she'd retreated into this dowdy school secretary, with clothes, hairstyle and shoes orchestrated to blend her into the background. She wore no rings or jewellery, other than a brooch in the form of a butterfly. A trinket of rare beauty, with wings of emerald green enamel laid on silver, delicate veins picked out in a deeper olive and two tiny glittering diamonds representing its eyes. It was deeply at odds with her otherwise conventional appearance and I wondered if another job, in another place, might free a butterfly hiding inside the nervous, mousy woman sitting in front of me.

We were in her office and the secretary shook throughout the first part of our interview. More than once I thought I'd have to administer smelling salts to stop her from fainting away.

'Oh, Inspector, what happened to that poor schoolgirl is spinning round and around in my head, lying dead down there in the dark for weeks and weeks and no-one knowing about it.' She shuddered. 'I heard she was in a terrible condition.'

We'd not progressed far in my questioning, despite my attempts to move forward from her shock about the murder. Miss Clements told me she only worked three mornings a week at the school. Her parents had died some years earlier, leaving her a small house and enough money to live on so she professed to only wanting to work for the social contact and to pay for the occasional holiday.

'I understand that the key for the crypt was kept here in your office — was it with the one for the chapel?'

She looked puzzled for a moment.

'Oh, the chapel is never locked, Inspector Given. There must be a key somewhere but I don't think I've ever seen it. The one for the crypt is usually hanging over there.'

She pointed to a board fixed to the wall just inside her office door.

'Are there any frequent users, Miss Clements?'

'I wouldn't really know. As I've said, I'm only part-time and the keys are freely available when I'm not here. The only ones I can think of would be the headmaster and Mr Sprigg, but even they'd not want it that often. Mr Neilson used to take it occasionally when he was still with us but obviously not since he left. Then again, people are at that board all the time so I'd not know which particular keys they were taking unless they told me.'

I asked her about the date in January when the caretaker found the door unlocked.

'I remember him coming in looking for the key to lock up. He asked me who'd had it last so he could have a word about their carelessness but I couldn't tell him. The board is such a fixture I'd never look at it unless someone comes in and wants help. When Mr Sprigg asked me I couldn't recall anyone in the previous week but they may have been in when I wasn't at work.'

This was leading me down a blind alley. I wasn't sure if the door being unlocked was even significant — it could have been so for ages before our French lady died in the crypt. The only certainty was that she didn't put the key back in the office afterwards.

Martha Clements confirmed that she kept the school accounts so I asked her to look for the receipt for the hammer which Sprigg told me he'd bought.

'Here it is. One shilling and tuppence on eleventh of January. Attached to the slip signed by Mr Sprigg to show he'd received it.'

I thanked her and moved on to explain that our earlier assumptions were wrong and that the body in the crypt was that of a young woman. I gave her description and asked the secretary if she recognised it.

'Actually, I have seen someone like her a couple of times; I assumed she was the older sister of one of our children.'

At last, a breakthrough.

'When was this?'

'The first time was around the beginning of December. I was leaving for home and the third-year boys were playing football on the field when I noticed someone walking away from them. At first I thought it was one of the girls.' She pointed to her glasses with a faint smile. 'My eyes aren't too good, and I was about to ask her what she was doing out of class when I realised it wasn't a child, so I simply nodded a hello when she walked past.'

'Could you describe her?'

'Not very well, I'm afraid, other than what you already know. She was pretty. Dark hair, I think. I could see she was quite nicely dressed when she was up close. She looked vaguely familiar but I couldn't place her, though, as I said, I thought she was a pupil's sister.'

'You said you saw her twice?'

'The next time would have been two or three weeks later.'

I pressed her to try to remember if it was two weeks or three. She thought for a few moments before answering.

'If I was pushed, Inspector, I'd say it would actually be three weeks after the first time. I seem to recall I was taking payslips to the cook and Mrs Johnston, and that's normally the third Friday of the month. They're paid every week but I only do the paperwork once a month when I bring the books up to date.'

'And where did you see her that second time?'

I wanted to shout at her when she gave me the answer. How can it be that people don't make the connections when they seem so blindingly obvious?

'Oh, Inspector, didn't I say? She was just going into the chapel.'

Mrs Spelding looked like she might be too over-fond of her own puddings. She was barely five foot and rotund as a barrel, though moved with an easy grace around her kitchen. Enormous pans of potatoes, carrots and beef stew bubbled on the stove whilst she mixed the ingredients for treacle sponge in the biggest bowl I'd ever seen. The smell was more than appetising and when the cook invited me to stay around for lunch I had to remind myself of my resolution to put such things behind me. If I was ever to lose weight it wouldn't come about by eating stodgy school dinners.

The cook was able to confirm it was the secretary's habit to distribute the payslips monthly so I asked if she remembered anything unusual on the day when our now-dead woman was seen going into the chapel.

'How would I see anything, Inspector? I'm shut away in here all day, every day, preparing food for all the children and teachers. I get time off between meals but I wouldn't be using that to wander round the school. Oh no, if I get chance I put my feet up.' She dropped to a conspiratorial whisper. 'Might even take a little nap in front of the cooker if I'm lucky.'

'Miss Clements described this woman as young, nice-looking, well-dressed. She'd have been about your height with dark hair. Does that ring any bells? An older sister or aunt of one of the children, perhaps?'

She said the description meant nothing to her because she had no contact with any of the children, other than in the dining hall. Mrs Spelding had nothing further to add to what Martha Clements had told me so I left her to finish her cooking.

It was almost lunchtime when I finished and there were lines of children queueing in the yard, waiting patiently to be let inside for their midday meal. The storms of the previous night had passed away and I decided to walk back home to eat something light rather than go up to the station canteen where the fare would be similar to Mrs Spelding's offering.

I walked this lane most days, and had done so for a number of years but every single time I'd see something new, whether it be the way the light was reflecting from the lake on Abbey Fields, a detail on one of the cottages dotting the roadside or a previously unnoticed turret on the castle at the bottom of the hill.

Fired by my determination to lose a few pounds I turned left, rather than right, planning to make a circuit of the castle before going home, though I hadn't accounted for the effect the previous evening's downpour had wrought on the footpath. I stepped over the first couple of puddles without a problem but soon I was slipping and sliding in the mud, almost losing my footing altogether on more than one occasion. The final straw came when I turned the corner close to Finham Brook and was faced with a newly formed lagoon fully twenty feet across. I had no alternative but to return the way I'd come, annoyed I'd not been able to complete my walk and because I'd now need to change my clothes before going back to work.

Oliver Neilson's net curtain moved enough to catch my eye as I crossed the road and put my key in the lock. I half expected him to pop out to assail me with another of his theories so I stepped inside, closing the door as quickly as I could.

The morning newspaper and two letters were lying on my mat and I could see from the envelope that one of them was a bill. I recognised the writing on the other but left it unopened until I'd prepared a sandwich. I scanned the headlines whilst making my cup of tea and on the fourth page was an article reporting the ongoing attacks on Jewish businesses in Birmingham. The number and severity of incidents were, in fact decreasing due, I believed, to disgust with Hitler's increased persecution of Jews in the ever-expanding Germany. Krystallnacht seemed to have been some kind of turning point in public opinion. Before that there'd been a gradual escalation in the Midlands leading up to the killing of a shopkeeper but over recent months the worst I'd seen was the fire at Goodman's warehouse. This wasn't to say things might not deteriorate again so efforts continued to be made to catch those behind the episodes, although it was unlikely Terry Gleeson would put in much time.

My second letter had a Lynton, Devon, postmark and a return address in Lynmouth written on the back. It was from Elizabeth Parry, my on-off girlfriend. Her parting note made it clear we'd probably no chance of a future together but still I held on to the hope she might change her mind.

Her letter began with the usual pleasantries; the weather, a holiday she'd taken in France and Italy, and how she was getting on with the solicitor's family for whom she now worked. Her new employer had clients in Germany and she'd heard many stories over recent months about the terrible things happening to Jews over there so enquired about my Uncle Gideon. My father had been receiving messages from him fairly regularly so we were satisfied he and his family were surviving despite widespread harassment by the Nazis. We knew Gideon wouldn't be safe forever but there was very little we could do, other than hope and pray for his family's safe keeping.

Elizabeth's letter finished with a few words which made me think I might see her again soon.

You'll remember Mrs Veasey, the cook from Grovestock House. She and I have kept in touch and she writes almost weekly. The poor woman has been increasingly ill since she stopped working at the House and so I've agreed to travel to Priors Allenford to stay with her for a few days. I don't have exact dates yet because I have to agree them with my employer, Mr Williams-Hogg, but I'll let you know when I'm there and perhaps we might meet if you happen to be in the area.

I returned to the station after lunch, where I found Sawyer, who had been busy in my absence. He'd found and visited every shop selling jewellery in the town, quizzing them about the crucifix.

'You know how many shops there are selling jewellery here in Kenilworth, sir?'

'Two or three at a guess.'

'Seven. You wouldn't think it, would you? Mind, they're not all proper jewellers — a couple are ladies' outfitters selling necklaces, brooches and bracelets as accessories and one sells bric-a-brac. There's also the pawn shop on that little street behind The Lion; he puts a few things in the window when they haven't been redeemed.'

'So did you find anything?'

'Well, I kept quiet why we were asking about it, as you'd suggested, sir — just said it was connected with a case we were looking at. Unfortunately, none of them recognised it. A couple looked at the hallmark and said they'd never ordered from that maker. In fact, they told me the cheaper jewellery often isn't hallmarked at all, so this must have been a bit more expensive. Did you know this stuff was made in Birmingham? Tons of it apparently.'

I did know this; I'd grown up only a stone's throw away from where most of it came from. Around twenty thousand people had been employed in jewellery manufacturing in Birmingham at the start of the Great War but they'd been badly hit in recent years, though it was still one of the major producers in the country. I asked Sawyer if he'd managed to interview all the shopkeepers.

'All except one. Watson's on the high street. There was a sign in the window saying they were closed due to illness. The young assistant in the shop next door said he was in hospital, expected out in the next few days but could be a bit longer before he gets back to work.' Sawyer thought for a moment. 'Have you considered it might not have been bought in Kenilworth, sir?'

'Well, of course I have, but we have to start somewhere, don't we? If there's so many possibilities in a small town like this just think how much walking you'll have to do if I send you off to check Warwick, Leamington and Coventry. Let's talk to Watson when he's back then see where we go from there.'

'This hallmark, sir?'

'What about it?'

'I was wondering, could we go at it the other way and contact the manufacturer? It should be easy enough to trace them from the marks. We could see if they might have a record of who they'd have supplied to in the area.'

'Good idea, John — you get on to it.'

Sawyer continued to justify my opinion that he'd make a good detective. He didn't just go through the motions on a case, he lived and breathed it, always trying to find that little bit of leverage to crack it open.

'Can I ask you something, sir?'

'Fire away.'

'You're working this other case in Coventry, aren't you?'

I was surprised he'd waited so long to ask me about it.

'I am.'

'Is it connected with this woman's murder?'

'No, why?'

'Well, I thought it might be, because Coventry's a different force, isn't it? I was thinking you were keeping me out of it for some reason.'

'Not at all. It's something I was assigned to before this one came up. Someone high up in the city police heard of the success I'd had in Birmingham with the attacks on Jewish businesses and asked Dyer if I could lend a hand with the ones in Coventry. It's only supposed to be one day a week and that's about as much as it takes just now.'

'Do you think they might have asked you because...' He struggled to finish when I raised my eyebrow. 'You know?'

'What, John? Come on, spit it out.'

'Because you're Jewish, sir. Could they have invited you because they know you're Jewish?'

It was something I'd considered, naturally.

'I don't think so. It's not something I put about and I'd think Dyer would be fairly discreet — I can't see me being his main topic of gossip at the monthly superintendents' meeting. Even if someone in Coventry did suspect, I'd hope they'd only invite me in because I have something to offer, either direct experience of similar cases or some kind of connection with the victims.'

I'm not sure if I sounded convincing to Sawyer but I was far from certain myself. I wanted to believe it was because a local senior officer knew the case might not get the attention it deserved if left to his own men, some of whom would carry the same prejudices as those committing the assaults. This would be bad enough, though I could live with it. Sadly, I was worried the motivation might be to simply pass the problem to the Jew boy from Kenilworth and let him clean up the mess. Not much I could do about it either way, other than attempting the best job possible.

I thanked him for his concern and asked if he had anything else. Sawyer passed me a list he'd collated of all the women reported missing over the previous three months within a twenty-five-mile radius of Kenilworth. I pointed out that the evidence from Walter Naismith about the French clothing might mean the victim wouldn't have been reported missing locally but we agreed to go ahead with what we had until we hit a brick wall. We excluded anyone over the age of thirty, then examined the files on each of the remaining eight. There were two matching the height of our victim but one of these was described as 'stout', leaving us with only one likely person, a Rose Spicer, whose father lived on the edge of the town.

EIGHT

Bill Webb's cottage was set back from the road, its long front garden still boasting a few remaining leeks, cabbages, kale and sprouts in immaculate beds. Most of the plot was now covered with a mulch of straw and horse manure, ready to be dug and planted when the ground warmed in the coming weeks. Several chickens pecked and clucked in a wire-enclosed run along one side where they were being used to clear and fertilise the soil for the new season just around the corner.

Rose's father invited Sawyer and me inside when I told him we were following up his daughter's disappearance. The house had the air of an older man living on his own. It wasn't a complete mess, simply not as well tended as it might be and I imagined he paid more attention to his vegetables than he did to dusting. I asked him to confirm the description we had from him on file.

'She's small, tiny really ... and skinny, like her Mum was, God rest her. Have you found Rose?'

'We don't know yet, sir, I'm afraid we need to ask you a few questions. How long since your wife died, Mr Webb?'

'She passed away three years ago, Inspector.' He shook his head. 'The wife and I had looked forward to spending more time together when Rose left home. Now all I have is work and my garden. Enough veg to feed an army and no-one to share it with. I thought I'd feel better when Rose came back but she was only here a few weeks then disappeared again.'

Sawyer glanced at me and I gave a brief shake of my head to tell him to keep quiet.

'Could you tell me why you reported your daughter missing?'

'One day in January I came back from work and she wasn't here. I didn't worry about it until the next day because she was a grown woman and, well, it wouldn't have been the first time she'd stayed out all night. When she hadn't come back by the next evening I checked her room and she didn't seem to have taken anything with her so I went into the police station. I haven't seen her since.'

'Was your daughter ever in France, Mr Webb?'

Webb clasped his hand over his mouth and closed his eyes for a few seconds.

'Something's happened to her, hasn't it? Is she —'

'Let's not jump to any conclusions yet. I take it she was in France?'

'Until early last year — March, I think. She'd been travelling for a while, a nanny to two boys in a place called Cassis in the south. I only remember it because she said it meant "blackcurrant" and brought me a bottle of cordial back as a present. The family returned to England so the children could start at boarding school. Didn't need Rose anymore and she came home. She seemed happy here, seemed to have lost the itchy feet, and even talked about settling down in Kenilworth. I told her she'd be welcome to stay here with me but she said she'd see. About a month later she picked up a shorthand typist's job at Coventry Council so lived over there for a while until she gave it up in November and moved in with me again.'

'You reported her as "Rose Spicer", not "Webb" — was she married?'

Webb hung his head. 'She was. To a no-good called Vincent Spicer.'

'Do you know where we might find him?'

'I wish I did, I'd give him a pasting for what he did to my little Rose.'

I asked him to explain and he told me he'd worked as an engineer before he retired. His specialism had been car gearboxes and he'd been offered good money to move with his family to Spain to use his expertise for a new manufacturer. When they'd been out there about three years Rose, who was only sixteen at the time, took up with Spicer, a man fifteen years her senior. The pair of them disappeared one weekend and came back married.

'I was livid. Tried to get it annulled but Rose would have none of it. I knew Spicer was no good the first time I clapped eyes on him but she wouldn't listen and even I didn't realise how much of a bad 'un he was. It turned out he drank like a fish and was a terrible womaniser with a fierce temper, though I never heard of him laying a hand on Rose 'cos if he had I'd have been strung up for him.'

'What happened?'

'Before long he and Rose were arguing all the time; then he just upped and left. Dumped her with a load of debts. I assumed he'd gone off with another woman stupid enough to take him. Rose told me that the night before he went he said if he ever found she'd been unfaithful he'd kill her.'

Webb confirmed that he hadn't seen Vincent Spicer since the day he disappeared. Then I showed him the crucifix. He turned it over several times in his mud-caked hands and I sensed he was trying to make some kind of connection with his daughter through it.

'Sorry, Inspector, I don't recognise it, but I wouldn't know all of my daughter's jewellery. What father would? I do know Rose had more or less given up on religion after her mum died so can't see why she'd want something like this.'

'Just one final thing, Mr Webb — could you tell me your wife's first name?'

I knew what the answer would be before he spoke.

'It was Josie, Inspector. Short for Josephine.'

The bracelet found on the woman's body only confirmed the inevitable. Our victim was Rose Spicer.

I sent Sawyer home to print photographs of Rose from a negative her father had dug out. My colleague had a darkroom in the spare bedroom of his father's house and because it was Friday afternoon it was much quicker to have him do it than mess about putting a request in through the station, then waiting until Monday when the photographer would be back. I'd told him to call to the school when he finished and ask if anyone recognised her.

For my part, I visited the library and dug up a guide to southern France. I discovered Cassis is a small town about twenty miles from Marseilles, not as fashionable as the resorts further along the coast but it has a pretty harbour and the Mediterranean sun shines down on it just the same.

I was in Marseilles once, but didn't venture far from the port. There was no need because every appetite was catered for on the dockside or in the street market selling everything from chickens to three-piece suits. If it wasn't available there amongst the lettuces, strawberries, wine and honey then it would be easy to find in the dozens of cafés, restaurants and seedy hotels within a ten-minute walk of our berth.

All I'd wanted was a drink or two and few hands of cards and I found both in the Café d'Angelique a couple of minutes from the docks. Sailors from all corners of the globe frequented the place and were, like me, happy to part with their money in the bar or in exchange for the favours of one of Angelique's girls in an upstairs room. The owner, Angelique herself, was a horror and tried to cover up her sixty-odd years with lipstick, rouge and revealing clothes, but she had a good sense of humour and took no nonsense from her customers. I was only in the city for a few days. I shed no tears when I left and never had a desire to return.

I walked back to the police station in the freezing cold and pouring rain, still thinking about the days I'd spent working and relaxing in climates far more pleasant than this cold, wet English winter. My reading about France made me yearn for sunshine on my face, heat on my back. I had the benefit of a brolly and a hat but my trousers were still drenched by the time I got back to my office and when Sawyer joined me he looked like he'd got it even worse than me.

He pulled off his cape and helmet and hung them on the radiator to dry.

'Cats and dogs out there, sir — for once I'm glad to be working inside.'

Sawyer loved the outdoors — one of the reasons he insisted in keeping his rural beat was it allowed him to spend his days wandering the countryside either on foot or by bicycle. When he wasn't working he'd be helping his father out on the farm, tending dairy cattle or ploughing near-perfect furrows in the fields. I couldn't work out if he'd make a better farmer or copper and doubted if he'd made a decision on which way he wanted his life to go. Perhaps that was another reason he was resisting a move to a detective, to avoid actually having to commit himself one way or the other. It wasn't that he wasn't already performing well in his police duties but he had the potential to go far and I just wished he'd see he couldn't achieve it unless he was prepared to give up his outside interests.

He sat down on the opposite side of the desk and flipped open his notebook.

'I've seen everyone again, all except Neilson, who wasn't in, and all of them say they don't know a Rose Spicer. The photo didn't help either, although one or two of the longer serving staff said she looked vaguely familiar. Miss Clements thought Rose was the woman she saw on the school playing field and going into the church.'

I asked if he believed them.

'Strange thing was, I did in the main, with the exception of Alan Johnston. There was something made me think he knew her. I didn't like him, you know — seemed to be laughing at me all the time, as if he thought he was getting one over on us.'

'Was it enough for us to bring him in?'

'I don't think so, sir — it was just the way he answered my questions. Have to say he didn't give a lot away.'

'All right, we'll leave him for now. Who was it said they recognised her?'

'Well, "recognise" would be a bit far. Only the headmaster and Mr Sprigg, the caretaker, said she reminded them of someone, but couldn't call to mind who it was. Later I wondered if she might have been a past pupil but, if she was, you'd have thought they'd have known her name.'

'Did you not tell them her maiden name?'

Sawyer spotted his error straight away and blushed. He'd have to learn to control that before he was much longer in the force.

'Sorry, sir, it was stupid but I didn't think about it. I'll telephone Mr Perelle when we've finished and ask him to check with the others.'

'What do you think about this Vincent Spicer character?'

'Well, I don't know — is it likely that he would come back from Spain just to have a go at Rose?'

'I suppose there's always a chance, isn't there? If he was as jealous as Bill Webb suggested and he heard she'd met a bloke here you wouldn't be surprised. You'd best see if you can trace him.'

Sawyer left my office, but was back only a few minutes later.

'By God, that man's an arrogant bugger, sir,' he said. He told me he'd spoken to Perelle on the phone, filling him in on Rose's maiden name. 'Can you believe he almost accused me of wasting his time? Said if I'd told him this earlier he could have saved a lot of messing about and needless conversations.'

'He knew her then?'

'Oh yes, sir. As soon as I gave him the name he remembered her. Said she'd been in his class for a time but left when her family moved to Spain. She'd have been about thirteen years old. He claimed not to have seen her since.'

'Any luck with the other staff?'

'Not so far. Perelle said he'd ask them and get back to me. None of the other teachers would have been around then. Possibly the cook and the caretaker were but I can't see either of them killing a young woman, can you?'

'Well, they'd be pretty low on my list of suspects, John, I agree. This is getting worse and worse. If we've got to find and interview everybody who worked at the school when Rose was there it will be a nightmare.'

'I'll see what I can dig up, sir. At least we know your neighbour was one of them, so he'll be easy to get to.'

He was right — I was sure to bump into Neilson again before too long, whether I wanted to or not.

I didn't have to wait too long for my neighbour to show up. I'd barely been home long enough to take off my coat and scarf when he knocked at my door.

'Evening, Mr Given — do you have a minute?'

Neilson had saved me the trouble of calling to him but I was getting a bit fed up with his interference in the case and wanted to tell him so. Before I could say anything he pulled a handwritten note from his pocket.

'Your colleague — Constable Sawyer, isn't it? — left this. Seems he called when I was up in the town. Says he wants to see me. I bumped into Mrs Perelle whilst I was out and she told me you'd identified the young woman who was killed. I thought I'd just call at your door and ask if you need to talk to me — or should I wait to see Constable Sawyer?'

I hoped my sigh would give him the hint that I really would have preferred it if he'd waited to see Sawyer rather than bothering me at home but I could hardly send him away.

'You'd best step inside, Mr Neilson — I'll show you her photograph. I have it in my jacket pocket.'

We went through to my sitting room. I didn't want him comparing my kitchen to his own, nor did I offer him a cup of tea.

'This is the woman. Rose Spicer's her name. Ring any bells? Webb was her maiden name, if that helps.'

Neilson gave the picture a quick look.

'I'm afraid the name "Spicer" means nothing to me, Inspector. I'd have known several Webbs but I can't recall a Rose just now. There's something niggling at the back of my mind but it won't come out.' He laughed. 'Old age, I suspect. I'm not quite in my dotage but the memory isn't what it was — I seem to forget more and more every day.'

'I understand she'd have attended Hannah's about nine or ten years ago. You'd have been there then?'

'Well I was, but I still don't remember the name. It's such a long time ago. Perhaps she wasn't in any of my classes.'

'Have another look at the photograph, Mr Neilson — anything there?'

He looked at it again, rising and taking it closer to my lamp. He examined it close to and at arm's length, both with and without his glasses. I had the distinct impression he was playing for effect. Eventually he sat down and handed the photograph back.

'There is something but I'm not sure I should say — it might be nothing and might cause trouble for someone who's not involved in her ... death.'

'You've carefully avoided the word "murder" twice, Mr Neilson, but that's what it is, you know. Not a game, not some vague intellectual exercise and not a story from some cheap detective novel. It's the cold-blooded murder of a young woman at the school where you used to work. Now, tell me what you know and I'll be the judge of whether it's relevant or not.'

Neilson looked taken aback by the harshness of my reply and could have clammed up but I was sure his appetite to be involved would outweigh any offence taken. I wasn't wrong.

'If that's your view, Inspector, I believe I saw this woman down by the castle just after I moved in here.'

'Can you be sure it was her?'

'Well, I wouldn't bet my pension on it, but I'd be quite confident. I noticed her particularly because she was walking arm in arm with a young man I'd know. I don't think he saw me, or just didn't recognise me out of school, paying too much notice of his little lady friend.'

I remembered the half-seen movement in Neilson's window when I'd been crossing the road at lunchtime and wondered if that's how he'd actually observed them, rather than being out on a walk. He'd have relished feeding me information but he wouldn't want me thinking of him a busybody.

'From school? Who?'

Neilson smiled. He now knew I'd have to pay attention to him.

'Oh, it was the groundsman, Inspector. Alan Johnston.'

NINE

Johnston didn't seem surprised when he was picked up. Sawyer said he'd acted as if he'd been expecting it. Sawyer and I, along with two other constables, had called to the groundsman's house soon after I'd spoken to Neilson. He wasn't there, though Stella was. After she'd asked why we wanted him, and after I wouldn't tell her, she told us he was still at work. I sent the others off to the school to find him and I waited with his wife in case he returned home before they got there.

Stella Johnston wasn't dressed as well as when I'd last seen her and I imagined she'd only recently arrived back from work herself. Even in headscarf and wraparound pinafore her good looks shone through. She ushered me into the front room and appeared a few minutes later with a tray of tea and sponge cake, the cups rattling in their saucers when she lowered it to the table.

'Alan's not in bad trouble, is he, Mr Given? Please tell me he isn't.'

'As I've already said, Mrs Johnston, I can't tell you why we need to talk to him. Is there something you think he might be in trouble for?'

She shook her head and spoke in a whisper.

'No, nothing.'

A layer of dust on the shelves and chair backs told me the Johnstons' parlour wasn't used very often and would only have been spruced up for visitors and treated to the occasional spring clean. I thought it a shame because the bay window offered a view of the small cottage garden where, even now, there was some colour from snowdrops and crocuses pushing through and daffodil buds waiting to burst. Alan Johnston, or his wife, kept the plot tidy and, even at this time of year, they'd dug a corner to prepare for new plants in the coming weeks.

A sideboard against one wall of the room held a number of photographs in cheap-looking frames, two of Stella Johnston in a wedding dress. The dresses and the men in each were different so she'd clearly been married twice. One of the photographs was with Alan but in the other Stella was younger and with a much older man. I took this to be her father but the rest of the photographs were family snaps and there was none with her and another groom, so perhaps her current husband didn't like to be reminded about his predecessor. I found it hard to believe, with the woman's good looks, she'd have married someone a lot older than herself.

I drank my tea and waited. And waited. Alan Johnston didn't appear and his wife talked incessantly about nothing: her cleaning job, new patterns she'd seen and was considering buying. She talked about her garden and how she tried to keep it colourful all through the year, Alan's love of the outdoors, days out they'd had and were planning, almost anything to avoid a silence. I asked her about the man in the wedding photograph.

'Is that your father?'

Stella chuckled. 'You'd think so, wouldn't you? Seems such an old man. Actually, he's my first husband, Dave Butler. He was in the Navy and we married when I was very young, just seventeen. Dad had to give his consent. Dave told me I'd get to travel all around the world but I didn't. Stuck in married quarters down south on my own most of the time, so eventually I came home, here, to stay with my Mum.'

'You're divorced?'

'No, he died.'

'I'm sorry to hear that.'

She laughed again, this time more grimly. 'Don't be, he was an animal. As soon as we were married he turned out to be drunk half the time and jealous all of the time. He'd come home from sea, rant and rave about who he thought I was seeing when he was away, then knock back too much rum and give me the back of his hand. He was all tears and apologies afterwards but I was glad when I was rid of him.'

I was shocked at how much bitterness she put into these words. It must have been very bad for her to be tied to a man who thought it his God-given right to beat her up, then blame alcohol and her imagined infidelity as an excuse.

'Did he die at sea?'

'No. Silly fool was drunk one night, as usual, and some fellers set on him in Portsmouth. Left him pretty bad they did, but they didn't kill him. He was in hospital for weeks and seemed to be recovering, but he took a turn and died, right out of the blue.'

'I was in a hospital down that way once — which one was it?'

'It was a Navy place near Gosport. Haslar, I think it was called. They seemed to look after him very well, but it was hard for me to get to from up here, so I only went a couple of times.'

I knew the place. A friend of mine had shifted from my boat to the service of the king and had ended up in the Royal Hospital Haslar when he slipped on the deck and badly broken his ankle. I happened to be docked in Southampton at the time so hitch-hiked over to see him. It's a massive and imposing building and its history alone would be enough to impress. The blood of thousands of sailors and other servicemen from

Trafalgar, Corunna, Waterloo, Crimea and the Great War had spilt on its floors.

'Any idea why he was attacked, or who did it?'

'It could have been anybody. Dave could upset a saint when he'd been drinking. The police said he'd probably had an argument in a pub and they'd followed him after he left. I don't think much effort was made to investigate though, even after he died. One more sailor in a fight on shore was hardly going to get much police attention, was it?'

I had to agree with her. We continued chatting about nothing in particular until a message arrived that Alan Johnston had been found and taken to the station. Stella Johnston wanted to come with me but I told her not to bother.

'We'll release him or send for you as soon as we've finished chatting with Alan, though I wouldn't wait up. It might be a long night.'

Alan Johnston was sprawled on an interview room chair with Sawyer and I across the table. He stubbed his cigarette in the ashtray when I asked my first question.

'Now, Mr Johnston, you've not been telling us the whole truth, have you?'

He obviously knew he'd been found out but tried to feign bewilderment.

'How do you mean?'

'You told Constable Sawyer here that you didn't know Rose Spicer, but a little birdie has led us to believe that's not the case. Do you want to change your story?'

Johnston gave what I'm sure he thought it was a disarming smile, one he knew worked with the ladies and hoped would show we were both men of the world.

'What else could I do? It was nothing, just a walk and a quick snog now and again. I thought if I'd said anything to you then Stella would have found out and she'd have crucified me.'

I asked him how long he'd been seeing Rose.

'Only a few weeks. She came up to me in the pub one evening in November when I was on my own and she was with a couple of friends. One minute we were just talking and the next she was pulling me into the lane at the back. She told me later she'd seen me around and fancied me so turned up that night on purpose, hoping I'd be there.'

It seemed Rose was no shrinking violet. If she was so forward and free with her affections she might easily court disaster if she got in with the wrong sort of man. Could Alan Johnston be one?

'And how often did you meet?'

He said it would have been only once a week, to avoid Stella Johnston guessing he was up to something, so they'd seen each other just four or five times. He claimed they always met on a Wednesday when his wife regularly went out for a couple of hours so he'd be able to slip away and be back with her none the wiser.

'And didn't you think it odd when Rose disappeared?'

'Not really. She'd arrived out of nowhere and I thought she'd just headed off again. I was a bit miffed she hadn't told me she was going, but that was all.'

'Did you try looking for Rose?'

I guessed he wasn't the kind of man who would be doing the chasing.

'As I said, I thought she'd just changed her mind, and when I didn't hear from her over the next day or so I assumed she'd moved on. I could hardly go calling round her house to check, could I?'

Sawyer interjected. 'Did you kill her, Johnston?'

'What? No, of course not. What kind of bloke do you think I am?'

'We don't know, do we? You're clearly the kind who'd cheat on his wife. You're also the kind who'd lie to the police. How do we know you're not lying again to save your skin?'

Johnston looked at Sawyer, then at me.

'I'm not lying, Mr Given — you have to believe me. I couldn't kill anyone. Rose and me had a good time for a few weeks then she didn't turn up one night. It's not the first time I've been dumped and I didn't think anything of it. Until she turned up under the chapel I thought she'd just got fed up of me.'

Sawyer and I pushed him for a while longer but he didn't budge from his story, though by the time we'd finished with him he was a lot less cocky than when we started. He had a real look of dread on his face as we let him go. 'You don't need to tell my wife anything about me and Rose, do you? I'm sure she hasn't guessed and my life won't be worth living if she finds out.' I found it amusing how he was still more frightened of Stella's reaction to his infidelity than of being a potential suspect in a murder case. It was something I might be able to use to my advantage.

'That's something I'll have to think about, Alan. If you've been a naughty boy then you'll have to take the consequences when your wife finds out, won't you?'

'Please, Mr Given, I had nothing to do with Rose's death, I promise. Don't say anything to Stella about why you had me back in.'

I couldn't really see any benefit in sharing his indiscretion any time soon with Stella Johnston, but it did no harm to keep him on his toes.

TEN

The next day should have been my first day off for almost two weeks but I spent the afternoon in my Coventry office, going through what we had on the attacks on Jewish homes and businesses. I had my personal reasons for searching for the "Italians". Strictly speaking they were Sicilian, a difference they'd told me they'd defend to their dying breaths, though one probably lost on most casual observers. There was no doubt in my mind that they were linked to the attacks on Dembowitz's shop and the Goodmans' warehouse, so I could have justified hunting them down in work time on that premise alone. But we had another history altogether, so I considered a few hours on my Saturday as time well spent.

I cross-checked the incident files against my personal ones on the Demma brothers' vicious careers stretching over a decade or more. At times I'd been close to putting them in the frame for Heather's murder, which they'd committed years before, but then they'd disappear again. Now they seemed to be popping up more and more, linked to this Fascist thuggery. Small hints in the reports started to slot into place. There were several references to men with 'black hair' and 'strange accents', and now Mueller's comments had given me the context they made sense.

It was growing dark when I made my way down the road to the Queen's Hotel on Hertford Street and though there were other drinking holes closer to my office, I was starving and knew I'd get a late lunch and cup of tea at the Queen's cafeteria with no bother. I thought it was quiet for a Saturday afternoon, though I'd never been in at the weekend before. On weekdays there'd usually be small groups of businessmen taking afternoon tea or something a little stronger and doing the deals which make the world go round.

My sandwich comprised fresh bread and somewhat older boiled eggs, judging by the smell. I was in two minds whether to chance them but my appetite got the better of me. I wolfed it down, avoiding contact with my taste buds as far as possible. I'd photographs of Benito and Paúlu Demma in my pocket but neither the doorman nor the bar manager recognised either of them. I can't say I was surprised; despite the dire food the place was probably still too upmarket for those two.

Criss-crossing the tramlines, I moved my search on to the Rose and Crown, then the Craven Arms, both on High Street, again without success. I spiralled outwards from Broadgate, pub after pub, hating every minute of fighting the temptation to sit down and play cards, to drink and joke with new-found companions, knowing that if I succumbed even once, it would be the slippery slope. There were a number of Temperance hotels around the city centre, where alcohol and gambling were off limits, but I couldn't imagine Benito Demma trying his recruitment in those, so there was no respite available.

No-one had anything to tell me until, on The Burges, I struck lucky when the landlord of the Coventry Cross recognised Benito's picture.

'He was in here a week or two back, looking for George Barber. I told him George hadn't been in for a while but I'd pass on a message if he liked.'

George Barber was a small-time thief and shoplifter, not known for his brain power. I wondered why Benito might have wanted him.

'And did he ask you to?'

'He said to tell George he was back in town and wanted to hook up with him.'

'So did you pass it on?'

'Not had a chance. George would only come in now and again, not really a regular, and I haven't seen him since this bloke came in.'

'Any idea where George usually takes a pint?'

'North end of the city, I think. That pub on Foleshill Road, you know the one. What's it called?'

I shook my head.

'The General Wolfe! That's it. I think George lives just around the corner from there.'

I asked for directions and realised it was only a few streets away from the Goodman's warehouse.

It was far too late to get out to Foleshill before closing time so I continued to trawl the pubs and hotels around the city centre, now asking about Barber as well as the Demmas. By ten o'clock I wasn't much further forward. A couple of barmen had seen either one or the other but not in the last few nights.

The door of the King's Head swung open as I was reaching for the handle to leave another fruitless enquiry and a tall man, head bowed, pushed in. It was the German I'd interviewed the previous week.

'Mr Mueller?'

He squinted whilst his eyes adjusted to the light.

'Ah, Inspector Given, it is you. Good evening. Will you join me in a drink? I would welcome some company.'

Even though his words were slurred, as if he'd been looking for company for a few hours, I agreed to sit with him on the off chance he might have seen the Demmas on his travels. I bought him a whisky and a cordial for myself and joined him at a table near the fire.

'You're celebrating something, Mr Mueller?'

'Celebrating? Or drowning my sorrows maybe?'

'Problems?'

'Only the problem we're all facing, Inspector, though for some the choices are more difficult. Everyone knows war is coming. And my country is the enemy. If I stay in England your people will lock me up. If I go back to Germany my people will force me to fight for a cause I despise.'

I acknowledged he was between a rock and a hard place.

'So what will you do?'

'This is what I'm trying to decide, though this —' he lifted his glass — 'is not making it simpler. I am thinking I might try to go to America but it would not be easy. I am not a skilled man, I sweep a factory floor, would I get a job there? And what happens if the Americans join in, would they lock me up too?'

There was nothing I could offer him in the way of advice. It occurred to me there must be many people like him here and in Germany who were against Hitler's thinking but couldn't escape what was coming. So it felt for many of us.

Mueller hadn't seen the Demmas since his last encounter in the Ragged Staff so we talked a little longer until he finished his drink and made for the bar. He offered to buy me another but I made my apologies and wished him well before trying one last possibility.

Harry Bates had just called last orders in the Clarendon when I walked in.

'Sorry, sir, I can't be serving you now, you should have been in earlier.'

I told him who I was looking for and he didn't seem best pleased by having the end of his night complicated by a policeman asking questions. He continued clearing glasses and wiping down the bar while he talked.

'They were in last week, all three of them, but not since. Sat in the corner talking for about an hour. Toe-rags, I knew they were up to something. George was chatting away and the older of the foreigners kept making notes. That's all I know. Can I get on now?'

I thanked Bates for his help then left him to put up the towels and clear out his stragglers. There were a few pubs I still hadn't visited and was sure they'd be serving after hours. However, I also suspected they were of the type who would never give anything away to a copper in a million years. Easier to call it a night than waste my time in places where I knew I'd get nothing.

ELEVEN

It was Sunday and I stayed in bed until late. Outside it was wet, windy and bitingly cold, so, after a comforting breakfast of sausages, bacon and eggs — the pork a guilty pleasure I'd developed since I started hiding my religion — I piled coal on the fire and settled down to catch up with the newspapers. So much for my resolve to cut down on the food and to take more exercise.

The *Sunday Express* was full of speculation about Adolph Hitler's plans, with more than one commentator siding with the Prime Minister's continuing aspirations for a peaceful settlement and a similar number banging the drum for a military solution. The debate was echoed in the *Leamington Courier* with reports of both the local 'Pals' Regiment reunion and the annual meeting of the Leamington branch of the League of Nations Union discussing the need for increasing armed forces recruitment. For my part, like Mueller, I was pretty sure there'd now be little chance of avoiding conflict with Germany, who seemed to desire total domination of Europe. Many feared the Nazis would soon be satisfying their appetite by swarming across the Channel if Britain didn't take action in the near future.

The news on the wireless was no better, with reports from Czechoslovakia about the imminent German invasion and the terrible loss of life at the siege of Madrid. Fortunately there was some lighter relief later with Freddie Grisewood and a gardening programme, though I even grew bored with these and turned my mind to Rose Spicer's death.

It was frustrating because we had so little to go on. Despite Walter's reluctance to commit to it being a murder, I was convinced it was because all the facts pointed that way so I'd treat it as such until it was shown not to be. So who did we have as suspects? No-one and everyone. Without a certain date and time for when she died we couldn't exclude anyone. In the last year the girl had lived in France, Coventry and Kenilworth and, if Alan Johnston's account was anything to go on, she could have had any number of male friends in any of those places. Rose had also attended the school where her body was found so it could be linked to her past there.

I scribbled ideas and scratched my head for an hour or two, getting nowhere and finally succumbing to my growing hunger for my midday meal. After a lunch of lamb cutlets, potatoes and cabbage, followed by apple tart and custard, I put work to one side, settled back and nodded off to the music of Grieg and the BBC Scottish Orchestra.

My snoozing was fitful, marred by dreams of churches, dead children and the Demma brothers, until I woke, shivering, with the fire all but extinct and a feeling that I'd been disturbed by the clatter of my letterbox.

It was murky in the hall with rain driving hard against the door and a note on my mat feebly reflecting the gaslight from the streetlamp outside. No envelope, no address, just a folded sheet from an exercise book.

I dashed out into the deluge and peered in both directions but there was no-one to be seen in the darkness. Along the street a light went out in Oliver Neilson's window. Could he have dropped the note in? Perhaps he'd knocked earlier and failed to wake me so decided to write a message instead.

Back inside I unfolded the paper and could see it wasn't from Neilson, unless he was trying to disguise his identity. The handwriting was tidy but immature, with some hints of the writer's own style. One particular feature was that he, or she, hadn't mastered the letter 's' and wherever it was used at the start of a word it was ill-formed, with no flow and much more like a printed letter than the usual cursive. It addressed me as 'Dear Inspector' and wasn't signed.

You do not know me but I know you. I heard that the dead lady was Rose and I thought I should tell you she was arguing with the man who looks after the school fields at Hannah's. I never heard what they was saying but he was shouting very loudly. I hope you catch whoever did it.

The more I looked at it the more curious it seemed. The vocabulary and syntax looked childish but there was something suggesting it was more adult, as if there was a crude effort at imitation. But was it a child trying to appear more grown up or vice versa? Then there was the use of the murdered woman's Christian name as if the writer knew her well. Was it familiarity or was it another attempt at obfuscation? I looked again at the paper, its ragged edge showing it had been torn, not cut with scissors, from its book. I thought I'd probably be able to buy a similar quality from half a dozen shops in the town so knew it wouldn't reveal anything to lead me to its owner.

I'd been convinced of Alan Johnston's truthfulness in his second interview but it was obvious we'd have to have him in again on the basis of this new information. We had put him under a lot of pressure last time so I was surprised he might still be lying. I couldn't fathom how he'd be so stupid as to assume we wouldn't find out. There was the chance, of course, that the note was a hoax of some kind, aimed to put us off the scent of whoever might be involved in Rose's death. I just hoped it wasn't some kind of child's silly joke, thinking it would be great fun to get the groundsman into trouble with the police.

After an almost sleepless night I walked up to the school to have a word with Laurence Perelle on my way to work. The wind and rain had battered my roof until the small hours but even without the racket I doubt if I'd have slept much better. It had been a mistake to spend so much time mulling over the case, and the note I'd received had only added to my restlessness. The weather had eased and most times my morning ramble would have lifted my spirits, especially with the sunlight bringing out the colours on the houses up the hill, but today it didn't. The sun was still too low to have penetrated the school yard and I shivered when I entered the gate then shivered again at the sight of schoolchildren already out on the playing fields in shorts and football kit, their shouts and shrieks bouncing off the school walls.

The headmaster was tied up in lessons but his wife invited me into the house and offered me a cup of tea.

'I'll not have one just now, Mrs Perelle. I just called in to ask your husband to cast an eye over a note I've received. See if he recognises the handwriting from one of the pupils. I've a feeling it is just some silly prank a child has thought would be funny.'

Once again I wondered how Perelle had landed such a beautiful younger woman for his wife. Her complexion was remarkably light for someone with such dark hair and her green silk blouse brought out the full effect of her hazel eyes. She agreed to ask the headmaster to have a look at the note and I started to leave.

'Oh, please don't go yet, Inspector. I get so few visitors — stay a little while and chat. Are you sure you won't have that tea?'

This time, I agreed. It was certainly a more appetising prospect than seeing the desk sergeant's ugly mug at this time of the morning.

'It's strange we haven't met before, Mrs Perelle — you'd have been in Kenilworth about as long as I have, and we're practically neighbours.'

'I'm afraid we don't socialise in the town much, my husband prefers to stay within the confines of his little world in the school.'

She was smiling when she spoke, though her tone suggested this wasn't the life she would have preferred.

'I suspect he carries a lot of responsibility with his job. And he does seem very dedicated to his research.'

'Research? Oh, you mean his biology. Oh dear, those things give me the shivers. I never go into his room. I tell him I can't understand how anyone could cut up and display poor little creatures like that. He always says that we'd have no medical knowledge unless someone was prepared to do it and I suppose he's right. But still.'

I admitted that I felt much the same about them.

'But you must be used to seeing dead bodies, Inspector.'

'You never get used to it, Mrs Perelle, or at least I never have. Even so, those specimens are different. Whether it's the preservative or the dissection I don't know but so many of them bear little resemblance to the living animals. In most cases a dead human body looks the same as a live one.'

Whilst we were talking, the headmaster's wife continually rubbed at her left wrist and at one point I caught a glimpse of a purplish-black bruise beneath her cuff. She noticed I'd seen and immediately covered it.

'I'm so clumsy, you know. I caught my coat sleeve on a door handle when I dashed through, giving my arm a tremendous clout when the door slammed shut. The pain made me sit on the stairs for ages with tears running down my face.'

I didn't believe her. They were more like wounds I'd seen where a person had been forcibly restrained and I suspected with distaste that Perelle was violent towards his wife.

She turned the conversation to lighter topics and I asked how she'd met her husband.

'My father was headmaster before Laurence. I was very young when he came to the school, about fourteen or fifteen, and Dad would invite him over in the evenings for a sherry and a game of chess. Laurence just became part of the furniture and it seemed natural to say yes when he asked me out. He was clever and witty — then — so I agreed to marry him when Dad announced his retirement and even though he's a good bit older it didn't bother me at the time. There was no-one else on the horizon so it was the obvious thing to do.'

She looked so sad and I thought was time for me to leave, before I strayed further into their troubled relationship. When I stood I remembered she had a box of correspondence from past pupils, so asked if she'd compare the note I'd left for Perelle with her cards and letters if she had a chance.

When I turned at the gate, Emily Perelle was still on the front step. She waved and called so quietly I could barely make out her words. Nonetheless, they stayed with me for all of the day.

'Do call again, Inspector, it was so lovely to talk with you.'

Sawyer was in the station and hard at work by the time I

arrived. He passed me a file before I sat down.

'Dr Naismith sent this round an hour ago. Don't know how he does that job; it fair put me off my breakfast just reading it. He's put "cardiac arrest" as his best guess at cause of death. Says he'd not even have been able to get that close if the body hadn't been so well preserved.'

'Cardiac arrest? That's damned unbelievable, John. She was only in her twenties. If that was the cause then why was her body posed like it was? She'd not have been likely to feel a heart attack coming on then simply lie down on a convenient mattress and say her prayers, now would she?'

I slammed the file down on my desk so hard poor Sawyer must have thought I was having a go at him.

'I'm sorry, sir, I'm only passing on what's in the report.'

'What? No, I know, I wasn't blaming you. This case is just getting to me. I'd bet my house that someone murdered the woman but now even the doctor won't confirm it. Did he say anything about the hammer?'

'Only reported what he'd suggested to you earlier; there was no significant damage to her skull and the flesh was so far gone he couldn't tell if there was any bruising. Said its presence at the scene was "unexplained though it could have contributed to rendering the woman unconscious". Bit scared of committing himself, isn't he, sir?'

'He's a good man so I suppose he's only doing his job, same as we have to do ours. He knows if we took the case to court without fool proof evidence the judge would throw the book at us. I'll phone Walter later for the unofficial version, the stuff he wouldn't put in the report. Was there anything else?'

'I was just coming to that, sir. There are a couple of things.'

Sawyer had followed up on Rose's first husband, Vincent Spicer, who had lived in Lincoln before moving to Spain. He had a string of offences to his name, most of them minor frauds committed against vulnerable women, and there were several warrants issued for his arrest, which is probably why he left the country. It seemed his mother was still in touch and he'd been in prison over there for the last nine months. Spicer had conned a considerable sum out of a lady friend, only to discover she was the wife of the local police superintendent. Comisario Principal Rafael Abascal was not best pleased with either the lady or Spicer and made sure he extracted the maximum sentence from the court.

'Seems like he can't have been our man, sir — he'd have been inside when Rose died.'

'So that's another possibility dried up. There was something else?'

'Yes, sir — it seems Alan Johnston has past form in the adultery department.'

'How so?'

'One or two people I've spoken to around the town have hinted he was involved with Stella while she was still married to her sailor boy.'

'Well, it wasn't hard to guess he'd an eye for the ladies, and them for him. Does that make him a potential murderer?'

I filled Sawyer in on the message I'd had through my letterbox. He seized on this to confirm the conclusion he was already forming.

'So if Johnston and Rose were fighting, perhaps he saw red and was not able to stop himself?'

'But the writer doesn't say they heard any more than an argument. Surely he, or she, would have been able to tell if it became violent. And even if Johnston had just lost his temper he'd have been more likely to have beaten her to death or strangled her. I assume Naismith would have spotted either of those.'

'The doctor does say Rose could have been hit on the head with the hammer we found.'

'Stop clutching at straws, John. You already said he doesn't have that as the cause of death, and why would Johnston have gone into the church, taken Arthur Sprigg's hammer and then gone out to the playing field to meet Rose? Don't you think he'd have enough tools of his own in his shed to have done the job just as well?'

'Unless he was planning to kill her but wanted to pin it on someone else?'

'But then your red mist argument falls down, John. This was premeditated. Someone knocked the woman out down in the crypt then finished her off, posing her on the mattress to leave a message. I can't see Johnston losing it, clobbering Rose over the head with a weapon he handily brought with him, dragging her body into the church and down the steps, somehow conjuring up a heart attack along the way, then calmly laying her out like she was some medieval knight.'

'But —'

'No "buts", John. I'm not striking Johnston out, just simply not agreeing with your version of events. You bring him back in and I'll see what else Dr Naismith can tell us.'

Walter was noncommittal when I rang, saying he'd put everything he'd found into his report. He said he'd looked for physical signs like strangulation, gunshot or knife wounds, and beating but there weren't any, other than the possibility of a hammer blow heavy enough to knock her out but too light to cause bone damage. Even this largely based on the presence of the hammer at the scene. Smothering had also been excluded, simply on the basis of lack of evidence. He insisted again that there was nothing to officially lead him to a firm conclusion she'd been murdered and he'd reflected this in his findings.

'Come on, Walter, I know you better than that. We both recognise this can't have been a plain and simple heart attack. Look at her age and the location. What about the way she was laid out? You even said yourself that she probably couldn't have wrapped the necklace round her hands on her own. You must have a theory.'

I heard him sigh at the other end of the line.

'Of course I've a theory, James, several in fact, but nothing I'm going to stake my reputation on.'

'I'm not asking you to do that. Just give me an idea of how such a young woman came to die.'

'Well, that bit's fairly straightforward. "Cardiac arrest" is the medical term but it's just another way of saying her heart stopped beating. Why it stopped beating is quite another matter. It could have been a problem she was born with, or a fright, or even poisoning.'

'Poison?'

'Quite a few poisons — cyanide, for example — can bring on a heart attack. Some do it quickly; some take hours or even days. I assume it would have needed to have been one of the fast ones, if it was done at all. There was no blood left in the body to check for toxins though most of them would be impossible to detect after such a long period anyway. Normally, I might also have expected to see other symptoms, like lung damage, if Rose Spicer had been poisoned, but none of the major organs were in a condition to carry out the necessary tests when I opened her up.'

'But it is a possibility?'

'Yes, James, it's possible. Other than that, she may have had a history of heart problems, diagnosed or not. If that's the case then the potential causes of the heart attack widen even further. For what it's worth, my money, like yours, is that it wasn't natural causes, but I can't say that without the evidence. I could refer it up the line if you don't think I'm up to it?'

'God no, Walter, don't do that. Of course I trust your judgement, I'm just frustrated by how difficult it is to get any progress on this one. On top of that, if you ask one of the higher-ups to take a look we'll have Scotland Yard down here in two shakes, poking their noses in where they're not wanted. Keep it local for now and see if you can find anything to give us a clue about what happened.'

'Alright, James, if you're so convinced then I'll do some digging through her medical records when I can get hold of them. I'll also check if there are any more tests I can do just in case we can find a poison. Will that keep you happy?'

'It will, Walter. Thanks.'

I put down the receiver and wondered where a break was going to come from on this case.

TWELVE

It took less than an hour to have Johnston picked up again and this time he was surly and demanding a solicitor.

'You're welcome to wait while we find you one, Alan. I assume you don't have one of your own at your beck and call?'

He didn't answer.

'No? Then it might take a while because we'll need to look for a kindly lawyer who'll take you on for free and there aren't too many of those around. Old Stubbins sometimes does but he's close to retirement and might not be keen to get involved in a murder case just now. Unless you want to spend a fortune paying for it yourself?'

Johnston dropped his head.

'I've already told you I didn't kill Rose, Mr Given. What else can I say?'

'I know what you told me but things have changed, haven't they? I don't think I'm going to have any option but to arrest you, especially if you're asking for legal representation. After all, that's bound to make me think you're guilty, isn't it?'

It was cruel but I didn't want a solicitor in with him yet. Having a brief in the room would only make him clam up, then we'd get nowhere and although I was threatening him with arrest I didn't really think it would be necessary.

'Alright, alright,' Johnston said, 'let's get on with it. What do you want to know?'

I passed him the note I'd received the night before.

'Read that.'

His lips moved as he traced each line with his fingertip and I thought for a moment he might hand it back for me to read it to him, simple as it was. When he'd finished he laid the paper down on the table then peered across at me defiantly.

'Anyone could have written this rubbish just to put the finger on me.'

I knew he was right but wasn't going to let him off the hook quite so easily.

'Are you saying you didn't have a fight with Rose, Alan?'

The resistance evaporated out of him, as if he knew he'd only get into more trouble by insisting on denial. He appeared a simple and honest enough man who might philander and not tell all of the truth but wouldn't intentionally lie.

'It looks bad, doesn't it?'

'I'm afraid it does, Alan. Do you want to tell me what happened now? All of it?'

'I didn't kill her, Inspector Given, honestly I didn't.'

'So what were you arguing about?'

Johnston paused only briefly before answering.

'The little bitch told me she was pregnant. Said I'd have to leave my wife and marry her or she'd just tell Stella and we'd be finished anyway. I lost my temper and said it couldn't be mine — we'd only done it a couple of times.'

Sawyer leaned over the table and jumped in before I could stop him.

'So you lost your temper and hit her with a hammer.'

Johnston was on his feet, shouting. 'I didn't kill Rose. She was nothing to me, just a bit of skirt out for a good time.' He stopped as soon as he realised what he'd said and sat down again shaking. 'I didn't kill her. We had a row and she stormed off. That was the last time I saw her.'

'I think the constable here needs to go and make us a cup of tea while we carry on with our chat, Alan.'

Sawyer's physical intimidation of Johnston wasn't going to get us anywhere so he was best out of it. He was a good copper but still inexperienced in how to interview subtly. Sometimes the heavy hand works best, though often it doesn't, and he couldn't yet tell the difference. I motioned to him to leave us for a while and waited until he'd reluctantly left the room.

'You told us earlier that Rose just didn't show up one night — are you now saying that wasn't the case?'

He thought long and hard before answering.

'Well, it is and it isn't. We had the row then she didn't turn up the next time we said we'd meet.'

Johnston dug deep into his memory and gave me the two dates when he'd last seen Rose and when she stood him up.

Sergeant Tommy Burns popped his head around the door before I could ask my next question.

'Excuse me, Inspector, could I have a word?'

Out in the corridor he told me that Rose Spicer's father had turned up wanting to see me and was waiting downstairs. I told Sawyer to go in and lock Johnston up until I could get back.

Bill Webb was sitting by the front desk with a package on his knee and his head in his hands. The poor man seemed to have lost weight since I last saw him and I considered the irony of him growing an abundance of food in his garden then not eating any of it.

'Mr Webb, are you all right?'

'Oh, hello, Mr Given. Not really. I found these and it's knocked me back a bit.' He handed me a bundle held in a thick rubber band. 'I was thinking about my Rose as a little girl and remembered a hiding place we'd made below the floorboards under her bed. We'd cut it out for her when she was a girl, just for a bit of fun, and I hoped to find some kid's stuff she'd left ages ago, not these. I thought you should see them.'

I took Rose's father into an interview room, asking Tommy Burns to bring us through a cup of tea. I removed the rubber band and spread the contents on the table: a diary, twenty crisp one-pound notes and four letters. The letters were revealing, in more ways than one. They were handwritten, dated in weekly intervals from around four months before Rose was murdered and went into significant details about what the writer would like to get up to next with the object of his lust. None were addressed, nor carried any names but each was signed with a single letter, 'A'.

I flipped through the period in the diary before Rose's body was discovered. Other than banalities such as make up all of our lives, the only entries of any interest were four of "Meet Alan, usual place" and one in early January of "Meet A. Chapel. 8pm. Not looking forward to it". This was the last significant entry in the diary and matched the date when Arthur Sprigg last used his hammer. At least this now gave us a likely date for when she was killed.

'What do you make of these letters, Mr Webb?'

'I don't know what to make of them. I've been thinking and thinking but can't come up with an answer. I didn't even know she was seeing anyone, let alone someone who'd write stuff like that.'

'What about the money?'

'The only thing I can think was that she was saving up from her wages.'

'It's an awful lot of cash to have saved over a few months; she can't have been earning more than a couple of quid a week. Why on earth would she have put aside so much?'

He said he hadn't a clue unless she was planning to go travelling again. I asked why she'd left her job if she was doing so well but he didn't know, though he suspected it might be something to do with a man working there. Neither could he shed any light on the mysterious "A" so I thanked him and said we'd be in touch.

Did the initial in the letters and the diary refer to the same person? Why would Rose write so clearly in her diary that she wasn't looking forward to meeting whoever it was? And why meet in the chapel?

I shared these thoughts with Sawyer.

'But surely, sir, it's got to be Alan Johnston. We know they were seeing each other — that's confirmed by other entries, isn't it? Perhaps she was breaking off with Johnston and she knew he wouldn't like it so that's why she wasn't looking forward to seeing him.'

'I'm not so sure. Why the switch from "Alan" to "A"? And does he strike you as the kind of bloke who'd be able to write letters like these? He could barely read.'

'Well my bet's on him. He's already lied to us twice. He was probably still mad that she was pregnant and when she said she was packing him in he grabbed the hammer from the caretaker's toolbox and clouted her with it. Then he dragged her downstairs and laid her out.'

'You're really keen that Johnston did this in a fit of temper, aren't you? I can't square that with the posing of her body. Why would Johnston do that and why would he take the hammer downstairs with him? It wasn't hidden anywhere, just lying on the floor. Also, he's already told us she was using her pregnancy to get him to marry her so why would she now be leaving him? Sorry, John, it doesn't add up.'

'Couldn't he have taken the hammer down to the crypt to delay Rose's body being found? And maybe he was lying about her saying she was expecting.'

'The posing?'

'Well, perhaps he ... oh, I don't know, sir. I can't get inside a murderer's head.'

'Well, we have to, John, otherwise we'll never be able to crack this.'

Another two hours of interviewing Alan Johnston got us nowhere. He stuck to his story about the argument and firmly denied he'd ever written to Rose in his life. I believed him on this last point. The letters were well penned, even eloquent in places, and Johnston hadn't the skill to write them. He was also adamant that he hadn't met Rose until November, after the last of the letters was sent and we had no evidence he'd met her when she was working in Coventry. He couldn't explain the final entry in Rose's diary but claimed it wasn't him and told us that he was at home that night and his wife would vouch for him. An alibi provided by a wife is worth next to nothing but we'd need to check it out anyway.

I moved to a different tack.

'You were seeing Stella whilst she was still married to Dave Butler, I hear.'

'Who told you that?'

'Doesn't matter. You were though, weren't you?'

He looked shamefaced. 'What of it?'

'Did you beat him up, you and some mates?'

'Me? Why would I have done that?'

'Come on, Alan, don't treat me like I'm stupid. You're sweet on his wife and he finds out so gives her a thumping. It would be only natural to give him some of his own medicine. Shame it killed him though.'

'Now wait a minute, Inspector. For one thing, I didn't do anything to him, and second, Dave Butler died of a heart attack. He was a pig but I didn't kill him.'

I hear these kinds of protestations every day from all sorts of toe-rags, but for some reason I believed Johnston, although I wasn't about to let him know it.

'Well, we'll need to check that, won't we, Alan? We'll just need to confirm when Butler was attacked then ask you where you were at the time. Now, do I lock you in the cells until we do the checking or do you have anything else to tell me?'

Johnston was panic-stricken at the thought of spending more time confined in a ten-by-ten box below the station and repeated his innocence over and over. He'd somehow managed to cope with being accused of one murder but when he realised there was a second one on the cards he fell to pieces. Unfortunately he didn't give us anything new.

Everything we had on him was mere supposition: he'd known the girl, had an affair and a row with her but had admitted it; he'd covered up on more than one occasion but had come clean when challenged; and he seemed to have an alibi, however flimsy, for the time she was murdered. Withholding the truth, on its own, doesn't yet constitute a crime, and it was pretty obvious why he'd done so. I could have held him longer, perhaps even charged him, but what would be the point? A decent solicitor would have him out in a flash so, despite Sawyer's obvious opposition, I let him go.

Sawyer and I carried on the discussion after we'd sent Johnston on his way.

'I know you think it's him but where would he have found the money Rose stashed away? It would be close on three months wages and why would he give it to her?'

'Rose told Johnston she was pregnant so he could have found the money somehow to ... you know ... pay her to get rid of it. Or perhaps he didn't give it to her, sir — maybe the money's not linked to the diary or her death.'

I had to concede he might be right, though I didn't want to discount the connection too soon. There would still be the unanswered question of how Rose did pull together that much cash.

'Have you considered his wife as a suspect, John?'

'Stella Johnston?'

'Well, why not? If she knew her husband was having a fling with Rose she might be a possibility.'

'But her name doesn't begin with an "A", sir, and we don't know if she had any idea about Rose, do we? Also, if her husband couldn't save up twenty pounds she'd hardly be able to do it out of the housekeeping money he gave her, would she?'

'But she has a job of her own. It's possible she was saving all of her wages for a rainy day and Rose made it start raining. We'd better ask her, hadn't we? You go round there tomorrow morning and bring her in. Probably best leave them to it for now; I think she and Alan might be having a few words.'

He was still convinced Alan Johnston was our man and couldn't see the point in questioning his wife but I sent Sawyer off, still grumbling, to follow up on everyone's alibis now we had a more or less firm time and date for the murder. I headed over to Coventry City Council to see what I could dig up on Rose's spell there.

The City Council offices were only next door to the police station where I had my office and I'd walked past them many times, though never been inside. From the reception desk I was pointed in the direction of the Housing Department on the first floor and, once in there, I was passed to a Miss Holt, head of the typing pool. With her pinned-back hair and pinched cheeks I'd have guessed she was in her late forties. Her desk held three trays, two with shorthand and longhand notes waiting to be typed and a third holding completed pages which she was probably checking for errors. I introduced myself and told her I was making enquiries about Rose.

'Rose Spicer? She seemed a nice enough girl, Inspector. What's she been up to?'

People often ask me that question and then never quite seem able to take in my reply when there's a death involved. Miss Holt was no exception. She drew even more deeply on the cigarette she'd been puffing since I arrived and I guessed from her yellowed fingers she had a serious habit.

'Dead?'

'Murdered.'

'My God. Who'd want to murder young Rose?'

The typewriters being hammered by the ten young women seated in front of Miss Holt rose to a crescendo, a mechanical scream. The supervisor beckoned one of the typists over and asked her to take charge whilst she chatted to me. She took me to a stationery storeroom in the corner of the office.

'It's quieter here, Inspector. I could hardly hear myself think in there. How can I help you?'

I asked her how long she'd known Rose.

'Well, she was only here a few months, started in April then left again in November. I can check the dates if you want me to.'

I asked if she'd do that before I left.

'What kind of worker was Rose, Miss Holt?'

'She was competent enough. A fairly fast typist, though not the most accurate. Sometimes I think these girls have their heads full of air, you know, thinking all the time about the young man they've just met, or the one they're hoping to meet soon. I did hear Rose had finished her schooling out of the country so perhaps that's why she made so many mistakes. Her shorthand was very good though, as well as her being pretty, and this made her a favourite with managers in the department who needed to dictate the odd letter.'

'Did she have any particular friends at work?'

'She got on well with the other girls but I only ever really saw her chatting at lunchtime with one, Elsie Manners. I think they might have been flat mates for a while. Elsie's in there, on the second row. She'll be devastated when she hears.'

'Do you know why Rose left the Council, Miss Holt?'

'They come and go all the time, Inspector. It's called a pool and sometimes I think it's just like one of those watering holes in Africa you see at the pictures when you're waiting for the main show. You know, the animals come along, wallow about a bit preening themselves, then go off in search of a mate. The ones who stay around end up like me, an old spinster looking after the pool until the next batch arrives.'

I had to smile at this image and the woman's self-deprecation. She must have been quite good-looking in her earlier years and a lot of this remained despite a slightly stern demeanour. I wondered if she'd ever been tempted to wander away with the herd and head for the wide-open grasslands to make baby shorthand-typists. Was this how I was going to find myself in ten years, still on my own with nothing but my case files for company and overseeing my own little watering hole?

With this sobering image of my future in my head I thanked Miss Holt for her assistance and asked if she'd send Elsie Manners in to see me.

Elsie Manners was a plain, skinny girl with glasses and thin auburn hair fashioned into a bun. She became almost hysterical when I told her why I wanted to talk to her, saying she'd heard in the newspapers about a body being found in Kenilworth.

'I never thought for a second it might be Rose; she was so young. How did she die?'

'That's something we're still trying to find out. Can you tell me anything about her?'

Elsie's sniffling had all but abated though she still didn't seem to comprehend what had happened.

'She was such a nice girl. A bit moody sometimes, but nice.'

'You knew her well?'

'We shared a flat for the last couple of months she was here. When she first came we sat next to each other in the office, then started having lunch together. Rose told me she'd taken the flat when she moved to Coventry but was finding it hard paying the rent on her own. I wanted to get out of my Mum and Dad's house, a bit of independence you know, so said I'd move in with her.'

'Did she have a boyfriend here?'

'I think she might have had one, or even two, but I wouldn't know their names and she wouldn't go out at night very often, only the odd occasion. We weren't in each other's pockets but there was never a man come to the house. My dad would have gone mad if he'd thought anything like that was happening.'

'Are you sure you don't know who they were? Anything, Elsie, anything at all?'

She screwed up her face in a most unattractive way whilst she tried to recall.

'I'm sorry, Inspector, there's nothing. Rose didn't tell me and I didn't ask. The only thing was, she asked me once if I knew how to get to Earlsdon on the bus, said she might be meeting someone there.'

'Do you know why she left the Council?'

'She didn't say. One day we came home and when we were having tea she told me she was leaving at the end of the week. Said she'd already given her notice into Miss Holt. I had a dreadful rush to try to find another girl to move in. I couldn't have afforded to stay in the flat if I hadn't.'

Elsie seemed on the verge of telling me something but then drew back. I asked her what it was. The girl popped her head out of the storeroom and looked around before coming back inside and pushing the door closed.

'It may be nothing, Inspector, but Rose seemed very nervous for the two weeks before she left and I thought she was scared of something.'

'What would she be scared of, Elsie?'

'Well, perhaps scared is the wrong word, just a bit on edge. I wondered if someone had been bullying her or trying it on.'

'Trying it on?'

Elsie blushed. 'You know. Like men do. Loads of the girls in here get their bottoms pinched, or worse. Think that because we're single and they're our bosses they can do what they like.'

'And did Rose mention anyone in particular?'

'Oh no, she never said anything — it was just a feeling I had. A few of them would ask for Rose if they wanted dictation. She'd been taking a lot from Councillor Gibbons in the few weeks before she left and I had wondered if perhaps he'd been making advances. In and out of his office all the time she was.'

At the reception desk I asked for an appointment with Councillor Gibbons and found he was, indeed, a powerful man — Chairman of the Housing Committee and Lord Mayor Elect. His first name was Andrew. Another "A".

On my way back from Coventry it occurred to me that Rose may have kept a diary for earlier periods if she'd kept one this year. In my experience people either keep a diary or they don't. Some need to do so because of their business or social engagements, others because they simply enjoy the act of writing, of recording every little incident in their life. I've never done it myself for pleasure and even the one I keep for work is scant, generally relying on others to tell me if I have to be in a meeting at a particular time.

I had to drive past Bill Webb's house to get to the police station so thought I'd call in. The dead girl's father was busy in the garden digging and turning the soil, preparing the ground for planting when the weather grew warmer. He asked me if I had any further news and I told him that I hadn't but it would be useful if he could let me have a look round Rose's bedroom. He followed me upstairs and stood in the corner looking as sad as ever a man can, until I asked if he'd leave me alone to do my investigation.

There was no point in looking again in the space under the bed where the young woman's father had discovered the hidden items so I examined the other floorboards to see if any were loose. There weren't. I looked in a small wardrobe but it contained, as might have been expected, only the woman's clothes. In a corner was a pile of cardboard boxes which I carefully went through but, again, they stored more clothes, mostly with labels from French makers.

Just when I was thinking it was a wild goose chase I noticed a biscuit tin, decorated with scenes of zoo animals, at the bottom of a bookshelf. Inside were six small volumes, each with its cover wrapped in brown paper and Rose's name and a year written on the spine. The latest was 1938. I pulled out this book and opened it. Unlike the one which her father had brought to the police station, this was simply a notebook rather than a printed diary. Every page had been divided, meticulously marked with the days of the week and the corresponding dates. Perhaps Rose hadn't been able to get hold of an English diary when she'd been in the south of France, so resorted to making her own.

There were entries on almost every page, the majority of them simply of the style of "Sunny day. Went for a walk". Early in the year, Rose had recorded returning from France and finding a new job, confirming it was mid-April. There was very little detail but in a small number of the entries names and initials had been included. I looked particularly at the period when Rose was living in Coventry, and there were several appointments with friends, usually alongside a girl's name. Most were with Elsie, the girl who worked with Rose with the council. Only two men's names were mentioned but each had several entries and it was obvious from the following day's scribblings that they were of a romantic nature.

One entry in late November particularly caught my eye.

Met him again and he gave me what I'd asked for. Perhaps I can now get away.

THIRTEEN

The bags under Stella Johnston's eyes showed she hadn't slept much the previous night. I guessed she and Alan had exchanged a few words.

'Thanks for coming in, Mrs Johnston.'

'I didn't really have much choice, did I, seeing as you sent the constable round to collect me? All you had to do was tell Alan to ask me and I'd have come in. God knows what the neighbours will think.'

I couldn't help but smile. Her husband was a possible suspect in a murder case, he'd been having a fling with the victim and she'd now been brought in for questioning, but all she could think about was how it looked to her neighbours.

'Can I ask you how well you knew Rose Spicer?'

'Clearly not as well as Alan. Actually, I didn't know her at all, never met her I don't think.'

'But you knew they were seeing each other. How did that make you feel?'

'I didn't know they were, at least not until last night. How do you think it made me feel?' She shook her head. 'I'd probably have killed her if she wasn't dead already.'

Not the right thing to say in the circumstances.

'And you're asking us to believe you had no idea about your husband's misbehaviour until he told you yesterday?'

'I honestly didn't. I've always trusted him but now I can see I was wrong and I've chucked him out. I never imagined he'd cheat on me.'

Sawyer stepped in.

'Why on earth would you trust him, Mrs Johnston? After all, he was seeing you while you were still married, wasn't he?'

This thought had clearly never occurred to her and she looked like she'd been slapped across the face now that Sawyer had suggested it. The cogs whirred in Stella's head for a long minute before she came up with an explanation she could accept as rational.

'That was different. Dave and I were almost split up. We both knew our marriage was over. He was living away all the time and I was up here on my own.'

'That might be your slant on the morals of it but what about Alan? Makes him look a bit of a "Jack the Lad" to me, out for what he can get.'

'Listen, I'm not defending him after what he's done but it was different. He didn't come chasing me. I don't think he even knew I was married, not at first anyway. We just met at a friend's birthday party and hit it off. I was feeling lonely and at the end of the evening told him I'd like to see him again if he felt like it. We went out a few times for a drink, nothing more, then we became more serious after Dave died.'

I took over again.

'Tell me about your first husband's death, Mrs Johnston.'

'I already told you once, Mr Given, he was beaten up then passed away a while later.'

'Did you have him beaten up?'

'What?'

'You heard me, Mrs Johnston, did you have your husband beaten up? Did Alan help you?'

'Of course not. What do you take me for? He was always getting into trouble through his drinking. He was a bully and I think this time he picked on the wrong person. Alan wasn't involved at all.' She seemed almost in tears. 'Despite everything, deep down I still loved him, you know. I was even at his bedside at the end.'

I find it hard to fathom how a woman can be so mistreated by a man and yet, in her heart, still feel a strong affection for him. Stella Johnston had earlier expressed the view she was happy her previous husband was dead and I could understand how she'd feel that way but one thing I've learnt in life is that people are full of contradictions. Several out-and-out villains I've known were the most likeable of characters when not engaged in criminal activity. Similarly, I've had work colleagues smile in my face then stab me in the back at the slightest opportunity to enhance their career. And a lady friend might profess to want to be with me forever then run away when difficult questions arose.

I moved on.

'Could we go back to the night Rose Spicer was murdered, Mrs Johnston? Can you remember where you were? It would have been Wednesday, fourth of January.'

'Wednesday's are my St John's Ambulance evening, so I would have been there. I've been a first aider with them since I got married to Dave and I go every week up to the parish hall.'

'So you wouldn't have been with Alan on that evening?'

For a moment she seemed uncertain how to answer.

'No ... I mean I'd have been with him at teatime, but then I'd leave about half past six and get home around half past nine. Alan's usually sitting listening to the wireless when I get back.'

'And was he that night?'

'I can't really remember.' She bit her lip. 'On the odd time he's not been at home when I've got in I'd always think he'd gone for a pint and so I'd just go to bed. But now he's admitted he'd sometimes go to see that woman when I was out. If I'd known what he was up to I might have taken more notice.'

The look on Sawyer's face told me he was far from happy.

Later, back at the office, I'd just finished another call to Walter Naismith when Sawyer came in to see me and he was still livid about what Stella Johnston had told us. Although he knew his place well enough not to show it too much he couldn't stop himself from raising his concerns.

'I said it was Alan Johnston didn't I, sir, and you've let him go. We don't even know where he is now his wife's thrown him out. I'll put the word out to have him picked up again.'

'Wait a minute, John — we still only have her word that she wasn't with him that night. Don't forget she's still mad as hell so isn't about to do him any favours.'

'Are you saying she'd be prepared to see him hang for murder just because he'd been seeing another woman?'

'Who knows what she'd do in those circumstances. Mrs Johnston probably wouldn't have thought it would go that far, and she'd get a great deal of satisfaction from the trouble it would cause him in the meantime. On top of that she admitted she'd have killed Rose Spicer herself if she'd known about his philandering.'

Even I didn't think her slip of the tongue meant anything, and I wasn't fooling Sawyer.

'That was just a turn of phrase, sir, something anyone might say when they're angry. It wasn't significant but if her husband can't account for where he was when the murder took place then that is significant.'

'I'm sorry John, but I still don't believe he did it. We've already questioned him three times and what have we got out of him? Only that he was seeing this girl on the side. I don't approve but it's not enough to get him into court. I'm sure we'll not move any further forward by pulling him in again. We'll keep asking questions until we have something more positive then, if we need to, we'll arrest him. You just find out where he's living now and warn him not to go anywhere else until we tell him he can.'

'But sir...'

'No, John. Leave it there. If something else comes up which puts Johnston in the frame then I'll be the first to apologise.'

I filled him in on what I'd picked up in Coventry but I could see he was still stuck with his opinion about Alan Johnston and wasn't about to be convinced anyone else could be a suspect.

'It's not always as it appears on the surface you know, John. People lie or get things wrong for all sorts of reasons. Everyone is economical with the truth occasionally if it prevents someone they care about being hurt. How often have you told a girlfriend she looks nice in a particular dress even though you don't like it at all? Sometimes people simply tell us what they think we want to hear to avoid getting into trouble themselves and they disregard the consequences for others. Sometimes they'll lie to get what they want, like Rose Spicer may have.'

'What did she lie about?'

I explained that I'd phoned Walter again after I'd interviewed Stella Johnston and asked if Rose had been pregnant. He'd said she didn't appear to be though if it had been in the early stages he'd not have been able to tell because she'd been dead for such a long time. Blood tests might have been able to show something if there'd been any blood left but there wasn't. Even though the body was in relatively good condition, the fluids had dried up inside the cadaver fairly quickly, so there was nothing left to test by the time he got to it.

'So, either she was lying to Johnston and wasn't expecting at all, just saying it to force him into leaving his wife, or she was only in the early stages. By his account they'd only been together about four weeks so she'd hardly know she was pregnant by the time she said it to him.'

'Unless,' Sawyer said, 'he was lying and knew her whilst she was still in Coventry.'

'Or maybe the child, if there was one, wasn't his. Perhaps it came from one of these boyfriends she had before she came back here and decided she could hang it on Johnston. That's it, you see, John, we're told a story and there could be any number of truths connected with it. We can't just arrest someone on the basis of the lack of an alibi. We'd all be in danger most of the time of being locked up if that was the case.'

Sawyer still wasn't convinced and continued arguing his corner more until I told him I wouldn't be budged on this one and he'd best get used to it. I left him in a sour mood and with a pile of paperwork to take his mind off it.

Foleshill Road was wide but still felt as closed in as the city streets in places, especially passing the enormous Courtauld's textile mill, which towered high above both sides of the street a mile and a half out of the centre. It was a busy thoroughfare and my progress was slow, needing to stop every few yards, or so it seemed, whilst the trams in front discharged their passengers before reloading to eventually trundle onwards.

The General Wolfe was an imposing red-brick building, three storeys tall and occupying a corner position, a far cry from the cosy Queen around the corner from my cottage. I picked up the landlord's name, Peter Weston, from the licence board over the front door. He was as imposing as his pub, at least six feet tall, broad in the beam and wearing an impressive handlebar moustache. He welcomed me like a long-time customer and asked what I'd like to drink. His expression lost only a little of its geniality when I explained I was a policeman.

'I'm looking for George Barber, Mr Weston. I believe he comes in here now and again.'

'You're a bit out of luck, Inspector. Our George was in earlier but he's gone off to put on a bet. He might be back later if you'd like to wait. Sure I can't get you something to drink?'

I refused and asked him for directions to the bookie, which he was reluctant to give at first until I said it would go no further. We've better things to do than lock up illegal bookmakers, knowing another will pop up as soon as we put one out of action. I sometimes think half their customers are policemen anyway.

The bookie's office was down a back entry, halfway along Station Street East. The yard was entered through a solid wooden gate, hiding the set-up from passing innocent or prying eyes. The place stank from the pigeon lofts lining both walls and when I walked by the air filled with feathers as the birds flapped into the corners of their cages. A man wearing a blue boiler suit peered through the back window of the house and then came round to take my bet. The upper half of the maroon back door swung open and he leant both elbows on the shelf fixed to the top of the bottom half.

'Can I help you?'

It never ceases to amaze me that I haven't the slightest interest in gambling on horses or dogs. If I let myself, I'd play cards all day and all night, losing or winning a fortune depending on how they fell but I've never seen the fascination in having a flutter on the races. Perhaps it's because I imagine I have some kind of control over the cards and I'd have no influence over the nags, other than trying to pick the right one. The odds are actually slightly better in racing I think, with only eight or so horses in a race whilst there are fifty-two cards in a pack, in a multiplicity of combinations. But obsessive gambling is never about the odds. Despite everything I know, when I'm playing, I believe every time that I can win.

'I'm looking for George Barber.' I showed him my warrant card.

The bookie looked over his shoulder and I heard a chair clatter to the ground inside. I leaned past him and saw Barber heading towards the front door.

'Come on, George, let's have none of that,' I shouted. 'It'll take me no time at all to have a bunch of coppers round at your house, then where will you be?'

He stopped in his tracks, turned and shrugged his shoulders.

'Alright, alright, I'm coming, Mr Given, no need for any trouble.'

Peter Weston let us use a small room behind the main public bar and Barber was sitting opposite me nursing a worried expression and a pint of mild. I could have pulled him into the local police station but decided the General Wolfe was nearer and would probably put Barber more at ease. It was pretty obvious after my first couple of questions that he thought he was being arrested for burglary or some such. I tried to get him to relax and open up.

'I'm not taking you in, George, at least not yet. I just want a little information.'

'I'm no snitch, Inspector.'

I laughed.

'I know you're not, George, wouldn't be worth it, would it? Not round here. But no-one would think badly of you helping the police with their enquiries, especially if it kept you out of trouble. That's all I'm asking.'

He thought it over for less than sixty seconds.

'Go on then, what do you want to know?'

I explained about the Demmas, how I'd been trying to have a word with them for a long time and that I'd heard he'd been talking to them recently. He didn't deny it but began to fidget as soon as their names were mentioned.

'They're nasty pieces of work, Mr Given. I know I'm no angel but that pair put the wind up me, the younger one in particular, and I wish I'd never got involved with them. I can't tell you where they are though.'

'Now, George, we've already agreed this isn't like being an informer.'

'No, it isn't that, I just don't know where they are. They find me when they want me — just like you did.'

'So why did they want to find you?'

'They were looking for fellers who'd help them with some business.'

'Business? You mean a robbery?'

'No, not this time. Someone told them I'd been shouting my mouth off about Jews one night after a few pints.'

I tightened my grip on my glass ever so slightly.

'And they were recruiting.'

'Sorry, Mr Given, that's not really how I feel but I'd been refused my old job and the boss was a Jew. You know how it is.'

The look I gave him would have left him in no doubt that I didn't know how it was. I asked him what the Demmas had been recruiting for.

'They'd heard about the place I'd worked and wanted to teach them a lesson. The younger one, Paúlu, kept spouting about how Adolf Hitler had it right and the whole lot should be kicked out.'

'So you joined them.'

'No, no, I didn't. All I did was give them some information. I was frightened of Benito but I didn't want any harm to come to the Goodmans. They were decent bosses when I worked for them, really decent.'

'The Goodmans? The ones with the warehouse that caught fire last week?'

'That's them. I felt really bad after it happened. They couldn't have given me my job back anyway; someone else had been taken on after I went inside last time.'

I asked him what information he'd passed on. He looked like he was about to be sick and drew a long draught from his glass.

'I told them when the place was likely to be empty and what the layout was inside. God, I wish none of this had ever happened.'

'You know I could arrest you as an accessory to arson, don't you? With your record you'd be inside for a very long time. This isn't like a bit of burglary or thieving from the market; people could have been killed.'

'I know, Mr Given. It's not what I do. I just couldn't get out of it. Don't get me sent down again. Please.'

The next part was easy. What I'd been building up to all along. Just soften him up with threats and pressure, and then go in with the sucker punch.

'You simply put the word around that you need to meet our Sicilian friends then leave the rest to me.'

I sent Barber on his way with the time and place for him to say he would meet the Demmas and then I headed back to my office to make some telephone calls. The first was to arrange for officers to be made available for where the Demmas would be if Barber did what he was told. I'd suggested a disused factory yard I knew with only a single route in and out and where we could keep out of sight until the right moment.

My second call was to Terry Gleeson to let him know my search for the Demmas had finally yielded a result. I might have guessed he'd not be grateful, his animosity towards me hadn't diminished in recent months.

'Why would that be of interest to me, Given? Thought you'd have better things to do than chase these fellers to settle old scores.'

'Don't you listen to anything I tell you, Gleeson? I'm not "settling old scores", these two are tied into the attacks on Jewish businesses both over here and in Birmingham.'

I went on to tell him, not for the first time, I thought he was idle and as bent as they come, and if he didn't get his finger out I'd be having a word with Dyer. Needless to say, that didn't go down well.

'You just be careful, Given. Don't get involved in something you'll regret later.'

'Are you threatening me, Gleeson?'

'Let's say it's a friendly warning, that's all. Just stay out of my business.'

FOURTEEN

I'd found the addresses of Rose's boyfriends in the back of her home-made 1938 diary. By chance they were both in the Earlsdon part of the city, one of the better areas and only a short distance from the centre. It contained two quite distinct neighbourhoods, one with row after row of small terraced housing, the other with larger properties, gardens and even some with servants' quarters. Joey Atkin's house was a recently built semi-detached on a road bordering Hearsall Common. The bonnet of the car on the drive was up, with a young man in overalls revving the engine beneath it.

'Mr Atkin? Joey Atkin?'

He didn't look up from the job he was engrossed in.

'Who wants to know?'

I introduced myself but he still carried on working, bringing the engine to a roar by pulling on a cable. I walked around the vehicle, opened the driver's door and switched off the ignition. He cursed and took two steps towards me.

'Stop right there, Joey. Wait, take a deep breath and think for a few seconds before you take another step. While you're doing that, remember that I'm police and it won't end happily for you if you make the wrong decision.'

He clearly reconsidered his options, wiped his oily hands on a rag then flung it on top of his toolbox.

'All right, what do you want?'

'Rose Spicer. You know her?'

'I did. Past tense. What's she been saying about me?'

'She's said nothing. When did you last see her?'

'Christ, I don't know. Months ago. Why?'

'A little more precise please, Joey, this is important.'

'October, I think.'

Atkin turned and smiled when he heard the front door open. A man in a blue pinstripe suit came out and approached us.

'Dad, this is Inspector Given. Inspector, this is my father. He's a solicitor.'

Atkin Senior demanded to see my credentials and asked why I was questioning his son.

'I wasn't "questioning" him, as you put it, sir, we were just having a chat, weren't we, Joey? If I'd wanted to question him I'd have taken him down to the police station. Perhaps I should if that's what you think the right thing would be, Mr Atkin, then you can represent him in your official capacity rather than as his father.'

The young man's father backed off and invited us inside but I declined, saying we would be fine where we were. He went back indoors and stood watching us from the front window.

'Now, where were we? Ah, yes, you were about to tell me more about the last time you saw Rose Spicer. October you said?'

'It would have been the early part of the month. I went away with Dad for a few days on the seventeenth and she'd chucked me in before that. We'd been to the pictures in town, the Gaumont, and I wanted to go back to her place afterwards but she told me she didn't want to see me any more. Said she was hoping to come into some money and probably leaving Coventry.'

'Did she say where she was getting it from?'

'No. I assumed a relative was on their last legs and leaving it to her.'

'And what did you think about her packing you in?'

He thought for a minute before answering. His father had taught him well.

'I was annoyed, angry I suppose, we'd seemed to be getting on so well. I liked her and we had a good laugh when we were out. So what has she been saying?'

'I'm sorry, Joey, she hasn't been saying anything for a little while. Rose is dead.'

'Oh.'

'You don't seem surprised.'

'I'm not sure that I am.' He glanced at the shadow behind the front window. 'Before I say anything else, do I need to get Dad out here again?'

'That's entirely up to you, Joey, but, as I've already said, we'd then need to finish this conversation down at the police station. Now, what were you saying?'

He sighed and continued.

'Rose was a good-time girl and would flirt with anything in trousers. I don't think she cheated on me but she was quite easy to pick up. We'd barely exchanged a few words when we first met and I could tell she'd say yes if I asked her out, so I did and she did. If she was like that with me then I suppose she could have got herself hurt if she did the same with other blokes.'

'Did you get her pregnant, Joey?'

'What? Now wait a minute.'

I sensed an outraged denial coming on but I could tell by the way he blushed that it was a distinct possibility. This time he did wave to his father to join us. It took the solicitor less than two minutes to establish I had nowhere near enough on his son to arrest him and offered to bring him in to help us further with our enquiries "at a mutually convenient time". Said Joey was a conscientious medical student, well respected in their local church, and I'd not have a cat in hell's chance of getting a magistrate to support him being hauled in for questioning. I could have forced the issue and demanded they come in immediately, though I was certain young Atkin would be home again in less than an hour if his father was as good as he'd just demonstrated.

Tom Marshall's house was completely different to the Atkin residence. An old terrace hard up against a large bicycle factory, which filled the street with the sounds of metalworking, and which doubtless provided an income to many local residents. A blond young man in work clothes answered the door and led me through to a back room which he said was Marshall's, explaining that three of them shared the house, splitting the rent and all the bills.

Marshall was dark-haired, very tall and bearded. An anchor tattooed on his forearm suggested he'd been at sea, like me, for a few years. I told Tom who I was and we went through the same questions I'd put to Joey Atkin. He said he'd only been out with Rose a couple of times after they'd been introduced and he'd liked her but she wasn't really his type. They agreed just to stay friends. He claimed they'd met in May, soon after Rose moved to Coventry, and he hadn't seen her since their last date, despite their promise to keep in touch. If he was telling the truth then he'd not have been the father of Rose's baby, unless she was considerably further advanced when she died, and Walter would have picked that up.

The young man seemed genuinely upset when I gave him the news of Rose's death and I had to ask his housemate to sit with him when I left. Unlike Atkin, I didn't think I'd bother putting Marshall on the list of suspects.

I was in a maze, with every path coming to a dead end rather than leading towards the heart of our puzzle. Walter Naismith hadn't come back to me with anything further I could use, none of the current suspects were straightforward, I was still waiting to make contact with the Coventry councillor and the trap I'd set up using George Barber needed time to ferment.

FIFTEEN

I spent all day Friday shuffling papers and kicking my heels around the office and I knew nothing would happen over the weekend. So, although I couldn't really spare the time to take a break I hadn't seen my family for weeks and decided to make the trip. My father was becoming more insistent on the telephone, saying my mother wanted to see me.

In January my mother had fallen down the last few stairs into the workshop and hurt her hip. She wasn't badly hurt, with her dignity more bruised than her body, but she'd needed to rest up for a while. Things had been quiet at work after I'd finished up in the Grovestock House murders, a case that had started and ended with a hanging, so I'd been able to take a few days off afterwards to help look after her.

Not that I was needed, really. Her neighbours and friends from the synagogue had clucked around my mother all the time I was there, even sparing time to ply me with chicken soup at every opportunity. By the end of the first night I felt like a spare part and was wishing I was back home.

My father was now telling me daily she still wasn't right and kept asking for me. I was fairly sure he was laying it on a bit thick to get me over, but what could I do? If I'd dismissed his pleas and there really was something wrong with her, I'd never forgive myself. Not to mention him probably never forgiving me. If she wasn't as bad as he was saying then what had I lost? Only a couple of days out of a murder investigation where we seemed to be going nowhere.

I packed a small case on Saturday morning and caught the train to Birmingham for the weekend. It was lucky for me that I did.

My mother was fine when I arrived but I could see the fall had aged her. Children take tumbles all the time and it never seems to bother them for more than a few minutes, perhaps because the distance to the ground is not so great. With adults it's different. I'd noticed she was more cautious in her step and a look of apprehension flickered across her face when we descended the stairs to take a walk to the shops. But she was happy to see me and the attention rained down on me by my little sister, Sarah, made me pleased I'd made the effort to visit. I still wasn't sure, however, why my father had wanted me to do so.

It was already dark and, as usual, after dinner on Saturday, he and I were in the parlour listening to the evening news on the wireless. There'd been a further report of Germany's expansion across Europe, gobbling up land wherever Hitler chose, with Austria, Czechoslovakia and, most recently, part of Lithuania all taken under Nazi control. All the talk was of Poland being next and it was clear to everyone that war wasn't far from our door. I could tell my father was worried.

'Have you heard from Uncle Gideon, Papa?' I asked.

Some months earlier we'd been told that my uncle's business had been confiscated by the Nazis and the family had fled from Bremen, trying to make their way to England or even to Switzerland. The last I'd heard from my father was that they still hadn't succeeded. It was almost impossible to move without papers in Germany. And their papers would show they were Jewish, which would mean beatings or worse. They'd been zigzagging across the country for hundreds of miles, keeping out of sight and hiding in barns or staying with friends, and friends of friends, wherever they thought it secure. Occasionally, one of these kind people would post a letter for Uncle Gideon to my father. The letters never had any detail, just the briefest of messages to let us know he was safe.

My father shook his head.

'I've had nothing, not for a month. He was writing regularly, perhaps once a fortnight. Then the letters stopped. I'm so worried, Jacob.' He knew I no longer used my birth name but insisted on doing so himself.

We both knew he had cause to be worried. The German Führer had recently made a speech promising the total annihilation of the Jewish race in Europe if war broke out and reports coming out of the country told of many killings had already been committed in the wake of Krystallnacht. There was little mention of them in the English newspapers but everyone in my father's community had relatives and friends sending them letters from countries under Nazi rule.

'You know how they were travelling, Papa, perhaps it's just become more difficult to get a letter away.'

'I know, I know, son, but I feel so helpless. I wondered if you might speak to your friend again. See if he can find anything out.'

He was talking about Mike Spencer, a Special Branch man who'd helped me find Uncle Gideon when he was first displaced.

'He's not really a friend, you know. I can't see how, with everything else happening in Germany, he'd be able to spare time to look for Uncle Gideon.'

'Will you try though, Jacob? Please?'

How could I refuse?

On Sunday morning, after a magnificent breakfast, I'd said my goodbyes and walked the half mile or so into the city centre. My train wasn't due until half past eleven so I wandered deserted streets looking for a newspaper shop. My mind was still full of the conversation with my father and I was concerned for him. When I did eventually manage to buy a paper it didn't help. Page after page held reports about Germany's aggression and it seemed strange how the arguments for appeasement dominating the discussion only a few months earlier had disappeared. Everyone, from politicians to letter writers, was now urging the Prime Minister to take action. I threw the newspaper in a bin before I arrived at New Street railway station, disgusted at the fickleness of public opinion.

Not long after I arrived home, Oliver Neilson's knock pulled me away from the pot of tea I was brewing.

'Good afternoon, Inspector. You've been away.'

'Just visiting my parents for a couple of days, Mr Neilson. How can I help?'

He looked up and down the street.

'May I have a word?'

I groaned inwardly and swung the front door wider.

'You'd best come in. I'm just making tea.'

This time I couldn't avoid taking him into my kitchen and I could see he was making comparisons with his own but I was beyond caring what he thought. I poured two cups and plonked a few biscuits onto a plate in front of him.

'Now, you have something to tell me?'

I was hoping he hadn't come round just to give me the benefit of his wisdom on the case of Rose Spicer's murder. I was disappointed.

'I heard you'd arrested young Mr Johnston again, Inspector, and remembered something you might be interested to hear.'

'You really should come into the police station with information, you know, not to my house. Especially if you think it's important and then I'm not here. Anyway, you'd best tell me now you've got me.'

Neilson explained how Alan Johnston had married Stella after her first husband had died. He seemed to know all the details of what had happened to Dave Butler, plus the rumours of Alan's affairs, but there wasn't anything new.

'I'm afraid we know all this already, Mr Neilson, we're carrying out a very thorough investigation. But thank you for bringing it to our attention.'

'It's a bit strange though, don't you think?'

'What is?'

'Well, he has an affair with Stella and her husband dies, then he has an affair with Rose and she is killed. I'm sure Mac Spielberg would make a connection.'

I snorted with derision.

'I'm sure he would, but that's not real life is it, Mr Neilson? It's easy to make neat connections though not always as easy to prove them. Your writer Terence Spelling only needs to please his readers. I have to convince a judge and jury. Quite a different prospect.'

Neilson seemed disappointed by my response. I was unsure if this was due to me ridiculing his amateur attempts at detective work or because he'd been hoping he could show Alan Johnston to be a more viable suspect.

Could he be trying to deflect attention from himself? After all, he'd worked at the school where Rose's body was found and left sometime between her being killed and the afternoon the unfortunate Benjamin Smith discovered her. He'd also told me he'd a good knowledge of the chapel and the crypt, as he'd been at the school for so long. It was becoming clear he lived in some kind of fantasy world, where he was a tough American private eye helping the cops to catch the bad guys. On top of this, or perhaps as part of it, he spied on his neighbours from behind closed curtains and, worst of all, appeared to be following me around. Alternatively, he might simply be a sad old man with nothing to occupy his time now he had retired.

I was about to ask Neilson about his time at Hannah's when there was another knock at the front door. Outside were a police car, two uniformed constables and a man in plainclothes who I immediately took to be a senior officer. He spoke first.

'Could you come along with us, Inspector? We need to talk to you about the murder of a friend of yours. A Mr Benito Demma.'

Inspector Harry Wilson looked every inch the hard-boiled detective. Late 40s, Brylcreemed dark hair and the amber-tinged fingertips of a 40-a-day smoker. A deep scar cutting across his right cheek only affirmed his no-nonsense credentials. The grey gabardine coat emphasised the squareness of his solidly-muscled frame and the deep shine on his black leather Oxfords hinted at an earlier career in his Majesty's forces.

My mind was racing. Who could have murdered Benito Demma, and why? The man was a thug and a murderer, someone I'd have happily killed for what he'd done to me in the past. But I didn't, so who else loathed him as much as I did?

SIXTEEN

'Can you tell us where you were last night, Inspector Given?'

The "us" in question were Wilson and a fresh-faced sergeant, introduced as Capstick, sitting beside him across the table. The view from the window told me we were, ironically, in a room directly below my own office in Coventry Police Station.

'Not until you tell me what this is about.'

'I already told you. A man you know well has been killed, stabbed to death to be precise, and we understand you'd been looking for him.'

'Who told you that?'

'Never mind who. You admit you had been looking for him?'

'Of course I had. For years.'

I explained my history with the Demma brothers, how I knew them to be rapists and involved in at least two murders, and how I now suspected them of being involved in the attacks on Jewish businesses in Coventry and Birmingham.

Capstick made a note and shook his head dismissively.

'So you had it in for the two of them, *Inspector*,' he said, stressing the last word so I'd understand that, despite our difference in rank, he was the one in charge at the minute.

'I can't pretend I'm not pleased that Benito Demma is dead, but I didn't kill him. If you check you'll find I had him in custody once before and let him go. Unharmed. Anyway, I was in Birmingham with my family last night and had only just arrived home when my neighbour called and then you two hammered on my door.'

'Who said Benito wasn't done in Birmingham? We didn't say where he was murdered, did we?'

'I know you didn't, *Sergeant* —' this time I stressed his rank — 'but I'm not stupid. If the killing had taken place over there then I'd have been taken to Birmingham nick, not here. By the way, you still haven't said who told you I was looking for the Demmas.'

He looked across at his boss for confirmation. Wilson's shake of the head was enough.

'And I'm not going to. Suffice it to say, it's a very credible source.'

Credible source? Who had I told? Sawyer, George Barber and Terry Gleeson were the most obvious, followed by half the pubs in Coventry. There's no way Sawyer would have said anything — he'd never met Wilson to my knowledge. I'd hardly imagine the Inspector could have cottoned on to Barber so quickly and, even if he had, George would hardly have been described as credible. Perhaps a landlord might have reported it but why would they?

It didn't take me long to work out that Capstick needed to say no more. It must have been Terry Gleeson. Who else would they have taken at face value? Gleeson must have heard what had happened to Benito then passed on information about my search in order to give me a headache, another warning not to mess around with him. He'd know nothing would come of it but it would amuse him to know I was up to my neck in manure for a day or two.

Wilson stood up and beckoned his colleague to join him outside. For a full five minutes I could hear raised voices in the corridor, too muffled to make much sense. When the pair came back the Sergeant's face was like thunder.

'We've had a little chat and decided to let you go.' Wilson turned and glared at Capstick. 'The Sergeant here doesn't agree with me but that's what's going to happen, though you'll be suspended until we've checked your story.'

'You don't have the authority to suspend me.'

'Actually, I do. I couldn't have pulled in a police Inspector without the say-so of my boss. Oatway and your Superintendent Dyer put their heads together and agreed you'd be put out to grass unless I was one hundred percent sure you couldn't have done it. From what I hear you seem like a decent copper and have a plausible enough alibi but you know I still have to follow it up. So just hand over your warrant card and you can be on your way.'

The next morning, I arrived early for my meeting with Superintendent Dyer so walked down to the shops to buy some bread and corned beef for lunch. On my way back, at the top of the rise, the police station stood solidly three storeys high, telling the local citizens that they were safe and secure. But how illusory was this? The square, tiered stone building hinted at permanence yet all over Europe the boundaries were changing beyond recognition. Even here in sleepy Warwickshire a young woman could be killed and no-one have a clue who murdered her, other than the person who did it. Our world changes every day, and how could this edifice, built for nothing more than housing police officers, prevent that? The best we could do would be to deliver a measure of justice when things inevitably went wrong. A bobby on the beat, and a villain put away, are all part of the pretence that we are protected, that the world won't come in and do us harm. I have enough experience to know that it just isn't like that. Consider what was happening to me now; I spend the weekend with my parents and come back to find I'm a suspect in a murder case. I am almost out of a job and there is hardly a thing I can do about it.

The boss had reluctantly agreed to meet me in force headquarters in Warwick even though he was planning to take the day off. He wasn't listening to any of my arguments, and his Fair isle pullover and tweed trousers told me he'd be on the golf course as soon as he could get away from our discussion.

'Look, Given, you know we can't have you on duty with a possible murder charge hanging over your head, so go home. Put your feet up for a few days and read a book, listen to the radio. Take up knitting, for God's sake, anything, just get out of here and don't leave the area.'

'But I wasn't even in Coventry when Demma was stabbed on Saturday, sir.'

'It doesn't matter. You're suspended until Inspector Wilson gives you the all clear and that's that.'

'This is madness, you can't actually believe I had anything to do with Benito Demma's murder.'

I might have thought for a second or two longer on my choice of words before trying to argue with Dyer.

'Madness, is it? We both know you've had a vendetta against him for years. You begged me to let the two brothers go last time we had them so how do I know it wasn't just so you could find them then finish the Demmas off for good? Even if you didn't kill him, it is your fault he was back out on the streets, allowing someone else the opportunity to bump him off, so go home, Inspector, and that's not a request.'

There was nothing else to be said so I took ten minutes more to telephone Sawyer to explain what had happened, then I did as Dyer had ordered.

Doing nothing at all just isn't in my makeup so after pacing the kitchen for quarter of an hour I tried relaxing with tea and a bun, then I started tidying up the house. Years spent in shared cabins on cramped merchant ships means I'm not used to spreading my few possessions around very much and this habit has stayed with me. I've always washed and put away my crockery immediately after every meal so, apart from the cup and plate I'd just used, the kitchen took hardly any time at all. Likewise my parlour and bedroom.

The only room where it looked a mess was my office and even here it was something of an illusion. I'd readily admit it could be tidier but there was a method in the apparent chaos. Few of my cases follow a logical sequence. Finding a murderer, or many other criminals, requires pulling together scraps of information, placing them first this way and then that way until a pattern emerges out of the confusion. In my view it's more important to have all the evidence in one place than it is to keep it orderly all of the time. Half an hour saw me file the few out of date scraps and put the rest of the material into neater piles, then I was at a loose end again.

Any of my acquaintances will know I'm not one for taking a walk without a purpose. I saunter to the police station most mornings and happily spend a lot of time tramping the streets following up witnesses, but the idea of stepping out of the house just to take the air leaves me cold. There was nothing on the wireless I fancied and it was the wrong time of year for doing anything in my tiny garden so I was just beginning to think I'd have to follow Dyer's advice to take up knitting when the telephone rang.

'James, is it you?' It was Elizabeth and she sounded on edge.

'Is there something wrong?'

'No, not at all. Well, not really. I arrived in Priors Allenford to visit Mrs Veasey last night. Poor dear is still not well so I came up to look after her for a few days. Are you free to meet?'

My first reaction was to refuse because I knew I didn't want to let myself get close to her and then be dumped. Our relationship over the years had been disjointed, at times romantic enough to put marriage on the cards, at others distant. We were in one of the arm's length phases at present.

'James, are you there? I really need to see you.'

Need. Not "want"? It's strange how we can be so imprecise in our attempts to try to describe our feelings and emotions, yet our day to day words cut directly to the quick of what we mean. Policemen watch for this when interviewing witnesses and suspects, a slip of the tongue often revealing more than they're prepared to tell. Elizabeth clearly wanted a favour. Had she concocted this visit to Mrs Veasey simply so she could ask?

'I thought you said there was nothing wrong.'

'There isn't. Not wrong exactly, there's something I need to discuss with you.' That word "need" again. 'So much has happened over the last few months, things I have to sort out.'

All the way out to Priors Allenford I wondered why I'd bothered. The rain was lashing down and the country roads were pitch black. More than once I almost ended up in a ditch when a bend materialised out of the gloom. My driving wasn't helped by my mind being elsewhere. Why did Elizabeth want to see me? Could it be she'd had a change of heart and decided we might have a future together despite our different religions? Somehow I doubted it. She'd been pretty firm in her views at the back end of last year and I wasn't aware of anything that might have changed her mind. Other than her telephone call earlier in the day, we hadn't spoken for months. She'd sent me the briefest of letters with her new address and that was the only correspondence I'd had from her until her recent note arrived. For my part, I hadn't written either, thinking it better to leave the ball in Elizabeth's court.

Perhaps I was being unkind in suspecting she'd visited the old cook in order to ask me for something. Maybe Mrs Veasey needed the favour and thought I'd be more receptive if Elizabeth made the approach. I really didn't know what to think and regardless of the rational side of me knowing Elizabeth was no longer interested, I couldn't help hoping I was wrong.

I parked as close to the entrance of The Victory as I could without actually driving inside. Even so, I was drenched and mud-splattered before I dived through the front door, which was hardly the impression I wanted to make on Elizabeth.

She was sitting at the counter in the snug, looking as pretty as she ever did, rosy-cheeked from the roaring fire and hanging on to the landlord's every word.

Mr Cudlip was ignoring his customers in the public bar, preferring to share gossip with my ex-girlfriend, much as he had with me when I'd stayed at the Victory sorting out the Grovestock House tragedy. He turned when I came in.

'Mr Given, how nice to see you. Miss Parry here was telling me you were driving over. Foul weather you've brought with you, I have to say.'

He continued to discuss the foulness of the night whilst he poured me a glass of Vimto, and then faded into the background. Cudlip had been in the pub trade long enough to know not to hang around when he wasn't wanted.

Other than a quick 'Hello James, lovely to see you' Elizabeth had remained quiet until Cudlip left us alone. I nodded towards a table in the corner.

'It will be more comfortable, don't you think?' I didn't add that it would also be hidden from prying eyes in the other bar and from Cudlip's greedy ears.

Even after we'd moved, Elizabeth didn't say anything for what seemed like an age, making a great show of taking off and folding her grey woollen cloak, then laying her hat, a style I believe is called a bolero, on top. She'd had her hair cut much shorter since the last time I'd seen her and she primped it before finally turning to me with a quiet smile. I couldn't tell if she was struggling to form the words or had changed her mind.

'You wanted to talk to me, Elizabeth?'

She reached across the table and placed her hand on top of mine.

'Oh, James, it is good of you to come.'

I almost pulled away, but half-controlled my annoyance.

'Please let's not pretend you asked to meet because you're missing me. I assume it's a favour you're after.'

Elizabeth took her hand away.

'I knew this was a mistake. I might as well leave now if you're going to be nasty to me, James.'

'I really don't want to be unpleasant, Elizabeth, but what do you expect? You left me, without a word of explanation, more than once. We even looked like we might spend the rest of our lives together then you just disappeared.'

'I'm so, so sorry.' She looked close to tears. 'I've never wanted to hurt you. I know it was all my fault but I just couldn't come to terms with what you'd told me. I panicked and took myself away. At first I'd hoped it would only be for a little while, until I worked out what to do, but the more I thought about it the more I realised I'd never be able to reconcile my faith with yours.'

I was about to say she was wrong, that my "faith", as she put it, was nowadays tenuous at best. My father, as always, continues to ask me to embrace it again but I haven't been able to give him what he wants. The only time I ever go near a synagogue is when I visit my family. Even these attacks I've been investigating haven't drawn me closer to my roots and I somehow feel they have no direct connection to me, other than being crimes which need to be solved. Perhaps I might feel differently if someone close to me had been targeted but I have to admit that, for now, they are remote. An intellectual exercise. Certainly, any affinity I've felt for my parent's religion takes a poor second place to what I've felt for Elizabeth. I found myself on the verge of explaining this to her and I think she sensed it.

'I must tell you, James, things have changed. I've met someone else and he's asked me to marry him.'

I drained my glass and thought seriously about getting it refilled. This time with rum.

'Is this why you asked to meet? So you could rub my nose in it?'

She tried to cover my hand again but this time I did recoil.

'Of course not. I'm fond of you, James, I'd never do such a thing. It's just that we can't be together.'

'So why are we meeting?'

Elizabeth bowed her head and rubbed her brow.

'I need your help.'

Elizabeth's request was straightforward. She'd met her fiancé, John Manning, at a Christmas party and they'd liked each other straight away. He was a widower with two children and had recently become a neighbour of her new employer. Something of a whirlwind romance followed, fuelled on her part, I imagined, by being on the rebound from our break-up, and he'd asked her to be his wife barely two months after they met.

'My only concern is that he never seems to have any money with him. Either he's forgotten his wallet or he has no small change, and he's always apologetic, but every time we're out I end up paying.'

My next question was obvious.

'Has he asked to borrow any cash?'

'No, nothing like that, at least not yet. It's just ... well, he lives in a fine house and says he has his own business but one hears such awful stories about confidence tricksters. I have a few pounds put aside and I wouldn't want to lose it. Apart from the money itself, I'd feel such a fool.'

There didn't seem any point refusing to have Manning checked out. I'd simply have seemed petulant and I was suspended anyway so what else was I doing with my time. Elizabeth gave me what information she had about him and I said I'd make a few enquiries, making it clear I couldn't promise anything.

I waited until she'd finished her drink and didn't prolong our mutual discomfort by offering to buy another. Instead, we walked to the car, then endured a silent drive to Mrs Veasey's cottage before I headed home through the storm.

SEVENTEEN

I now had two things to do to stave off the boredom. The next morning, I telephoned Spencer, my Special Branch contact. He'd pulled me in for questioning when I was working on a previous case and we'd since become friends. We didn't see each other much, he was working all over the country and in these difficult times had his work cut out keeping up with all the reports of German spies, real and imagined. When he happened to be close by he'd ring to meet up for a meal. It was unfortunate that the only time I'd ever phoned him was to ask for a favour. His greeting was wary when he heard my voice.

'Good morning, James. An unexpected pleasure.' He laughed. 'What do you need today?'

'I'm sorry to bother you, Mike, but you are still working alongside Mitchell in MI5?'

'Yes, for my sins. Why?'

'It's just that my father hasn't heard from his brother, Gideon, for a while. We were receiving letters regularly after you located my uncle last time but they've stopped. The family seemed to be heading towards Switzerland or France.'

'All the way across Germany? Why on earth didn't they try to get out through the north?'

'I don't really know. Perhaps they thought it would be easier to escape the country on land than try to board a ship. Is there any chance your associates might have a clue what's become of them?'

'Afraid not, James, the whole Jewish population is in turmoil with thousands on the move. Some are doing as Hitler has demanded and trying to get back to the countries their families came from, others, like your uncle, are fleeing anywhere. From what I hear, there are queues at every port, railway station and embassy in the country with the poor sods trying to get out. I know Mitchell still has men on the ground but they'd be far too busy to spend time looking for one family, especially if you haven't a clue where they might be.'

'I understand, Mike, and thanks for your honesty; you could have said you'd follow it up, to keep me happy, but then not bothered.'

The first time we met hadn't been the easiest of circumstances, at least not for me, but I'd been able to tell straight away that Spencer was solid and would be a good man to have at your back. Definitely not a person to have as an enemy. He reminded me of Harry Wilson, the same air of toughness and determination. They'd be similar ages, Wilson a tad younger, and I wondered if they'd both seen action in the War.

We exchanged news for a few more minutes and agreed to meet as soon as we could, finishing with me vowing to phone Mike when I didn't need something from him. I hung up, not knowing how I'd break the news to my father.

My second call was to the police headquarters in Devon, trying to find anyone who'd have contacts able to vouch for John Manning. I was eventually pointed in the direction of an Inspector Sydney Britton, now based in Barnstaple but having spent lots of his working life in Lynton, near where the new man in Elizabeth's affections lived. Britton was out of his office, so I left a message for him to call me back when he had a minute.

I'd barely put the receiver down when the phone rang and it was Sawyer.

'Could you come up to the station, sir? There's been a call for you.'

'Well, pass it on to Reynolds or Gould and let them deal with it. You know I'm suspended?'

He snorted.

'Of course I know, everyone does, but none of us believe a word of it.'

'That's kind of you, John, thanks. Though it doesn't alter the fact that I'm under suspicion and not working, so pass on the message as I've asked.'

'Anything you say, sir. I just thought if a member of the public contacted us with information about where to find Paúlu Demma, you'd want to be the first to know.'

In ten minutes, I'd hot-footed it up the hill to meet Sawyer in the canteen. He was nursing a steaming mug of tea and a self-satisfied grin, which I told him to remove as I collapsed on the seat opposite him. My wheezing only caused his smile to broaden. I really do need to get fitter.

'Come on then,' I gasped, 'what have you got for me?'

'About half past twelve WPC Merrion passed a caller up to me. Wouldn't give his name but said he'd heard you were looking for the Demma brothers and knew where you might find Paúlu. Also said he'd be willing to give evidence but only when Paúlu was behind bars. He left me a number where you can contact him between six and seven tonight.'

A roar of derision rose up when a young constable dropped his lunch over in the corner and we paused our conversation until the mayhem had died down. Sawyer passed me the informant's number then looked around to see if anyone might be in earshot.

'You're not going to do anything silly, are you, sir?'

'Like what?'

'Like trying to catch Demma.'

I didn't answer.

'At least let me come with you when you go looking for him.'

Why do we not welcome offers of help when they come along and make perfect sense? I don't think of myself as a proud man, nor as some kind of heroic tough guy who doesn't need back up, yet the idea of accepting Sawyer's assistance never crossed my mind for a moment. It just shows how stupid I can be at times. I shook my head.

'Sorry, John, but I can't let you do that. I'm not prepared to let you get into trouble.'

'But sir, you're not even supposed to be working. You won't be able to formally take him into custody and if anything was to happen to him...'

Written on his face, in letters ten feet tall, was his final understanding of why I'd been suspended. I can't say that I blamed him, what would I have done in his shoes? No smoke without fire, isn't that what they say? There wasn't a man in the station, probably in the entire force, who didn't know I hated the two Sicilians and, despite Sawyer's protestations, I was sure at least half would think I had something to do with the older brother's death. Some would be certain, others, like Sawyer, would be much more sceptical. It was pretty clear now that I couldn't take him along. He was right that I'd need him to arrest Demma but he'd only ever have one eye on Paúlu. The other would be firmly fixed on me and I wasn't prepared to have him doing it.

'I'll phone this chap later and we'll see if it leads anywhere. In the meantime, don't mention this to anyone else and I'll give you a shout if I need you.'

The afternoon dragged remorselessly. On the off chance the informant might be there early, I rang his number several times without an answer. I also phoned Inspector Britton again but was told he was still away and wouldn't be back until next day. The newspaper crossword held no interest and I gave up on the Terence Spelling novel I'd taken out of the library on Oliver Neilson's advice, fifty pages before the end. I couldn't see how the obviously intelligent retired teacher could find it remotely worthwhile. The book's hero, Max Spielberg, seemed to have no clue about reasoning or deduction, simply beating up all his suspects in equal measure until the guilty party coughed up a confession. I'd found it fairly obvious by the third chapter who the villain was. I only stuck with the damned book until Spielberg's strong-arm tactics produced the required result because I had nothing better to do.

Somehow I managed to survive the ticking of the clock until preparing my dinner, eating it as slowly as I could. This and the washing up took me to half past five. The next three-quarters of an hour almost drove me to distraction. I dialled our snitch at least another dozen times until he finally answered at quarter past six.

'I hear you're looking for our friend Mr Demma,' he said in a strong Coventry accent.

'Do you know where he is, Mr...?'

'You can call me ... err ... Mr Chamberlain for now — like the Prime Minister,' he chuckled, 'and I want to know what it's worth first.'

'Before we get into that, I want to be sure you're not just spinning me a line. How do you know Demma?'

'I've worked with them a while, him and his brother.'

'Doing what?'

'This and that. Does it matter? All you need to know is that I can lead you to Paúlu.'

'So why so public spirited all of a sudden?'

'You and I both know Paúlu's an unpleasant bugger, very unpleasant indeed if he's crossed. Benito kept him in check but now he's gone there's no stopping the brother. Takes everything a bit too far for my liking. I want to make sure he'll be out of the way for keeps if I tell you where to find him. I can't have him being free to come after me. I also want a decent payment to get out of here myself, somewhere warm and sunny.'

I asked him how much "a decent payment" was and he named his price. It's amazing how little it took for him to agree to deliver up his partner in crime. The amount might have paid for a one-way train ticket to the Continent and a couple of weeks' rent. Not enough for him to retire. I only took a minute to agree, hoping that I'd be able to get the cash back from Dyer when the time came, though perfectly happy to find it out of my savings if it would guarantee putting Paúlu Demma behind bars. "Chamberlain" gave me an address in one of the seedier parts of Coventry, to meet at lunchtime next day. He'd then take me to where I'd find Paúlu. My head told me again to contact Sawyer and ask him to set up reinforcements. I didn't.

EIGHTEEN

I drove out to Mrs Veasey's cottage again after I'd spoken to Inspector Britton on the telephone at breakfast time. It was in the opposite direction to my planned rendezvous with Chamberlain but the Inspector had what I wanted at his fingertips, so it made sense to make an early start rather than sit twiddling my thumbs all morning. Britton had seemed like a nice bloke, with a soft West Country burr and a ready chuckle, and he couldn't have been more helpful.

Elizabeth greeted me.

'You've got some information for me, James?'

'I'm afraid it's good news, Elizabeth.'

'Afraid? How?'

'Well, if it's good for you and this Manning chap then it's not so good for me, is it?'

Elizabeth gave me her gentlest smile.

'I expect not. I am sorry, James.'

A part of me was pleased that Manning had turned out to be above board; at least I'd know for certain there was no chance of getting back with Elizabeth.

'It seems your new boyfriend is what he says he is, and actually quite wealthy. I'm told he has a string of shops and businesses. Apparently, he's in the process of buying a hotel on the promenade in Newquay but has had to throw all of his own money in the pot until the bank loan comes through. That's probably why he's been a bit short of ready cash.'

Elizabeth still looked concerned.

'And you're positive there's not a problem? You've checked?'

'I'm a policeman, Elizabeth, it's what I do for a living. Isn't that why you asked me? Do you think I'd be slapdash, especially for you?'

'No, of course not, James, that's not what I was trying to say. I'm sorry, it's just that I've been so concerned. I think so much of John and I wouldn't want to find he's been less than honest with me.'

I could see she wouldn't be content until I told her the whole story.

'After we spoke I contacted the police headquarters in Barnstaple. They cover the whole area where you're living and put me on to an Inspector Britton. He seemed to know a lot about your John, quite the local worthy, and I'd think Manning is sound enough if Britton vouches for him.'

The relief on Elizabeth's face was obvious.

'Oh, thank God,' she said, 'and thank you, James, you've made me very happy.'

'It sounds like the poor man's had a hard time of it over the past few years. Britton told me the wife had been killed and left him with two young children, and that's why he moved to Lynton, to get away from the memories.'

'It was a terrible tragedy for John. He's a lovely man; I think you'd like him.'

True. I might have liked him if circumstances were different, he was probably a really nice bloke. I couldn't imagine Elizabeth falling for anyone who wasn't. But the situation was what it was. I knew Manning didn't steal her from me, it just felt like he did. We sat quietly, each finding the wallpaper fascinating, no longer knowing where to go with our conversation, or our relationship, until I stood and told her I had to leave. I said my final goodbyes to Mrs Veasey at the gate then walked with Elizabeth to my car.

'Be happy, Elizabeth, but one request.'

'Anything, James. What is it?'

'Please don't invite me to the wedding.'

I hadn't intended to hurt her, it was simply a silly quip, but her face told me it had stung.

'Oh, James, don't be like that. You're a good friend, you must come to our wedding.'

So that was it, clear as day. A "friend". Elizabeth was over our break-up and I needed to get to the same place or I would see that watering-hole described by Miss Holt filling in front of my eyes. Did I want to be one of those beasts left there because it appeared safer than venturing across the savanna into the unknown?

Outside of my family there's only been two women in my life I've ever cared about. One was butchered and the other was unable to see beyond a two-thousand-year-old schism. Perhaps I would be better off on my own after all. As this thought faded another woman's face came into my head. Attractive, emotionally bruised and asking me to call on her again.

I made my way to the meeting point Chamberlain had given me. The only sound was a child crying on one of the upper floors of the dilapidated St George's Terrace. The three storey buildings on both sides hid much of the grey day but at least they provided some respite from the biting wind which had picked up throughout the morning. From my vantage point at the corner I had a good view of the house I was looking for, number fifteen, and hoped the occupant wouldn't be able to see me. Halfway along, the frontage was broken by an arch the width of at least one house which I knew would lead to a series of courtyards at the back. There was little chance of reaching it without being spotted if I walked past the window where

Chamberlain would be, so I circled the block and slipped through a similar passageway on the other side, hoping to go unnoticed. True, I'd arranged to meet my informant here, but I wasn't about to simply walk up and knock on his front door. I wanted it to be on my terms, not his. I'd some vague notion of sneaking in through the back door and catching Chamberlain unawares, once I'd made sure it was safe to do so.

The house was in a terrace of what were known as topshops, which had once been silk-weaving factories, the top floor divided into individual workshops, the lower ones housing the weavers. There were row after row of them in Hillfields, still providing accommodation for poorer families, though the industry had largely died away. For a time after the looms had become redundant due to more efficient methods and cheap imports, the machinery had been committed to making bicycle or watch parts but even this industry had now crumbled.

This particular complex had been built as a huge triangle and inside, as I'd suspected, the grim walls bounded a cavernous open space with communal washing lines and a water pump, and three long rear entries leading to several dozen smaller private yards, each house having its own. I wondered what it would have been like when the gigantic steam engine at the end of each block was pumping power for the machines in every loft. The entire place would have rattled and echoed with a deafening noise, even though it was now empty and quiet.

I counted back to the house I was looking for. In a corner of its yard was a makeshift wooden shed with a shattered pane of glass in the door facing the house. I slipped inside and was almost overcome by spirit fumes. By the look of it, Chamberlain was a house painter. Wooden shelves on three sides and much of the floor were stacked with tins, every conceivable colour dribbling down their sides, leaving no need for the labels which were obliterated on every one. The side wall without shelving was hung with brushes, rollers, blowlamps and scrapers, all the paraphernalia of a painter's trade. Below these was a steel bin full of fading rolls of wallpaper, their edges nibbled by probably long-dead relatives of the mice who'd scattered when I'd shoved open the door. I perched on the edge of this container, able to see the back of the intended rendezvous through the glass and hoping I was far enough back to escape notice from the other side.

Less than two minutes into my vigil a fist thumped the side of the shed, then rapped on the door. I leapt up only to hear a padlock snap and see Paúlu Demma sneering at me through the broken window.

NINETEEN

Two men whispering? Three? How far away? It might have been twenty feet or forty. A smell of cigarette smoke and damp certainly. What else? A spirit of some sort. And hessian.

A slap on the table I've heard a million times. Two glasses clink. A man laughs.

They're playing cards and drinking, using a paraffin stove to keep warm. Are they whispering because they imagine I'm asleep? Or because they know I'm not?

I can't see but it can't be dark because they couldn't play if it was as black as this. Coarseness against my face. A sack over my head? I gradually become aware of a rope chaffing my wrists. My skull hurts like stink.

What happened? I remember being pulled, kicking and gouging, from the shed, by Paúlu Demma and two others; doubtless one was "Mr Chamberlain". They got in a few thumps and kicks but I'd landed some good blows before a fourth man knocked me cold.

I shudder when it strikes me that I'd been snatched because they thought I'd murdered Benito. Paúlu wasn't about to forgive anyone who'd stabbed his brother.

'He's awake.'

'Thank God for that — I thought you'd killed him.'

Laughter.

'You'd best go fetch Paúlu.'

A chair is pushed back, a door unlocked and one of my guards grunts up a flight of stone steps. So I'm in a cellar. What seems like an hour passes, actually only a few minutes, when I hear three pairs of feet come back down. One person walks across the room, stopping close in front of me. I brace for another blow. Instead, Demma's heavy accent whispers in my left ear.

'You've been looking for me, Given, and now you've found me. I hear from our friend Mr Barber you were setting up some kind of a trap you were so keen. Instead it was you caught in the trap, yes? So what you want to talk about?'

He laughs heartily but without humour. A cruel, chilling sound. I make a mental note to put Barber away when all this is over.

'I wanted to pass on my condolences, Paúlu, when I heard about your brother; couldn't have happened to a nicer bloke.'

I expect the slap and I'm not disappointed, though it still makes my teeth rattle. Warm blood dribbles down my chin. Demma calls to one of his accomplices.

'Here, Jez, come and take this thing off his head.'

'But he'll see our faces.' He sounds like the one I'd spoken to on the telephone.

'Well, he already knows mine, don't you, Inspector? And he won't be telling anyone because he won't be able to where he's going.'

So he does suspect I stabbed Benito. Another voice joins in the debate.

'Now wait a minute, a bit of Jew-baiting is one thing but I didn't sign up to killing coppers. Rough him up and warn him off you said. No mention of doing him in altogether.'

'You shut your mouth, Madeley.' Demma steps away and I sense they're squaring up. 'Or I'll stick you before I do him.'

'Try it and see how far you get. As I said, we're not murdering a copper.'

The seconds tick and I hear Demma clenching and unclenching his fists. Finally, he barks at the one he'd called Madeley.

'Have it your own way. But you're going to have to work out how to keep his mouth shut. He's like a pit bull, once he's got his teeth into you he won't let go. He was after Benito and me for a lifetime.'

No mention of his brother's death. Perhaps it is simply the old vendetta being played out yet again, the same reason we'd played cat and mouse for so many years. He'd never, ever, let Madeley get in his way if he believed I was guilty. Not that his motive matters much; he is still intent on getting rid of me. My only hope is that Madeley might be my saviour. My optimism is short-lived when he speaks again.

'Don't you worry, Paúlu, he'll not be coming after us after I've finished with him, he'll be far too scared. In fact, they might need to pension him off when he can't walk any longer.'

Demma's horselaugh tells me the storm has passed as quickly as it blew up.

There were times over the next two hours when I half-wished Demma had won the argument.

Madeley was no stranger to violence, despite his objections to going the final furlong. His demands were simple. Lay off my investigations into the attacks on Jewish businesses and forget all about Demma, the house in Hillfields and himself. I told him where he could go, so he slowly drew on his cigarette and placed the glowing tip on the space between the knuckles on my bound fingers. Each time I refused he burned another finger. Then the other hand. Then back again. I started bravely enough, telling him what I thought of him and his parents for the first few burns. By the second cycle, with pain on top of pain, I was just shaking my head and gritting my teeth. He called out to someone across the room.

'Kev, put the kettle on, will you?'

I imagined he'd grown tired of his little game and decided to take a well-earned rest. The other man struck a match and, a few minutes later, the boiling kettle whistled.

My tormentor walked away.

'Keep it good and hot 'til we're ready.'

The whistling continued. Their conversation dropped to a whisper.

'Will he break?' asked the one called Kev.

'He'd better. If he doesn't then I wouldn't fancy his chances when Demma comes back. That madman won't care if he kills one copper or two.'

'Do you think he'll really go ahead with topping that Birmingham one?'

Madeley laughed grimly. 'Of course he will. Demma's not going to let him get away with killing Benito, now, is he? I'd say that bloke's as good as done for.'

'Do you know why the copper did it?'

'From what I hear he was taking a back-hander to look the other way then he asked for more money. Benito told him to bugger off. There was a scrap and Benito got stabbed.'

'Can we stop Paúlu finishing off this feller? I'm with you on it, I'm not up for killing coppers, even if they deserve it.'

'I reckon the best we can do is make Given agree to stay off our backs, then Demma will likely let him go. What happens after that I wouldn't want to guess.'

For the next half hour I thought I'd died and gone to hell. Madeley and his partner removed my shoes but left on my socks, so the water stayed on my feet, burning, and didn't run off on to the floor.

A question from Madeley. 'Are you going to let this go?'

'Sod off,' followed by a yelp, from me, when he did his work, half emptying the kettle on to my ankle.

A repeated demand, with the same reply from me and the same response from Madeley.

I knew I wouldn't withstand the searing pain for long. Madeley left enough time between each pouring to allow my skin to cool, to fool the nerve endings to the edge of sensitivity again. Even after two treatments I was going into shock, gasping for breath, my head swirling into a deep pit. As with the cigarette burns, I soon stopped replying to his questions, using all my energy to stifle my desire to scream and scream.

I tried to travel away from the torture; to Elizabeth in happier times, to days picking fruit in the Kent sunshine, to weeks at sea in Mediterranean warmth. I even mused that Madeley's methods were amateurish compared to Harry Wilson's, who intimidated by his very presence, his voice implying so much dominance he didn't actually have to resort to violence to get what he wanted. Top class interrogators are like that. I'd watched and envied them whenever I came across one.

These meanderings would only stave off the agony for so long. They boiled the kettle twice more. Halfway through the fifth assault I dropped my chin and nodded.

'Stop, please stop.'

We'd been driving for about twenty minutes and I was curled on the back seat of the car with the bag still over my head, Demma beside me and Madeley at the wheel. I'd heard no-one else.

Paúlu muttered the whole time: 'You're a very lucky man, Given'. Then he'd squeeze my still-soaking foot, making me feel far less lucky than he imagined. I could feel my skin slip like an extra sock before the excruciating pain kicked in.

The car slowed, turning onto a much bumpier road then jerking to a halt. It seemed to be a dead end because there was much swearing as the car swung backwards and forwards, with Demma shouting 'right hand down', 'two feet', 'plenty of room' and similar instructions until Madeley switched off the ignition. The brief ensuing silence told me we were no longer in the middle of the city. Demma leaned close over me.

'Now listen, Given, we can find you any time, and don't you forget it. If you want more of Mr Madeley's pampering, you keep looking out for our Jew friends. We think they're only getting what's due to them and shouldn't be receiving help from the likes of you. Good Christians like us need to stick together, isn't that so?'

Demma shuffled on his seat and I heard a click close to my face. The point of a penknife, warm from his pocket, grazed the length of my throat through the sacking. I imagined that he'd changed his mind and any moment would push the blade through an artery before dumping me in a field to bleed to death. Instead, he just slashed the bonds from my wrists and pushed me out on to a verge of sodden grass.

'Now, off you go and enjoy your walk home.'

The two of them laughed as the car door slammed and when their engine faded into the distance there was no sound other than birdsong. I lay still for a long time, the smell of wet soil seeping through the sack before I finally ripped it from my head, wincing as the daylight fractured my eyes. I was lying in a field entrance, a five-bar gate behind me and a rutted farm track in front. Three large, black and white, horned heads peered over that gate, oblivious to my predicament.

I tried to stand and cried out, falling down again to lie gasping for a while longer. Gingerly, I lifted myself to my knees, edging forward on all fours to the track, trying to get some bearings. If I was as lucky as Demma had suggested there would be a farmhouse a few yards away. Needless to say, there wasn't. In one direction lay another field, covered by some winter crop I didn't recognise. In the other direction, about three hundred yards distant, several vehicles passed the end whilst I watched, suggesting there was a road. I dragged myself through the mud on hands and knees, cursing and squealing each time I slipped and a foot made contact with the ground. I needed to rest every few yards so it took nearly an hour to cover the short distance to the roadside, every inch and every second punctuated by an explosion of pain.

Despite the earlier flurry of activity no vehicles appeared for the first five minutes, then a gleaming Rover 10 slowed, only to speed away when the driver saw the state of my clothes. His startled face through the windscreen told me he thought I must be mad, or drunk, or both. A couple more minutes dripped away before a Royal Mail van slammed on his brakes and I passed out.

TWENTY

I awoke to find a hopelessly beautiful nurse cutting off my socks, the insides of which glistened with damp skin as they peeled away. Strangely, there was no pain despite the scarlet stumps now revealed at the ends of my legs. Beside her stood a doctor running a hand through his silver-grey mane, introducing himself as Doctor Baines, and explaining I'd been dosed with morphine in the ambulance called by the postman. The scene was surreal and I considered if it could have been an illusion brought on by the narcotic.

'You're very lucky, Inspector,' said the doctor. I heard myself giggling at the thought that this wasn't the first time I'd been told this today. The effects of the drugs were certainly interesting. 'If you'd not managed to make your way to the main road you may not have been found for days, then you might have lost your legs. As it is, you're bruised, you've two broken ribs and you'll be scarred for life unless this lovely nurse's lotion works its magic.'

Doctor Baines supervised as the nurse smeared thick white cream over my wounds and gently bandaged them. All through the process he continued to talk, although only occasional words managed to penetrate the fog drifting in and out of my head. A thick wave of nausea swept over me.

'I'm sorry to say you'll be in pain a few days, Inspector. The morphine will help but it might make you feel a bit sick. Call Nurse Ingram here if it gets too bad.'

I garbled something which the nurse correctly interpreted as me asking how they knew I was a police officer.

'Your papers were in your pocket. We've contacted the police station in town and they've said they'll send someone down straight away.'

I asked if she'd also contact Sawyer to let him know where I was. She gave me a devastating smile and said that she would telephone him as soon as she'd finished looking after my feet.

The doctor looked at his watch and it was pretty obvious he had other patients to attend to. The last words I heard him say before I floated into my morphine abyss was him explaining I'd need to stay in hospital for a while until I was fit to walk again.

The next thing I knew, Wilson was standing beside my bed. I'd been too dopey to make much sense to him so sent him away. Now, almost twenty-four hours later, I was more compos mentis and he was back with a vengeance. I'd had my drugs reduced in the afternoon so now my feet were throbbing like a ship's engine pushing against the tide but I knew I had to face Wilson sometime. I filled him in on how I'd ended up on the side of a country road covered in mud.

'You're never going to learn, are you? What the hell did you think you were doing?' Harry Wilson growled at me from the end of my bed. 'Suspended, under suspicion of murder, and still you're out there chasing the dead man's brother. Am I to assume you were trying to kill him as well?'

There was nothing I could say which might lessen his anger because I'd been stupid. The sort of incompetence you'd expect from a raw recruit, charging in without any back up, just to show what a brave and clever copper he was. In Wilson's shoes I'd have been as mad as he was. If I hadn't been blinded by my desire to get to Paúlu so quickly I'd have made sure I had enough reinforcements in place to cover my back, then we'd have caught the lot of them and I wouldn't have ended up in here.

'Even that little toe-rag, George Barber, is trying to use your vendetta as a bargaining chip.'

'Barber?'

'He was picked up at the end of last week for breaking into a shop. Told the lad who arrested him he would lead us to Benito's murderer, then came up with a story that you'd been looking everywhere for the Demmas before the older brother was killed. I gave Barber a boot up his backside, partly because he wasn't telling me anything new. What would you do in my position?'

I told him he was right, and that I was sorry, though I'd hoped he'd have a bit more trust in a fellow police officer.

'The fact that I do have some trust in you is the only reason you're not behind bars already. You know as well as I that I have to follow up any lead, however slim, and right now you're actually the only one we've got.'

'Perhaps I can help. You don't have to believe this, especially as I've no proof, but Benito Demma was killed by a copper, though it wasn't me.'

'A copper? How do you know?'

'When I was tied up I overheard two of Paúlu's men discussing it. The one called Madeley said this policeman had tried turning the screw, they'd fought and that's when Benito was killed.'

'What do you think he meant?'

'It's hard to say. As far as I could make out the killer was tipping them off about investigations in exchange for cash and he wanted more. Apparently, Benito threatened to expose him.

'And they didn't give his name?'

'I only wish they had. Only that he was from Birmingham. That could have been the force he was on, or he might be a Brummie working somewhere else. Have you any here in Coventry? It might be anybody. You don't go around acting like the Demmas without attracting a few enemies along the way.'

'Like you?'

'Yes, if that's how you see it, like me. Only difference is that I wouldn't take the law into my own hands and kill Benito Demma myself, I'd let the courts do their job and put him at the end of a rope. Now, I think we're finished, I need my rest.'

Wilson paused and stretched.

'You know, Given, you can be a very difficult man to work with. I followed up your story about being at your parents' house and it checked out.'

'Don't sound so surprised.'

'I'm not surprised, it's what I expected. I told you I believed you, even if you are the only person we've found who has motive and opportunity. But you know I have to follow the rules every step of the way on this. The important thing now is that my boss and yours have decided to reinstate you. We'll sort this mess out much more quickly if we work together. Agreed?'

I could hardly say no.

'Agreed, but listen, I meant what I said about needing my rest, and my damned feet are hurting so much I'm not thinking straight. Can we talk again when I'm a bit better? I promise I'll rack my brains to see if any clues come back to me about who our copper could be.'

As he walked from the ward I thought back to the conversation I'd heard in the cellar and knew I had a very good idea who'd killed Demma, though I wasn't prepared to share it with Wilson until I'd made a few enquiries.

The boss came in not long after Wilson left and gave me the official reinstatement speech. He wasn't a happy man.

'I should suspend you again, Given. Straight away for the embarrassment you've caused.'

If I thought Wilson had been tearing me off a strip it was nothing compared to what Dyer said. I couldn't argue with him. Sometimes I think he can, like many managers, get caught up with petty rules and regulations, forgetting what it's like in the real world where people like me do our job. But not this time, even I'd have had trouble letting this one pass if it had been one of my subordinates. After all, the Superintendent would be the one having to explain to his superiors how one of his senior officers had come to be suspected of murder in the first place and then, not content with that, had gone looking for the victim's brother and got himself abducted.

After the hurricane had blown itself out Dyer asked me how Rose's murder investigation was going.

'It's a bit like wading through treacle, sir, the delay in finding her body, and the state it was in, means we've not much to go on. There are a few teachers, who wouldn't say boo to a goose, a couple of boyfriends and the greenkeeper. None of them really stand out.' I ran through the possibilities with him, finishing with the most likely suspect. 'Sawyer thinks it was Alan Johnston but I can't see it. All the evidence so far points at him but there's something that doesn't stack up. He has a motive, knew Rose, and was more than familiar with where she was found, though I don't think he's the type.'

'James...'

'I know, sir. There isn't a type. I've said it often enough myself. But this feller is too easy going, hardly seems to have a temper on him. I simply can't see him killing a young woman in a fit of passion.'

'Well, you'd better get some kind of idea of who did it as soon as you get out of here or I'm pulling the plug. There's plenty of other cases you could be working on, ones where you stand half a chance of solving them.'

Dyer left this hanging in the air until I lay back and looked at the ceiling.

'I'm sorry, James, but you seem to have got yourself tied up with this one. You're a good man and I don't like to see you beating yourself up. Let's leave that to Demma and his mates.' I couldn't help smiling at his little joke. 'Sawyer tells me you're thinking of pulling in a councillor from Coventry — Gibbons, isn't it? Had something to do with the dead girl. Is that right?

'I wasn't going to have him in, not just yet. I do need to have a word with him when I eventually get out of this place. Unless you want to send someone else round, sir?'

'Not a chance. It's enough to have you and Sawyer tied up on this damned thing without me putting extra manpower on it. I just wanted to say to be careful. If you thought the Demma brothers were vicious then you'll find these political types are like piranhas if you start stirring their pool.'

Dyer was demonstrating how he could combine concern for his men whilst looking after the wider interests of the force. In a younger, more ambitious, boss I'd have suspected him of watching out for his career but I knew this wasn't the case with Dyer — he'd be retired in less than a year. He knew Gibbons was influential and even though the councillor was in a different area, he'd still have powerful contacts in ours who could make life difficult if we overstepped the mark.

I reassured Dyer that I'd tread carefully and thanked him for coming in. He left me with a parting shot.

'Remember, James, I want some results. Quickly. I'll give you two more weeks when you leave hospital, then this case is put to bed.'

TWENTY-ONE

'You look like you've been in the wars,' I said to Sawyer.

A first hint of spring was enticing buds skywards and Sawyer had pushed me out into the late-March sunshine in a wheelchair. He was sitting opposite me on a bench, the ugly red-brick lump of Gulson Road hospital looming up behind him, and he was picking at a bandaged hand.

'It's nothing really, sir. A stupid accident when I called round to talk to Stella Johnston. I'd gone round to ask if she'd any suspicions that Alan might have been seeing Rose in Coventry, before she moved back here. She said she didn't know but thought it unlikely. She said she thought she'd have noticed if he'd disappeared for that long and someone at school would have mentioned it if he'd taken a day off. Whilst I was there she gave me tea and I dropped the cup on the kitchen floor, then stabbed my palm trying to clean it up. Bled like a pig but she fixed it up in a flash.'

'Good job she knows her first-aid.'

'She certainly does. Fetched a bag from the kitchen stacked with plasters, creams, liniments, the lot. Patched me up then sent me to the hospital for a few stitches. She made me laugh when she said she knew how to do them but would probably get in trouble with the St John's if she practised on me.'

'Sounds like you got on like a house on fire.'

Sawyer blushed.

'Stella — Mrs Johnston — has a good sense of humour.'

'And quite easy on the eye for you, I'd say.'

He went even redder. Would he chance his arm there if we put Alan Johnston away for Rose Spicer's murder?

'Sorry, John, only teasing. Let's have a look at where we are.'

'As far as I'm concerned it's still Alan Johnston at the top of the list, sir. He knew the victim well, very well in fact. He'd argued with her, he needed to shut her up to save his marriage, and he probably knew where he could hide her in the school without her being discovered. No-one else comes even close.'

'Look, we've been through this a couple of times. I agree he's a suspect but I'm not convinced and until I am we need to look at the alternatives. Are you sure you don't just want him out of the way?'

I regretted it as soon as the words were out of my mouth. Sawyer glowered at me as coldly as ever I'd seen him.

'What do you mean by that, sir?'

I should have backed off straight away, but I didn't.

'Only that you've been round to see his wife, at least once, for God-knows what reason, while I've been away, chatting and supping tea, and then all of a sudden you're all gooey-eyed and on first name terms. She has to be a suspect as well, John, and I can't have your judgement being clouded because you're sweet on her.'

I thought he was going to get up and walk off but he didn't. Instead, he settled back down, still scowling.

'It's a shame you'd think I would do that, sir, I wish you'd give me more credit. You know damn well I've believed Johnston was our man right from the start. The only reason I went round to the house was in case he'd been back and I thought if I asked her a few questions I might get something more on him. As for me and her, though it's really none of your business, there isn't anything. Yes, I think she's attractive and, yes, we had a laugh over a cuppa but that's it. She's the wife of a suspect in a murder case, might even be one herself, so why would I even consider jeopardising my career over her?'

Now he did stand and turn to leave.

'Wait a minute, John, sit down. I admit I was out of order. This pain and the painkillers are making me stupid, not to mention being cooped up in this place. Let's start again.'

I was relieved when he complied. The last thing I wanted was to have to work this case on my own. Sawyer would need to do a lot of the legwork until I was fit and I also needed him by my side in case Paúlu Demma came looking for me again. We agreed to differ on the Johnstons and I filled him in on my latest thoughts on the current crop of suspects. I asked if anyone else had emerged.

'Not so far, sir.'

'Could it be someone from Rose's past, before she even moved back to Kenilworth? I need to talk to that Councillor chap, Gibbons, but I really mean from her time in France. Smith and Spicer fit the bill but both are unlikely. It did occur to me there's someone from that period in Rose's life we haven't come across yet.'

'But why wait until she's in England?'

'Oh, I don't know, any number of reasons, I suppose. Perhaps they only recently found out where she was. Perhaps they thought they'd stand a better chance of getting away with it in another country. Perhaps there's some significance in the place she was left.'

'Like what?'

'You tell me. None of this makes much sense. Not the murder itself, they happen all the time, but the posing of her body, leaving it under a church, wrapping a crucifix round her hands. In some ways we don't even know it was murder because Dr Naismith can't confirm a cause of death other than heart failure. Could it simply be that whoever was with her when she died thought they were showing respect by laying her out that way and now they're too scared to own up to it?'

'Who would do such a thing?'

'Well, imagine Alan Johnston, your prime suspect, for instance. I'm not conceding he did it, just using him as an example, but if he and Rose happened to be using that mattress for some hanky-panky and she took a heart attack, he's hardly going to raise the alarm and let his wife know what he was up to, is he? There could be half a dozen reasons why whoever was with Rose didn't want anyone to know, even if they didn't actually kill her.'

'So what do we do?'

'We carry on as before. I'll interview Gibbons as soon as I can get out of this place, you ask around to see if anyone has any ideas about Rose's time in France and we'll see what develops on the other leads.' I passed him a sheet of paper from my dressing gown pocket. 'Meanwhile, could you telephone these people and ask them these questions, no more, no less. If they want to know why you're asking just tell them it's a favour for me.'

TWENTY-TWO

What is it about hospitals that stops me from sleeping? It was dark and I was in bed, relatively free of pain, but still sleep wouldn't come. The night sister had put the lights out hours ago and the only sound was gentle snoring from my fellow prisoners. Try as I might, the pieces of the Rose Spicer jigsaw swirled round and round in my head, in that strange fashion where they're all disconnected and transitory. My concentration would stick with one piece until, for a split second, I thought I'd glimpse a link, then my mind would veer off to another totally different part of the puzzle.

A nearby church bell struck two o'clock shortly before a nurse came in and quietly checked on my neighbour. I asked if there was any chance of a cup of tea.

'I shouldn't, you know,' she whispered, then gave me a wink and disappeared for a few minutes before returning with two cups. She sat on the side of my bed. 'Can't sleep, Mr Given?'

'Afraid not.'

'Are your feet hurting? Can I get you some aspirin?'

'No, thanks, I'm fine, nurse. It's just work keeping me awake.'

'Anything you want to talk about?'

'Did you ever keep a diary, Nurse — sorry, I don't know your name?'

'Call me Beryl when Sister's out of earshot, otherwise it's Nurse Peters. I don't keep one myself, though my brother does, always has. He doesn't need it, I don't think, not for appointments and that, I imagine he uses it to keep his thoughts in order. I haven't even seen one of his for a while, he's getting a bit too old to let his big sister peek into his private world, but he'd show it to me when he was younger. Always full of scraps he wanted remember, what the weather was like, how many fish he'd caught, that kind of thing.'

'Would he keep secrets in it?'

'Well, in a way, it was all secret, wasn't it? Youngsters are full of them, I know I was, I just didn't write them down. How about you?'

She was right, of course. We all have things we don't want to share and I imagine a diary might be a useful way of having a conversation with oneself, not simply recording memories but trying to make sense of them as well. Was I missing something in Rose's? Was there a clue hidden in the day to day, the outwardly mundane, that I wasn't seeing?

Beryl sipped the final dregs from her cup, plumped my pillow and wished me goodnight before tiptoeing out of the ward. I swallowed the sleeping tablet she'd left behind and my thoughts returned to Rose's diary.

She'd been meticulous in naming people she was meeting except on a single occasion, her last, when one person was only denoted by their initial. This secrecy can't have come from a fear of a casual reader finding out. After all she'd named Alan Johnston, Joey Atkin and Tom Marshall then retrospectively recorded what they'd done together. Was it because Rose was afraid "A" might get hold of the journal? But there was nothing incriminating in it. Maybe the girl had expected to make an entry after their rendezvous but had died before she was able to do so. Then it struck me that the ones after the night she was planning to meet him had only been appointments, with no report the following day. Did this mean I was right in my assumption that this was the time and date she was killed? It was as good as anything else I had to go on.

I'd already suspected it was correct because if Rose had died earlier in the day then "A" would probably have found her and reported it if he'd been innocent. Her father had also seen her the previous night so it had to be after that. I wasn't sure how I could discount a later date but then Rose would have had to either be staying away from home for some reason or held in the crypt up to the time she died.

So far we had three people we knew of in Rose's life who had a name beginning with "A": Alan Johnston, Joey Atkin and Andrew Gibbons, and I had good reasons to suspect any of them. Unfortunately, I had only reasons, not evidence and, in fact, it could be none of them. "A" might be someone we'd not even come into contact with yet or be completely spurious. Rose might have met them and then been killed by someone else.

Who else did we have? In addition to the three "A"s there was Oliver Neilson. He'd been at the school for years and might have known Rose but he'd denied it when I'd asked him. He also played the amateur detective and was a bit too quick off the mark in pointing the finger at other possible suspects. There was no doubt in my mind that Neilson was a little strange but was he a murderer? If strangeness were enough to convict then the headmaster, Laurence Perelle, might also be close to the top of the list. He was arrogant and dismissive, showed little concern about a potentially missing child or relief when it turned out not to be one of his charges and his collection of dead creatures topped Oliver Neilson's assortment of relics for weirdness by a country mile. There was a remote chance that Stella Johnston and Benjamin Smith might also be in the frame, she because she may have found out about her husband's adultery and he because he could have been on the Riviera at the same time as Rose. Could he have met her there and followed her back to Kenilworth to conclude some unfinished business? He'd have known someone would eventually discover the corpse so reported finding it himself, just to put us off the scent.

Possibility after possibility swirled around, each seeming more likely than the last for a few short seconds, until being replaced by the next one that my sleep-deprived mind could dredge up. *Alan, Atkin, Andrew, Anyone.* The words spun in my head until the sleeping tablet finally did its work.

There are those who'd welcome with open arms the opportunity to stay in bed for a few days. I'm not one of them. Each time a nurse came to change my dressings I'd ask the same question: "When can I go home?" She'd always respond with the same answer: "When the doctor says you can." The doctor, in turn, replied, "When you're well enough", and round and round it went.

By the afternoon of the fifth day I'd had enough.

'Tell me something, Dr Baines, can I discharge myself?'

'You could, but you'd be very silly to do so and I won't take responsibility for what happens if you do.'

'Fine. Bring me the papers.'

'Inspector Given, what you need is bed rest. I can easily arrange for your dressings to be changed by the district nurse but you must stay off your feet to let them heal, and I suspect you won't do that if we let you out of hospital.'

'But I'm going mad in here, doctor.'

'Better to briefly lose your mind than permanently lose your feet, don't you think? You don't seem to appreciate how badly you've been burnt.'

I appreciated it alright. It was bad enough when Madeley was doing his work but now, with my skin crisp and dry despite copious applications of cream, the pain seared from my toes to my groin at every contact with the floor.

I've always had a nails-down-the blackboard fear of losing a limb, ever since seeing a deckhand mangle his arm in a winch on a boat we were working. By the time we got him into port it was too late to save it and when we picked him up again on our return journey to take him home his stump attracted my morbid gaze each time I met him. He drank and drank the whole journey and, when he was in his cups, he cried for fear of what was going to become of him and his young family if he couldn't work.

Regardless of this dread, I knew I couldn't stay in hospital much longer. The isolation and boredom were driving me crazy and I needed to get back to work. Sawyer could only do so much without direction and Dyer wouldn't assign anyone senior to Rose's case in my absence. The boss barely believed she'd been murdered anyway and the trail would be getting cold three weeks into our investigations. On top of that, I wanted my revenge and I'd been laid up five days already, so how much chance would there be of catching up with Paúlu Demma? I made my decision.

'Thank you for your concern, doctor, but please just bring me whatever it is I have to sign.'

An hour later, with paperwork out of the way and a stack of painkillers in my bag, I was being helped into a taxi by the nurse, Beryl Peters. She repeated what she'd been telling me from the moment I'd last spoken to the doctor.

'You're a fool to yourself you know, Mr Given. You might catch whoever you're after but what possible use will that be if you're back in here having your legs amputated?'

I squeezed her hand both in pain and in gratitude for her kindness.

'Don't you worry, Beryl, I'll be fine. You go back inside and carry on the good work. I'll call in to see you again when I'm passing.'

I gave the driver directions to where I was hoping my car was still parked. I settled back in my seat, gripping an armrest whilst waving a last time to Beryl, wishing with all my heart that her prediction wouldn't materialise.

It was less than a mile in the taxi and, in normal circumstances, I'd have walked it in a quarter of an hour, but these weren't normal circumstances. Climbing all over my car were half a dozen lads, who headed for the hills when we drew up. Other than dust, handprints and footprints the motor didn't seem any the worse for wear and I relaxed when the engine started first time — I couldn't have faced a walk to find a mechanic.

I drove home, gingerly manipulating the pedals as infrequently as possible, staying in low gears and pulling on the handbrake whenever that was an option. This resulted in the journey to Kenilworth taking twice as long and at least twenty times the usual effort. I parked and dragged my screaming feet into the house before throwing back double my prescribed dose of painkillers, then collapsing, fully clothed, onto the sofa, wishing for sleep to come.

TWENTY-THREE

The short ride up the hill to the station the next morning was quicker and less painful than the previous night's drive and Sergeant Tommy Burns greeted me like a long-lost friend when I got in. At least like a friend who'd been missing for a while and quietly connected to rumours that he'd been inside for crimes unspecified. Not really his fault, I suppose — as a policeman he's expected to be suspicious, to look beyond face value, and he wouldn't be the only one in the building glancing at me sideways over the next few days and weeks.

We chatted for five minutes, he trying to appear supportive, me shifting weight from one foot to the other and scanning around for a chair. My eyes were watering when I eventually hobbled up the stairs to telephone Councillor Gibbons.

The mess on my desk told me no-one had picked up my work while I was away, so I had to clear a space to put down my notebook. There were no reports of further incidents with Jewish businesses over the past week, but this could simply be because no one had bothered carrying the files upstairs. There were two brief notes from Sawyer telling me he'd made the calls for me but that he hadn't had any luck. Both notes seemed to have been written the previous night.

I swallowed my second dose of codeine of the morning whilst I found Gibbons' number. The telephone rang for a long time before he answered. I introduced myself and apologised for my delay in getting to him.

'We need to have a chat — when would be convenient?'

Secrets don't remain secret for very long in a typing pool. Even if Miss Holt could be relied on to keep our conversation confidential I'd be less sure about her colleague, Elsie. All the typists would want every juicy detail of what we'd discussed and she'd be happy to tell them, basking in the spotlight for as long as it kept burning. Still, the good councillor pretended he didn't know why I was calling.

'Could you be more specific, Inspector? I can't think of anything the police would want to talk to me about.'

I made it clear I wouldn't discuss it on the phone and he reluctantly offered to meet me in the Council offices.

'I think we — sorry you — might find it better to meet somewhere a little more private.'

'I'm sorry, Inspector, I'm a very busy man. If you can't tell me more then perhaps I'll have to call the station and speak to your supervisor. Could you please tell me his name?'

'It is Dyer, Superintendent Dyer, and I think you'll find he'll give you the same answer. So let's not play around here Mr Gibbons.' I deliberately missed out his title. 'You may carry some weight in the Council, but not with me. I'll tell you more when we meet and that can be in the police station, where a reporter might spot you, or at your home where we'll not be disturbed by such distractions. Where is it to be?'

Gibbons blustered for another minute or two but he capitulated pretty quickly. I've always found these types of men are bullies within their own fiefdom but cowards outside the safety of its walls. We agreed I'd drive out to him that evening. With luck, the throbbing feet would have subsided by then.

The Councillor lived well. His stretch of the Kenilworth Road rose long and straight out of the city, its grand houses on both sides hidden behind a curtain of manicured woodland. The area was known as Gibbet Hill but, perversely, only the very wealthiest and upstanding of Coventry's residents could afford to live there. The screen of trees offered privacy to the road's inhabitants and the discreet signs on gateposts whispering "Raven's Nest", "The Willows", "Yew Tree Lodge", only served to heighten the sense of detached affluence.

Gibbons' house was perhaps twenty or twenty-five years old, considerably younger than many of the trees surrounding it, and I have to say I was impressed. I'd speculated where his money had come from and imagined he must, like many of the local nouveau riche, be involved in the motor car industry in some way. So I'd done some digging and it turned out the father of our man, a watchmaker and keen car enthusiast, had invented a method of making carburettor jets more efficiently. He'd never done anything with it but his son saw the potential and put it to good use.

His factory now produced thousands upon thousands of precision motor parts and sold them throughout England and beyond. Although the modern motor car is built on a production line, with every vehicle the same as the next, all manufacturers seek to be different to their competitors, making their product faster, cheaper, more comfortable — anything to give them a competitive edge. As a result the patterns for parts change constantly and this provides an endless flow of orders to Gibbons and his like.

I rang the doorbell and even though he'd been expecting me and would have heard my car arrive, crunching on the gravel drive, I was left waiting just long enough to put me in my place. If I'd anticipated Gibbons being the archetypal businessman, overweight and flouting an enormous cigar, I'd have been disappointed. A short, thin man in a brown wool suit and carpet slippers opened the door, then led me through an oak-panelled hallway to a beautifully decorated sitting room.

A middle-aged woman, inches taller than him, popped her head round the door. His housekeeper?

'Ah, Marjorie, this is Inspector Gibbons, he wants a few words. Inspector, this is my wife, Marjorie.'

Mrs Gibbons was what might be generously described as plain; bespectacled, skinny and no figure to speak of. She offered a cup of tea and returned a few moments later with a tray, complete with two plates of sandwiches and cakes. I wondered how much he'd told her of my visit and if he'd insisted she try to make a good impression. After she left the room he settled back in a leather armchair, hands clasped on his lap.

'Now, how may I help you, Inspector?' He seemed calm, composed.

'I believe you knew Rose Spicer, Mr Gibbons.'

A look of puzzlement.

'She was a shorthand typist at the Council. I'm told you called her in for dictation quite often.'

'Oh, that Rose, the girl who died. You quite had me there for a minute. I don't believe I knew her second name.'

His answer was too pat.

'I find that hard to believe, sir. I understand you asked for her every time you wanted something typed. It's rumoured you even asked her out — and you a married man.'

His composure slipped a little.

'What nonsense — who told you that?'

'You know how it is in offices, Councillor, gossip and innuendo. Personally, I often find there's something behind it. Smoke and fire, that kind of thing. After all, she was quite attractive by all accounts. So, how well did you know Rose Spicer?'

He spat out his next words.

'Not in the way you're suggesting. Now, I think we're done here.'

'She's dead, Mr Gibbons, and you spent lots of time with her.' His reaction told me nothing. 'Dead, with money and very explicit love letters hidden in her bedroom. Did you write them to Rose?'

'No. I've told you, Inspector. I didn't know the girl in that way.'

Though he denied it, his face told me he knew about the letters. I looked around at the antique furniture, the chandelier, the Oriental rugs, the expensive new gramophone in the corner.

'You look like you could afford to drop a few pounds to a willing young woman. Did you give her the money?'

Gibbons paused for a few seconds, sighed, and nodded his head.

'Yes. Yes I did.'

Taking Gibbons into the station in Kenilworth was closer than Coventry so he was now residing in the cells two floors below us. Marjorie Gibbons had insisted we wait at their home until his solicitor arrived but the councillor had requested there be no fuss and came with me quietly. He kissed his wife gently on the cheek and whispered something in her ear before joining me in the car. I'd imagined he was apologising for the scene being played out before her.

Sawyer and I were catching up.

'He says she was blackmailing him, John. That's why he gave her the cash and why she left her job at the Council. No need to work if you've a steady supply of funds from someone as well-heeled as Gibbons.'

'But it can't have been worth his while giving in to blackmail. He's not the first married man to have fling with a secretary and I doubt he'll be the last. Why didn't he just own up to his wife and take the consequences?'

'That's the point though — it wasn't Rose he was seeing.'

'Then who?'

'It was a young man in the Town Clerk's office.'

Sawyer's face was a picture.

'A poof? Gibbons? But he's married.'

I laughed and told him he had a lot to learn about the ways of men.

'Christ, sir, they disgust me. Makes my skin crawl thinking about what they do to each other. Are we going to charge him with gross indecency?'

Sawyer also had a lot to learn about tolerance, about when to do the legal thing and when to do the right thing. Perhaps I'd travelled more and seen more than he had, but it seemed to me that his prejudice against homosexuals was only a small step away from condoning Hitler's persecution of the Jews. It was the German people's mindless acceptance of his message of intolerance that was letting their leader get away with it.

'Why would we do that, John? We've bigger fish to fry. Anyway, I'm not sure we could, we've only the letters and he'd withdraw his admission if it ever went to court.'

'So how could Rose Spicer blackmail him?'

'She'd have been a witness. Gibbons says she came into his office one day without knocking and caught them.'

'So he has a motive to get rid of her.'

'He certainly does. We'd better get on down there and talk to him some more but before we do there's one thing you need to be clear about.'

'What's that, sir?'

'This is a murder investigation, and only a murder investigation. If I think you're letting your feelings about Gibbons being a homosexual cloud your judgement I'll throw you out of there so quickly your feet won't touch the ground. Do you understand me?'

To his credit, Sawyer accepted my warning without argument and I asked if his phone calls had led anywhere.

'Actually, I did have some luck this morning when you were out,' Sawyer replied. 'The records clerk over in Birmingham nick had a look through Inspector Gleeson's log and there's no entry for the time and date you mentioned, even though he was on duty. Are you going to tell me what this is about?'

'Not just now, John. I'll fill you in when I'm a bit more certain what I'm looking at. Anything on the others?'

'Nothing at all. No-one has seen or heard from Paúlu Demma since he put you in hospital. Perhaps he's done a runner.'

'I'd doubt it. His connections are all up here in the Midlands now. Benito wasn't bright but he did have the lion's share of the brains. Without him Paúlu wouldn't have a clue how to manage anything other than basic thuggery and, believe me, he's still around here somewhere.'

Across the interview room table Gibbons looked completely dejected. I put the letters in front of him, one at a time, and told him to look at them. Beside him, in an expensive three-piece grey suit, his solicitor peered over Gibbons' shoulder. I knew Partridge to be top man in one of the best practices in Coventry and both the suit and his reputation told me he wouldn't come cheap. He'd tried to push me into releasing Gibbons by saying we had no evidence to hold him. I'd told him we'd wait and see.

'You're telling me these weren't from you to Rose Spicer? They were in her possession and all signed with an "A". For Andrew?' I asked.

'I don't know why you're making me go through all this again,' Gibbons replied. 'I've already said they weren't to her and I wrote them to a male friend. I know I've been stupid but that damned woman went through his desk after she'd seen us together and found them there.'

'So you killed her.'

'No. No, I didn't. God, this is a nightmare. Rose ambushed me next time I called her into my office and told me what she'd found. Said she wasn't going after him because he had nothing she wanted. At first, she just insisted I ask for her every time I wanted some dictation but to make sure it was outside her normal hours, that way she'd be paid overtime. Soon afterwards she decided it wasn't enough so demanded I pay her to keep her mouth shut.'

'And how long was this going on?'

'Only a couple of months — the first few weeks were just the extra hours dictation, then she asked for a hundred and fifty quid. Two weeks later she asked for the same again but I told her I could only raise fifty in cash without my wife noticing. Rose said she'd take it to be going on with and it would probably be enough for her to go travelling again.'

'When was the last time you saw her?'

'I went into my office one day and found a note from her asking to meet me in Kenilworth. We met in a teashop and she apologised for what she'd done. She said she would give me the money and letters back.'

Sawyer leaned across the table, his face only inches from Gibbons'.

'But she didn't, did she?' he asked. 'They were found in her bedroom after you murdered her. We know she was frightened of you and that's why she left her job, so why don't you just come clean? Get it off your chest and save us all a lot of trouble.'

Gibbons leaned back again in the chair and rubbed his forehead. 'I didn't kill her. When I didn't hear from her any more I thought she'd kept the cash and gone travelling as she said she would.'

'How convenient,' said Sawyer. 'I don't believe a word of it. Perhaps you weren't on your own. Did your boyfriend give you a hand? Shall we pull him in and ask him some questions as well?'

Gibbons immediately looked terrified. 'No, please don't, he hasn't anything to do with this.'

I stepped in. 'But you do?'

'No. That's not what I meant. Why can't you believe me? I'd been angry with Rose but I didn't kill her. I couldn't. I couldn't kill anyone.'

'In Rose Spicer's diary there's an entry that she's meeting someone called "A". That's how you signed your letters. You've admitted she was blackmailing you and there's nothing else new in her diary after that date, the day we think she was murdered. How else would you explain it if it wasn't you?'

Gibbons looked at me as if resigned to his fate.

'I can't, but I didn't do it. You know, Inspector, the day Rose promised to give back my money she was crying. She said she didn't know why she'd done such a terrible thing. She was so contrite. I knew I could never forgive her but I stopped hating her. I couldn't harm her after that.'

Partridge intervened. 'Now, Councillor Gibbons has told you what he knows, Inspector, he's co-operated fully with your questions and I believe it to be time you release him.'

'I'm afraid I don't think I'm convinced, Mr Partridge, and neither is Constable Sawyer here.' I looked at Sawyer. 'Are you?'

Sawyer dutifully shook his head and I turned back to Gibbons.

'So you'll tell us your story one more time, then you'll go back in the cells until we can check it. If you're telling us the truth you should be out in the morning.'

'Any news, Walter?'

'Not really, James, I just rang to tell you I've finally received Rose's medical records, they were tied up in France and it took the devil of a job to get them. I've been through everything and the odd thing is there's no mention of any heart problems. No problems of any significance at all, at least nothing that would explain a sudden death.'

'So you agree she was murdered?'

'I'm not saying that. What I am saying is I can't now see how she died of natural causes.'

'Well, you'd better come down on one side of the argument soon, doc. I've a very credible suspect locked up in the cells downstairs and I don't want him walking free just because we can't show Rose Spicer was actually murdered. Isn't there anything you can come up with?'

'I have to have good reason to suggest murder as a possibility, even if I'm not one hundred percent sure. The problem is, I haven't found anything which convincingly leads to that conclusion medically. It's true the body was found in unusual circumstances but the posing alone doesn't necessarily point to foul play. The girl could have felt unwell and lay down, not knowing she was having a heart attack and needed help. Then she could have been found dead by someone who didn't want to be identified and they posed her out of respect. If you, or I, had to stand up in court all we could say was that in our opinion the balance of probabilities is that Rose was killed.'

Walter was a good friend. I'd met him years earlier when I was still a sergeant and working a case where my Inspector wasn't too keen on attending the post-mortem. I called in one day looking for extra information and came across him swigging gin from a bottle he kept in his desk. He tried to cover it up by saying it was nothing, just a bad morning, but I disagreed and said that I'd been there. We talked for ages about why he drank, and why I used to drink, and agreed to get together again soon. As I got to know him I could tell that despite his problem he was good at his job, always committed to finding the right answer.

Walter once told me he thought he owed thoroughness to the individuals finding their way on to his slab. He still took the odd tipple but, as far as I knew, it was under control and he wasn't bringing booze into work any longer. I was sorry to push him but I couldn't let our friendship get in the way of the case. I had my job to do and he had his, so I pressed him further on what might have killed Rose.

'All right, James, if you must. I've been looking at the possibilities of what could cause almost instant death and leave no trace. As we've discussed, there are plenty of poisons which would finish you off in seconds but all of the easily accessible ones would be detected by the tests I've carried out. One other option which has occurred to me has been an embolism.'

'What's an embolism?'

'It's a blockage in a vein or an artery. If it's serious enough it can cause all sorts of problems, including a heart attack or stroke.'

'So how would Rose have one?'

'They usually come about through blood clots but there are cases where they've been induced through pumping a massive air bubble into the person's bloodstream.'

'Could that be done?'

'Oh, very easily. Just whack an empty syringe into a vein and press the plunger. Piece of cake. The only problem being you'd need quite a big syringe, with a thick needle, to achieve the desired effect and you'd not get that into someone without them noticing.'

'But we think Rose might have been unconscious at the time, correct?'

'I can't say that, James. She seems like she may have been knocked out by the hammer but we don't have any way of knowing if that was five minutes or five hours before she died.'

'But if it was done that way, or through poison for that matter, it would mean it was premeditated, wouldn't it — not a spur of the moment thing?'

'Steady on, James, we haven't shown this was how she died yet. I'm only considering options. There's a long way to go before I'd stand up in that court and put my reputation on the line. Leave it with me and I'll keep looking until I find something.'

A gaggle of laughing drinkers were paying court to Wilson when I pushed my way into the public bar. It's easy for a copper to find "friends" in his favourite watering hole. There are always those who think they'll establish an aura of respectability by association, or less savoury individuals who believe they'll get immunity from prosecution. Undoubtedly, with some of my colleagues, it works, though I guessed with Wilson they'd be out of luck. He was different. He had a presence and would command an audience in any setting regardless of his station in life.

'Inspector Given, come here and sit down,' he boomed. 'Give the man a seat, lads, and make yourselves scarce while he and I have a chat.'

The hangers-on drifted away and he offered a drink so I asked for a Vimto. Wilson stared at me, turning up his nose before calling for mine and a pint with whisky chaser for himself. I guessed it might have been his fourth or fifth of the evening. When the drinks were served, Wilson asked the inevitable question.

'You don't drink then?'

'I try not to.'

I remembered my last bender with a shudder. Possibly it led me to a multiple killer, but still wasn't a place I wanted to return to any time soon.

Wilson raised his glass. 'I reckon I could cut down a bit myself, wouldn't do me any harm. So what can I do for you, Inspector?'

'It's James, call me James.'

'And you can call me Inspector Wilson.'

He laughed so hard I thought he'd fall off his chair. I've noticed how drink makes our own jokes so much funnier. When he stopped he gulped down his whisky, told me to call him Harry and repeated his question.

'I was just in town and wanted to ask if you'd had any leads on Benito Demma's killer.'

I wasn't telling him the entire truth. I'd had a call to an incident in Coventry where a Jewish tailor, the same trade and roughly the same age as my father, had been pushed around in the street by four men. They'd spat and called him names but not hurt him. Every time I went out to investigate one of these cases I became more and more worried about my family and this event made me even more uneasy for them. I resolved to give my father a call when I got home. One of the men harassing the tailor had an Italian accent and told him to get his wife and children out of the country or it would be worse next time. Luckily, a policeman came upon them so the men ran off shouting abuse. I'd interviewed the victim but he had nothing to add to what I'd already been told, although his description seemed to fit Paúlu Demma.

Whilst at the police station I asked for Wilson but he'd left for the night and I was told where I might find him for the next few hours. So I'd taken the opportunity to repeat my search for Demma and his gang round the pubs in the city centre, though I had no more luck than I did last time. I thought it best not to mention the final part of my afternoon in the city centre to my erstwhile colleague.

Initially he wouldn't give me any information on Benito Demma's stabbing.

'You know I can't do it, James, you're too closely involved.'

'Come on, Harry, we're both off duty. It's why I looked you up, I've asked around and, putting two and two together, I think I know who stabbed Benito.'

'Who?'

'I believe it could have been Terry Gleeson.'

'Inspector Terry Gleeson?'

'You know him?'

The alcohol-induced mellowness evaporated from Wilson in an instant.

'Let's just say our paths have crossed. Not one of my favourite people. You've worked with him, right?'

'I still am, in theory. He's supposed to be handling the Birmingham end of these Jewish attacks. There's been no progress over there and I've suspected for a while that the gang have someone on the inside looking out for them. Gleeson's anti-Semitic himself and totally dishonest. Quite apart from his own leanings, he would have no conscience at all about looking the other way if they slipped him enough cash.'

'He wouldn't be the only one up to that game, would he? But we can't go after him simply on your hunch, James.'

'Of course you can't. I had Sawyer do a couple of discreet checks and no-one can vouch for Gleeson's whereabouts at the time Benito was stabbed. He was supposed to be on duty but wasn't in the station and there's nothing in the book to say where he was.'

'That's still not enough.'

'I know it isn't. I'm just telling you what I think and suggesting you keep your eyes open with Gleeson in mind.'

'I'll do that, James, and thanks for the lead. However, I'm not the only one who needs to watch out for Gleeson.' Then he told me what I'd already guessed. 'Terry Gleeson was the one who gave us the tip you'd been looking for the Demmas.'

TWENTY-FOUR

My telephone rattled me awake. Although I hadn't been drinking it had been a late session with Harry Wilson. His coterie had returned after we'd finished our business and we swapped stories and joked until the early hours. It turned out Wilson worked alongside Terry Gleeson for a short time when they were both sergeants. He'd discovered his colleague was taking backhanders and reported him but he wasn't the only one, as Harry had said, so Gleeson was simply moved on to a neighbouring force.

A pub never closes when there's a policeman at the bar so it was around two when I flopped into bed; a glance at the clock when the phone rang told me it was still only twenty past seven. It was the duty sergeant.

'You'd better get down here, Inspector, we have a problem.'

Fifteen minutes later I hobbled into the station. Sergeant Ted Pickering was waiting for me.

'I've called the doc, sir, but there's nothing to be done. He's stiff as a board.'

Pickering had found Andrew Gibbons hanging in his cell when he did his morning wake-up call at seven o'clock. He'd last looked in on the councillor before putting out the lights at midnight and Gibbons had been lying on his bunk, reading. They'd bid each other goodnight and the sergeant hadn't detected anything to preface what Gibbons had in mind. He'd managed to tear his sheet into strips, twisting them to add strength, and then tie one end round the window bars, the other round his throat.

Gibbons was slumped underneath the window from where Pickering had cut him down, the remains of the makeshift noose limp around his neck. He looked like he'd choked to death, not having enough height to manage an effective, and quick, hanging. The man must have kicked and spluttered for an age and I wondered if he'd changed his mind in his dying minutes.

Pickering pointed to a note on the bed.

'It's addressed to you, sir.'

My hands were shaking as I read his words. I'd interviewed him so recently I could even hear his voice speaking the words in my head.

Dear Inspector Given. I'm calm now and ready to do what I must. I'm not a brave man and thought I'd be frightened, but I can see this is really the only way out. I want you to know, most truthfully, that I didn't kill Rose or harm her in any way. When I first knew her I liked her, she was irreverent and funny, and that's why I used to ask for her in particular. But then she did that awful thing to me. One time in my life I've seriously strayed, despite the odd encounter and knowing for years that I was different, then Rose Spicer finds out and my world comes tumbling down. I dearly love my wife and couldn't face her being hurt if this all came out. I'm begging you to believe my suicide has no connection with Rose's death so please, please, keep my transgression out of the newspapers if it's in your power. Tell Marjorie I'm sorry.

I crumpled the paper in my fist and dropped it to the ground. I couldn't begin to comprehend the fear which had driven Gibbons down this path. He was successful in business and in politics, he had a nice house and a pleasant wife, and I suspected his alibi would even check out if we now bothered to make the calls. The implications of being exposed must have seemed overwhelming to him.

In this job I meet villains and victims every day and often I'd feel sorry for both; the criminals because they'd been driven to it by poverty or stupidity, or a mixture of the two, the injured party for a hundred and one reasons. Then there were those like Gibbons, basically law-abiding but making one mistake which ruins their life and the lives of all around them. A pool of sadness we'd all struggle to escape from. Sometimes I wonder how I can face it day after day.

I did what I had to do over the next couple of hours; meeting with the doctor, arranging for removal of Gibbons' body, writing a report, waiting for the time I was due to meet his wife. Someone from Coventry station had been sent out to break the bad news and to bring her to Kenilworth to make the formal identification.

When she arrived, Marjorie Gibbons was pale and shaking. I led her to her husband's body and she nodded to affirm it was him.

'I'm sorry for your loss, Mrs Gibbons.'

She looked straight through me.

'Why would he do such a thing, Inspector?'

I thought about Gibbon's suicide note and decided to lie.

'I don't know. We had him in custody but may have released him today once we'd questioned him again. The evidence wasn't really strong enough to charge him with Rose Spicer's murder.'

'Murder? I thought you'd arrested him over his —' she struggled to find the words — 'indiscretion.'

'You know about it?'

She shook her head slowly.

'I'm his wife, Mr Given, do you think I'd not know that Andrew preferred men? Soon after we met I heard rumours but he seemed keen on me and, you know, I was young and didn't know much about the world. Later, almost from the first night we were married, it became clear he was just keeping up appearances. He had his little crushes from time to time but he always took good care of me and it was never anything serious until this latest one. I've plenty of friends whose husbands do the same but it's with their pretty young secretaries or women they meet at the tennis club.'

Sometimes we're faced with a truth which is so overpowering we have no choice but to hide it away in order to survive. Whether she'd done it out of love, or to keep the lifestyle her husband could provide, or simply because she couldn't comprehend it, I had no way of knowing. But Marjorie Gibbons had hidden the truth, perhaps not from herself but certainly from those around her as far as she could. And now she was faced with a reality which would see the finger pointed by those who couldn't see beyond their prejudices.

'Well, I'm afraid it was this recent situation which seems to have led to his death, Mrs Gibbons. He'd been blackmailed by the young woman whose killing we're investigating; we found some letters in her bedroom and my enquiries steered me to your husband. He'd written them to his friend at the Council and she'd got hold of them.'

She gave a bitter laugh. 'The poor, poor, fool. How could my dear Andrew have been so silly? And you think he murdered this girl to stop her?'

'Actually I don't, not any more.'

I shared his final words with her, there was no reason not to. She broke down in tears when she read the last line and I nearly joined her.

It hadn't taken long for news of Gibbons' death to reach Dyer and by the time I'd finished with the widow he was already ensconced in my office. He'd interviewed every copper who'd been on duty or in the station between midnight and the body being found. Tommy Burns came out just as I arrived.

'Christ, James, he's hopping mad in there. I only called in this morning on my way home from the papershop. I wasn't even working, and he's had me in there for twenty minutes.'

Tommy marched off down the corridor and I was left waiting until the boss barked for me to join him. A WPC who I recognised from Dyer's team in Warwick sat beside him, poised to take notes of our conversation. He didn't bother with an introduction.

'What the hell's happened here, Given? Didn't I warn you to be careful? The press are going to be all over this and how do you think I can explain it? A respected member of the community, a pillar of society, for God's sake, kept in the cells overnight so he hangs himself. Your story had better be good.'

'Last night we had a case against him, sir. If we'd let him go he had the cash to do a runner, then you'd have been down on me like a ton of bricks. Just because he had a bob or two and friends in high places there was no reason to treat him any differently to any other viable suspect we'd pull in, was there?'

'Actually, Inspector, that's exactly what you should have done. I'll get bucket loads of the proverbial manure thrown at me for this, and if it's coming my way then it's definitely coming yours.'

I'd heard enough.

'Begging your pardon, sir, but it's already come my way. In case you've forgotten, I'm the one who's just had to take the man's wife to identify his body. Do you think it was easier to explain to her than it will be to one of his fat-cat mates at your golf club?'

Dyer's face went redder than I'd ever seen it, so red I worried for a second that Gibbons might not be the only casualty in the station that morning. He gripped the edge of the desk.

'Now you be sensible, Inspector. Think very, very carefully before you open your mouth again and you tell me, step by step, why you had him in here and why you didn't let him out for the night when his solicitor asked you.'

We glared at each other for a few moments, with the WPC trying to find something on the wall to distract her attention, but the storm had passed. I knew Dyer would have questions to answer and wouldn't be prepared to carry the can for any mistakes I might have made, so I told him what he needed to know. He rubbed his forehead when I told him about the letters and who the recipient had been.

'So you're telling me he was a homosexual?'

'Yes, he was, sir, and I don't think releasing him would have saved his life. He knew his secret would be out before long, even if he never went to court. Rose Spicer found out and we found out — how long could it be before it became public knowledge? I believe he'd have topped himself at home if he hadn't done it in the cells.'

When Dyer finished and left me alone in my office, I couldn't settle. I hadn't wanted to admit it to the boss but I kept thinking about Gibbons and how he might still be alive if I'd trodden a bit more carefully. I'd warned Sawyer against jumping to conclusions yet I'd done the same thing. I tried telling myself that it wasn't my fault; that Gibbons had been a credible suspect and I had no alternative but to lock him up for the night, but it didn't help. The man was dead and there was no reason for him to die. Deep down I did believe what I'd said to Dyer but it was meagre consolation.

After shuffling papers for an hour I rang Terry Gleeson, saying I wanted to give him an update on Paúlu Demma. He wasn't interested.

'I heard the older one had been killed.' He laughed. 'Good riddance, I'd say. What's his brother got to do with me?'

'Up until last week he was still up to his tricks in Coventry but now he's disappeared. I thought he might show up in Birmingham.'

'Tricks? Oh, the Jew thing? Not very high up my list of priorities, I'm afraid, Given, or is it Geffen again these days?'

So he'd been digging around in Birmingham and picked up my original family name. It made me uncomfortable that he was poking around in my background quite so much. Gleeson was unpleasant but he also knew some very nasty customers who'd be quite happy to do dirty work for him in exchange for the occasional blind eye.

'Then let's say I'm giving you a little warning, Gleeson. Paúlu, without Benito, is like a mad dog and he thinks you killed his brother.'

The bravado slipped out of Gleeson's voice, though he tried to keep up the pretence.

'I'm not afraid of him. If he comes looking for me he'll get more than he bargained for.'

It was my turn to laugh.

'You're a fool, you know. Demma's not going to let you get away with murdering Benito. You must have heard what he did to me, and that was only to warn me off. The only thing stopping him just now is that some of his gang don't have the stomach for killing a copper, and I can't see that holding him back for long. He'll either convince them or ignore them. One thing's for certain though, Terry.'

'What's that?'

'If Paúlu doesn't finish you off then I certainly will. When I can prove it was you who stabbed Benito then I'll have you hanged or behind bars until you're a very old man.'

Without giving him chance to reply, I wished him good luck with Paúlu then hung up just as Sawyer knocked at my door and popped his head inside.

'Mind if I have a quick word?'

I told him to come in and fire away.

'I've been following up alibis, sir, and I checked out what Gibbons told us. It took a while to track down his so-called friend, Gerald Wallace, but he's now confirmed Gibbons' story. The night of the murder they were sharing a cosy night at his home. Wallace remembered the date particularly because it was the first time the councillor had been round there. He said they were celebrating Rose Spicer's decision to let them off the hook and his sister called round. The three of them sat round finishing a bottle of champagne before she left around nine o'clock. I spoke to her on the phone and she substantiated what he said.'

'Crying shame we couldn't get to Wallace yesterday.'

'It is, sir. He was devastated to hear about Gibbons and he seemed like a really nice bloke. Well, apart from ... you know.'

I shook my head and tutted.

'What are we to do with you, John? Anything else?'

'Well, it also looks like the teachers, Jenkins and Rosebury, are in the clear — two parents have now come forward and said they'd seen them around eight on the night Rose died.'

'So that leaves us with the Perelles, who vouch for each other, the other teacher, Smith, who claims he wasn't even in Kenilworth that day, Neilson and Alan Johnston and we've still got Joey Atkin to follow up.'

'You've not mentioned Stella Johnston, sir.'

'I thought you'd said she was at her weekly meeting.'

'Well, that's really why I came in. I spoke to the St John Ambulance chap running the group. It seems she wasn't there on the night Rose Spicer was murdered.'

TWENTY-FIVE

I sent Sawyer to check on Stella Johnston's story and an hour later he walked into my office looking like the cat who'd got the cream.

'I went round to see her like you said and she had a perfectly reasonable explanation.'

'Oh?'

'She apparently had a bad headache one time so couldn't face the class. Said she hadn't realised it was the night we were asking about but it must have been because she doesn't miss her training very often.'

'And can anyone back up that she was at home all evening?'

The wind went from his sails.

'Well, no, but what she did say was she now remembered that her husband came home for his tea and it wasn't ready so they'd had an argument and this is what gave her the headache. She'd taken to her bed with a book and left him downstairs in the kitchen. She thought she heard the back door go at about half past seven, so he might have gone out, but she didn't bother to check. If he did go out then she probably wouldn't have noticed what time he got back because she said she dosed herself up with aspirin and nodded off around eight.'

'You believe her?'

I didn't need to ask. Sawyer was so taken with Stella Johnston he'd have accepted anything she said, almost without question. I thought Sawyer had little experience of women. He'd been seeing someone in his village a few months earlier but she'd gone back to Birmingham and he'd told me they were remaining friends, nothing more. Not that I'd be much more experienced. A string of one-night stands in ports around the world before I met and lost Heather, and now this recent debacle with Elizabeth.

Sawyer reddened. 'I do think she's telling us the truth, sir. You've said yourself that not having an alibi doesn't prove you're guilty.'

'No, but it certainly doesn't show you're innocent either. You'd better put your feelings for that young woman to one side, Constable, or I'll take you off this case. You told me in no uncertain terms it wasn't an issue, but now I'm having my doubts again.'

'It's not an issue, sir. I'm not sure what I can do to convince you but if I thought she was lying I'd be the first to pull her in for more questioning.'

'I'm glad to hear that. What else?'

'If we do believe Stella, then Alan Johnston's back at the top of the list, isn't he?'

'Not really. The only change is that now she says he went out when earlier she said she was the one who had gone out. He already couldn't prove where he was at the time the murder took place.'

I could see there was actually a big difference between the two, but I wasn't about to hand that to Sawyer. It would do him good to figure it out for himself.

'There's something else Stella said which was interesting, sir. Out of the blue she suggested we should talk to Oliver Neilson.'

'Why him?'

'She said he was creepy. Said being a cleaner made her invisible and she'd often see him hanging round the girls when he was still working at the school, inviting them to join his clubs, asking them round for tea, that kind of thing. Perhaps he met Rose, tried it on and then lost it when she rejected him.'

Stella Johnston's accusation confirmed my own suspicion that something wasn't quite right about Neilson. I'd put it down to him being a leech, sucking every ounce of gratification out of a murder enquiry, but perhaps there was something darker. Something altogether more unpleasant lying under the surface.

'And you're saying he still has no alibi?'

'He's not really offered one, has he, sir? Appeared to have kept himself apart from the other staff, spent most of his time with the pupils or in his house with his books. I can see why that might seem weird.'

'Weird enough to commit murder?'

'Maybe. Should I go and pick him up?'

Sawyer and I discussed the teacher for a few more minutes and we agreed I'd call in to see him on my way home. I didn't want to put another innocent in the cells for questioning until I was on firmer ground.

I thought we'd finished but Sawyer seemed reluctant to leave.

'What is it, John?'

'I wanted to clear up this thing with Stella — sorry, Mrs Johnston, sir — I don't want you to get the wrong idea.'

'Go on.'

'As I said, I do find her attractive and good fun to be with. She's had such a hard time of it. Even though her first husband, Dave Butler, treated her badly, she was still there at his bedside until he died. Now she's got all of this to contend with. A murder at the school where she works, her husband having an affair with the victim, and him being pulled in as a suspect. Some people just seem to attract bad luck, don't they, sir? I just feel sorry for her.'

Some people make their own luck. Good or bad. Was it bad luck that Rose Spicer discovered Andrew Gibbons' letter, or was it inevitable as soon as he put pen to paper? Was the young woman simply unlucky to have her life snuffed out down in that crypt or was it bound to happen once she'd set in motion the events that took her down there?

Christians believe they'll be punished or rewarded for their actions in the afterlife, some Eastern religions teach an endless cycle of reincarnation where one's place in a new life after death depends on how you've behaved in the previous one. Different branches of Judaism reflect a version of both of these. Yet other faiths offer a kind of balance, where good things and bad things offset each other and are actually inter-dependent. There is a sense of harmony in this philosophy which I find appealing, linked to my sense of justice where I, as a policeman, try to catch the criminals who've done harm to others.

Sawyer was impatient for my response. 'Sir?'

'Sorry, John, I was just thinking. I can't say I blame you for fancying Stella Johnston. She is good-looking and chatty. You do need to keep it separate though. She's a possible suspect in a murder enquiry, as is her husband. If it turns out to be him, the defence would rip us to shreds when it emerged you were up to something with Johnston's wife behind his back.'

I wasn't sure I should be the one giving him this advice. It was only a few months since I'd found myself in a very similar predicament with Elizabeth. I'd been certain she couldn't have been involved in a case but had no more evidence than Sawyer had about Stella Johnston. I'd been lucky it turned out the way it did. I'd been even luckier that my boss hadn't found out.

'But I'm not "up to something" as you put it, sir, that's what I'm trying to tell you. We're not even friends. Not really. I've only met her a few times and that was either with you or to ask her more questions. We seem to get on, that's all. I won't say I haven't thought about how it might be if things were different, but they're not. If the situation changes then we might get together, or we might not, we'll just have to see. Until then, I'm a copper investigating a death at a school where Mrs Johnston works and she, like a number of others, is still in the frame.'

I believed he meant what he said and told him so, then sent him on his way. I'd still be keeping my eye on him — my own experience told me I had to.

I noticed a light on in Watson's jewellery shop when a detour took me past and wondered how long since he'd reopened. My daily walk to the station usually took me along the high street but I'd been driving up since Madeley did his work and used a different route to get to the car park. The distance really wasn't worth using the car, but it couldn't be helped and this enforced suspension of my daily exercise was undermining my resolve to become fitter. I'd just have to try twice as hard when I was back to normal.

The man behind the counter looked up when the doorbell clattered. He was in his late sixties, wearing a pin-striped suit and glasses and I asked if he'd stay in the shop until I fetched something from the station to show him. He said not to be too long because it was his first day in the shop since his heart attack.

'I'll be no more than twenty minutes, I promise.'

'Well, please don't be any longer, Inspector. I shouldn't really be here this late — my wife will give me a proper telling off.'

'Actually, Mr Watson, it will be much quicker if you could let me use your telephone.'

It wasn't only speed which prompted my request. The thought of walking from the car park then up and down several flights of stairs again gave me the cold sweats. Fortunately, there was someone available to bring the evidence round straightaway so, shortly afterwards, Watson had the crucifix under his expert eye, aided by a jeweller's glass.

In stark contrast to Dembowitz's shop in Coventry, Watson's was well lit and uncluttered. His clocks, watches and baubles were in glass fronted wooden shelves, displaying beauty or utility to best effect, rather than how they were made. I suspected he produced none of the items himself, simply buying his stock directly from the manufacturers. Watson carried a wide range of necklaces, rings and brooches, and one cabinet held nothing but crucifixes; gold, silver, jewelled, jet and amber.

'Sell a lot of these, Mr Watson?'

'They're steady, you know. Two churches nearby and even folk who don't attend regularly still believe in the power of the cross.'

He was right. Even though the second commandment demands that images of God aren't worshipped, Christians still cling to their symbols. There is something pagan about the crucifix worn around a person's neck, like a lucky charm or amulet, where the power is vested in the thing itself, not necessarily in what it represents.

'Any thoughts on this one, Mr Watson?'

'Trouble is, these smaller items are often not hallmarked, though I can see this one is — it's very nice quality. Just give me a minute.'

Watson held the piece closer to his lamp and squinted even harder.

'Ah, that confirms it, Inspector, the tiny mark of Henry Sparrow is stamped on the back. He's one of my suppliers from Birmingham.'

'Would you know who you'd sold it to, Mr Watson?'

He shuffled in a drawer then leafed through the carbon copies in his receipt book until finding the one he was looking for.

'This is it. Sold on Christmas Eve to a Mrs Johnston. I remember her now. Pretty young lady, well dressed, said she was buying it as a gift.'

TWENTY-SIX

I sat in my car outside Watson's with my head against the steering wheel. Even the short time I'd stood in the shop made my feet sting and I needed to rest before wrestling with the pedals. I took the opportunity to consider the implications of what the jeweller had just said. Should I call in reinforcements and arrest Stella Johnston, or bide my time and just go round to question her again? She might have lost the trinket, or given it as a gift as she'd told Watson, so would there be any point rushing in with all guns blazing?

I closed my eyes momentarily, snapping them wide again when I heard my passenger door open. I tensed at the thought it might be Paúlu Demma then relaxed when I saw the concerned smile of Emily Perelle.

'Are you all right, Mr Given?'

I laughed. 'I'm fine, Mrs Perelle, you made me jump there.'

'Sorry. You just looked so ... still. Anyway, I'm glad we've bumped into each other, now I can tell you how we're getting on with the handwriting thing. Do you mind if I climb inside? It's bitter out here.'

Without waiting for an answer she slid onto the seat beside me and I caught the fragrance of lavender. I started the engine and turned on the heater.

'It'll take a few minutes but should soon warm up. So you've had some luck with that note?'

'Not so far. If we had I'd have called in to the station to tell you earlier. I've been through about half the cards and letters, and Laurence has been looking at exercise books and the like when he can, but neither of us has found anything. It can be

218

quite slow, you know, so many children would have similar writing. You see one that looks right then spot a couple of characters that are different.'

I thanked her for her efforts so far.

'Oh, don't thank me, Mr Given, it's quite exciting really, playing the detective.' She gave a nervous giggle. 'You must think me very silly.'

Normally I would consider it vaguely childish, but it made me happy it was giving Emily Perelle some pleasure.

'Not at all, I'm grateful for your help.' I paused, desperately trying to think of something to say which would keep her and her perfume in the car a while longer. I failed. 'Just let me know if you find anything.' Inspiration. 'Can I drop you off at home?'

'No thanks. I've only arrived just before I saw you. I've a few things to get from the shops. I hope I'm not too late.' She slid out as quickly and elegantly as she'd slid in, then leant through the door again. 'I'll be in touch soon, Mr Given. Promise.'

I watched as she crossed the front of the car and followed her pale ankles until they disappeared into the darkness.

I didn't immediately see Oliver Neilson looking in the Catholic Repository a few doors up from Watson's until he turned and waved. I was annoyed that he still seemed to be following me and imagined his mind would be working overtime if he'd observed the headmaster's wife in my car. I'd planned on going to talk to him anyway so I bit my tongue and beckoned him over to the window.

'Good evening, Mr Neilson, were you waiting for me?'

He looked puzzled.

'Oh, no, Inspector, I was just doing a little window shopping.' He turned and looked back into the window. 'Some of the things in here are quite beautiful, don't you think?'

I shrugged and gestured for him to climb in.

'Can I give you a lift?' I said. 'There are a couple things I want to check with you.'

We chatted about the weather and what he was doing in his retirement whilst we drove down the hill to his house. He asked me in for a cup of tea so I accepted, welcoming this opportunity to ask my questions.

He clattered a tray of teapot, cups and cakes into the front room where I'd been sitting alone for five minutes, feeling most bemused. On every surface there was some kind of icon, a Russian triptych here, a Greek orthodox cross there, and any number of religious texts. There seemed to be no link between them other than belief in a higher power, a multitude of emblems of faith in uneasy proximity.

'How do you like my collection, Inspector?'

I told him the truth. I was impressed by the range and quality of what he'd put together, though it wasn't really something I'd collect myself. What I was thinking was that it showed he'd almost certainly understand the significance of the crucifix and the way the dead woman was laid out.

'Now, what was it that you wanted to talk to me about?' he asked.

'There's a couple of things really, Mr Neilson. Firstly, I wanted to check again when you were last in the school church — in fact, more specifically, when you were last in the crypt? You told me earlier that it hadn't been for a couple of months. Can you be more precise?'

'I've been thinking about that since you asked me. It would've been in the week after I stopped working. I was clearing the last few things from my house and thought I'd take a last look around.'

'And you left at the end of December?'

'Yes, at the end of term.'

'You finished part way through the school year, Mr Neilson? Why was that?'

'Simply because it was convenient for all concerned. My birthday was over the Christmas holidays so it made sense to retire then and the headmaster had already appointed my successor, Mr Smith, even though he wasn't starting until later. I think you've met him. Mr Perelle said he could manage the first few weeks of the new term without me, so I left.'

'That must have been hurtful. You'd been at the school a long time, hadn't you?'

'Well, when one's time is done, it's done, I suppose. I was a little upset but I can't imagine he meant anything by it. He and Mrs Perelle have been very nice to me since I retired.'

'So you've not been down inside the crypt since, say, the first week in January? Would that be right?'

Neilson thought for a moment before answering.

'Yes, that would be correct.'

This placed the teacher below the church around the same time Rose Spicer was killed. Either he didn't know this or it was a double bluff, intended to demonstrate his innocence.

It was time to move on to the accusations made by Stella Johnston, though I wasn't sure how I'd get into the discussion without upsetting him to the point where he'd stop volunteering information.

'Could I ask you, Mr Neilson, if you are aware of any rumours about you at the school?'

His knuckles tightened on the arm of his chair.

'There are always some. What kind of rumours have you heard?'

I bit the bullet.

'We've been told you might be a mite too fond of the little girls.'

Neilson relaxed and chuckled like a drain.

'That old one, Inspector. It's the teacher's curse. Some child gets a crush or the teacher says something nice about a piece of homework and the next thing you know the story starts that the poor man is chasing the girls. I always tried to avoid being in that position but it shows you can't be too cautious.'

It was a plausible explanation. Should I believe him?

'I can see how it might happen. A close community, lonely young people away from home and you never having married. Ripe for unkind gossip, isn't it?'

'You're right there, Mr Given.'

'So there's nothing in it?'

The smile departed.

'No, there's nothing in it.'

I knew I'd gone as far as I could with our informal chat and would need him in the station if I wanted to push him further. He'd then have the right to have a solicitor present and I'd get nothing else. I drained my cup and rose to leave but Neilson spoke before I could slip on my coat.

'Could I ask you something, Inspector?'

'Fire away.'

'I wondered if you are Jewish?'

Where did that come from? I was at a loss how to proceed with this conversation. I didn't shout my religion from the rooftops, though there was no reason for me to try to keep it secret any longer. The events of recent months had seen to that but I wasn't sure I wanted Neilson to know. He was a neighbour, a potential suspect and seemed the sort to suck up juicy morsels to gossip about later.

'Please don't take offence, Mr Given, there's just something about you made me wonder.' He gestured around the room. 'As you can see, I'm fascinated by all religions: the artefacts, the rituals, the hierarchies, the subtle differences. Unfortunately, I rarely get the opportunity to meet non-Christians. It would be wonderful if a friend could give me an insider's view on another faith.'

The very idea made my skin crawl.

'That wouldn't be appropriate, would it, Mr Neilson? We might be neighbours but we're not friends. I'm here to ask you about the death of a young woman, not religion, mine or anyone else's. She died — seems to have been murdered — in the school where you worked, in a place you knew well, and you, like it or not, are on the list of suspects. Perhaps you'll try to remember that when we meet again.'

I left him, open-mouthed, and let myself out. It was now sleeting, with a bitter wind, and my feet were shooting razor blades into my core. I decided to call it a night and question Stella Johnston on my next shift.

TWENTY-SEVEN

'Stella bought it? Are you sure?' Sawyer asked me the next morning.

'According to old Watson. He had pretty good records and gave a fairly accurate description of her.'

'So what do we do now? Are *you* going to arrest her?'

The emphasis on "you" told me Sawyer wasn't too keen.

'I don't think so. I'll call round later and ask her about it. Unless you want to do it?'

He declined, which was a good thing because I had no intention of letting him. I knew he'd turn down the offer; he'd not want to mess up his chances with Stella Johnston by asking her awkward questions.

I filled him in on my conversation with Emily Perelle then moved on to Neilson.

'So you didn't get anything out of him?'

'No, not much, I didn't really expect to. Naturally enough, he denied all knowledge of fancying young girls.'

'Did you believe him?'

'Not entirely, but even if he does have a fondness for children why would he bother with Rose, she wasn't young?'

'She looked young though, didn't she? Maybe that was enough. Or perhaps she saw him up to something with one of the girls at school and threatened to report him? We know she was hanging round the grounds quite a bit, particularly near the chapel where it would have been deserted most of the time. Maybe he took his conquests down to the crypt as well and she spotted him.'

I was pleased Sawyer continued to consider all the options. He might have one suspect he favoured but wasn't closing off his mind to others.

'Good thinking, John, that's a possibility, but he may just be the victim of rumour, as he suggested. Strange man, though. House full of religious stuff.'

'Well, he did teach religious instruction; you'd expect him to be very devout.'

'It was more than that. He'd be Church of England, I suspect, teaching in that school, but his collection seemed to cover almost every faith. Could that be associated with the crucifix draped around Rose's fingers? If anyone would know about the religious symbolism around Rose's posing, he would.'

'Did you ask him about it?'

'I didn't want to give him any more information than he already has. We'll continue to keep details as vague as we can and hope someone trips up by revealing facts they shouldn't know. Neilson, by his own admission, knew the crypt well and was down there around the date Rose was killed, so he's as likely a suspect as anyone.'

'Are you still sure I shouldn't bring him in for more formal questioning, sir?'

I considered the implications for a minute. I wasn't sure we had enough on Neilson yet to justify arresting him — no more, really, than a slightly odd collecting habit and an unsubstantiated accusation of his attraction to his female pupils. And my distinct dislike of the man.

'Let's leave him where he is for now, John — I can't imagine he's going anywhere.'

I sent Sawyer off to get on with his work. It would have been helpful if he could have followed up Stella Johnston's purchase of the crucifix but I still didn't trust him to make an unbiased assessment of her responses. There's a fine line between being courteous, friendly even, towards witnesses or potential suspects, and stepping over to a place which would jeopardise your judgement or a case going to court. I wasn't sure how close Sawyer was standing to that line so I'd need to make the time to interview her myself. Meanwhile, I couldn't help thinking that Neilson might be playing a game of cat and mouse, getting a thrill from being my neighbour and following me about the town, whilst all the time knowing he'd murdered Rose Spicer. Was leaving him free the right thing to do?

Over breakfast I'd seen that *The Times* reported Andrew Gibbons' "tragic" death with due respect and the minimum of fuss, mentioning his position on the Council, his charitable works and the names of his close family. Later in the day the local press, as Dyer predicted, had a ball. Someone had tracked down Elsie Manners, who was more than happy to reignite the flame which had hovered over her for the few days after my visit, and she had provided lots of details about Rose Spicer. So many were either different to, or missing from, the account she gave to me that I suspected she was making them up as she went along.

One newspaper mentioned that Gibbons' name had been linked to a "close friendship" with a male Council employee who had resigned and moved on in recent weeks. It didn't go so far as to suggest a romantic attachment, but the inference was clear. At least they hadn't yet got hold of Wallace's name, though I imagined it would only be a matter of time before they unearthed it. I only hoped that Marjorie Gibbons wasn't reading the papers and was leaving her telephone firmly off the hook.

Reporters had tried phoning me, in both Coventry and Kenilworth, but got nowhere. I'd left firm instructions at both stations that I wouldn't speak to them and they should ring Superintendent Dyer for the official line. He'd enjoy seeing his name in the papers and would give them nothing other than police-speak platitudes.

Last time I was at the cinema I'd endured a short film about the Serengeti before the main feature, where a pack of hyenas tore at the still-kicking carcass of a zebra, their snouts dark with blood as they ripped away its flesh. Our upstanding local reporters seemed to have embarked on an equally vicious feeding frenzy now they'd seen a man down. I despaired for the future of humanity.

A call from headquarters reminded me that reports were needed urgently for two cases I was taking to court so the remainder of my day was spent writing them and delivering the finished products to Warwick. Both were related to local burglaries and should have been straightforward, until I noticed discrepancies in the notes of the arresting officer in one. It meant I had to read the whole file in detail then get hold of the copper concerned to put them right. He was on his beat on the edge of the town so I had to drive out to find him, bring him back then drop him off again before I could finish.

There were no lights on in the Johnstons' house when I arrived, even though the afternoon was gloomy and I hoped I'd not had a wasted journey. A key had been left in the front door and, after pondering for a moment, I turned the lock and stepped inside. The light trickling through the doorway illuminated the rose-patterned wallpaper in a hallway leading to the open door of the kitchen.

I didn't call out even though I should have done. Here was I, a policeman, creeping uninvited round the house of a woman who I knew to be living alone. A woman who was now a possible murder suspect. However, Alan Johnston was definitely under suspicion. What if he'd come home and done away with his wife because he'd figured out she might know he'd killed Rose Spicer? Stella had thrown him out and already undermined his alibi. Perhaps she'd goaded him with this and he'd reacted.

On my left was the living room where I'd talked to Stella Johnston whilst we waited for her husband to return. A hinge complained as I pushed the door. The room was empty and had been for a few hours, judging from the dying embers in the grate. I'd already had a good look in this room on my previous visit so I left and went through to the kitchen.

My pulse quickened when I saw the young woman in a chair, head slumped on her chest. I shook her shoulder.

'Mrs Johnston. Mrs Johnston.'

She gasped and drew back, eyes wide from her broken sleep.

'Oh, Mr Given, what is it? What are you doing here? I'd only intended sitting down for a minute, then next thing it's going dark and you're standing there. About scared the life out of me.'

I apologised for startling her and explained I'd come in when I'd seen no lights in the house and an unlocked door. She made the challenge I knew she would from the minute I'd stepped into her home uninvited.

'I didn't hear you shout out.'

'Didn't you, Mrs Johnston? I knocked several times and called you when I came inside. You must have been well away.'

Stella rubbed the sleep from her eyes and acknowledged not sleeping well since her split with Alan. She said she'd nodded off when she arrived home from work and I couldn't tell if she believed that I'd called out but if she didn't then she simply let it rest. She offered to make tea and a sandwich but I refused anything to eat, even though I was peckish. If I settled down for a feed and a cosy chat then I'd soon be as biased as Sawyer in my assessment of Stella Johnston.

'I need to ask you about a piece of jewellery, a gold crucifix. Do you own one?'

She looked mystified.

'No.'

'But you bought one recently?'

She clearly wasn't sure how to respond and didn't reply until I prompted her.

'Mrs Johnston? The crucifix?'

'Did I?'

'You bought it from Watson's, on the high street. Christmas Eve.'

'Oh, that one, I'd almost forgotten. It was a present for Alan.'

There was a softness in her eyes and a catch in her throat when she used her husband's name, as if remembering better times whilst still being angry with him for two-timing.

'It wasn't cheap — are you in the habit of buying such expensive gifts?'

'Of course not. Look around you, Inspector, we could hardly afford such things on our wages, but I'd been putting a few pennies by for a rainy-day kind of thing. Alan can be a bit distant sometimes — I think it might be to do with him being on his own in the outdoors so much. Then, just before Christmas, he changed and was so nice to me for a couple of weeks, I thought I'd get him something special. I didn't know he was just trying to cover up his affair with that woman.'

She began shaking as she told me this and I couldn't help feeling sorry for her. Here was a woman who loved her husband despite what he'd done and couldn't come to terms with being betrayed.

'Do you know if he still has it?'

'He doesn't.'

'You seem very sure. A few minutes ago you didn't even recall having a crucifix.'

'That was before you reminded me where I'd bought it. And why. The reason I'm so certain he doesn't have it is that about a fortnight after I gave it to him he told me he'd lost it. Did he give it to that Rose?'

'What makes you think that, Mrs Johnston?'

'Well, he was seeing her then, wasn't he? If she'd seen it and asked him for it he's so soft he wouldn't be able to refuse.' She burst into tears. 'Please tell me he didn't give my present to her, Mr Given. Please.'

After she'd calmed down Stella Johnston had told me she'd given her husband the present on Christmas morning, this was a little over two weeks before the "meet A" entry in Rose's diary. So Alan Johnston had supposedly mislaid the crucifix round about the time Rose was killed. He could have lost it only for it to be found by the person who then murdered her, who just happened to want such an item to leave a message, but the coincidences were stacking up a little too strongly around the gardener.

I called back to the station to collect Sawyer so we could go to arrest Johnston when I received a message to get over to Superintendent Dyer's office at headquarters as quickly as I could. His secretary couldn't tell me what it was about but said there was a big flap on and Dyer had said he'd not accept any excuses if I wasn't there within the half hour. I grabbed my coat and dispatched Sawyer with a couple of men to pick up Alan Johnston again.

When I arrived in Warwick, Dyer had two others with him, Harry Wilson and an officer who was introduced as Superintendent Ben Oatway, Harry's boss. There must be something common in the manufacturing of senior police officers because Oatway was an almost carbon copy of Dyer. Tall and well-built but going to seed due to too many hours behind a desk and good lunches. Doubtless they both made vain attempts at keeping fit by knocking a ball around the same golf course every weekend, only to finish off the afternoon swallowing gin and tonics at the nineteenth hole before a meat and two veg dinner prepared by the loving wife at home. Disturbingly I could easily see myself on the same downward path in a few years' time.

Dyer kicked off.

'Have you heard about Gleeson, Inspector?'

'Sir?'

'He was stabbed last night. Pretty bad. He'll survive but he's in hospital in Coventry.'

Gleeson stabbed? Had Paúlu Demma caught up with him? If he had then Gleeson was lucky to be still breathing. But if it happened in Coventry and not Birmingham then Gleeson must have gone looking for the Sicilian. Why would he do such a stupid thing? Dyer knew that Gleeson and I weren't exactly pals, so what had this to do with me?

'I'm sorry, sir, but why have you dragged me all the way over here to tell me this?'

Dyer shot a look at Oatway as if he'd already told him I could be awkward.

'Don't take that tone with me, Inspector, you were supposedly working alongside Terry on these attacks on Jews. Could it have anything to do with that?'

How much had Harry Wilson told them of our conversation in the pub?

'I spoke to Inspector Gleeson a couple of days ago, sir. I told him to be careful because I believed Paúlu Demma might be after him.'

'Why?'

'Because Demma thinks his brother was killed by Gleeson.'

Dyer's reaction told me Harry hadn't said anything about my suspicions; he must have just been pulled in because Gleeson was attacked on his patch.

'What? And you didn't think you'd bother to tell me about this? A fellow officer is under threat from a known thug and you keep it quiet?'

'I didn't keep it quiet, as you put it, I rang Terry Gleeson and passed it on to him. He told me, in no uncertain terms, where I should stick my suspicions.'

Dyer now wanted the full story so I let him have it. He didn't seem particularly surprised about my allegations of how bent Gleeson was, nor of his anti-Semitism.

'But murder, Given? Would he have gone as far as that? You're not saying this just because he reported you to Inspector Wilson here?'

I ignored his accusation. 'Perhaps Gleeson demanded more of a back-hander and Benito Demma threatened to expose him. He'd lose his job, his pension, everything. Gleeson is as crooked as they come. Always has been and always will be, and it wouldn't take much, in my view, to push him into taking any steps he needed to protect himself.'

If I'd expected these revelations to finally bring Gleeson to justice then I was going to be disappointed. Dyer turned to Oatway.

'So what will do about all of this, Ben?'

'Well, we can't have criminals attempting to kill policemen and getting away with it, can we? It's up to you how you deal with your man Gleeson but if it was me I'd pension him off. I'd say the last thing we need is the spectacle of a wayward copper being dragged through the courts, the papers would love it.'

They were clearly going to sweep as much of the dirt under the carpet as was possible. The boss returned his attention to me.

'I agree with Superintendent Oatway, so this is what we'll do. Inspector Wilson will pull as many men together as he needs, including some from over this way if he wants them, and he'll find Demma. You'll go and visit Terry Gleeson in hospital. Take him some flowers. A bunch of grapes. Even a bloody get-well-soon card. And tell him you're sorry to hear he's retiring.'

Normally you'd never get to a hospital bedside before two o'clock but a policeman's warrant card tends to open doors locked to most people. Dyer must have been secretly chuckling at the irony of making me visit Gleeson, knowing I disliked him so much. I'd have much preferred to be back at the station questioning Alan Johnston and would have objected more strongly if it hadn't been for the satisfaction I'd feel when telling Gleeson he was on his way out.

He was in a private ward, with a uniform at the door making sure he wouldn't be attacked again. This lone defender was smoking and reading the racing pages, doubtless making his selections for the afternoon, and he barely acknowledged me when I walked towards him. I felt like tearing a strip off him, telling him to pay more attention to who was about, but I couldn't be bothered. It would be no skin off my nose if Demma or one of his boys got in to finish off Gleeson.

The room was painted the same light grey as the corridors, a grey which almost matched my injured colleague's complexion and for a passing moment I almost felt sorry for him. His eyes flickered open when I pulled my chair up to the bed, scraping it just enough to make sure it disturbed him. He struggled to focus for a moment before recognising me.

'Given? What are you doing here?'

'Hello, Terry, how are you feeling?'

'Dreadful, you'll be pleased to know, but I can't believe you've come because you're concerned about my health, so what is it?'

I'd practised my speech all the way to the hospital and took great pleasure in explaining that the boss had believed what I'd said about Gleeson's corruption and his involvement in Benito's murder. I took him through it step by step, finishing with what Dyer had decided to do about him.

'To my mind it's unfortunate you're not going to be prosecuted. But you've had it as a copper. No fanfare, no party and no suspension. Just fade away into early retirement with your pension.'

Gleeson sneered weakly.

'That's perfect, Given, I couldn't have wished for anything more. Getting paid for doing nothing is my idea of a cushy life.'

'Well, you've managed it for years, Gleeson, so why change now? At least you'll be out of my hair. Though I doubt you'll be able to relax for a while.'

He looked baffled. 'How come?'

'Oh, didn't I say? The boss is certain you murdered Demma and is only avoiding going to court because he doesn't have the evidence. Yet. But I'll be doing my best to find it for him. How many of your villains will keep quiet after you're out on your ear? None, I suspect. Then all I have to do is find a way to make sure Dyer uses what I dig up. Apart from having me on your tail all the time, Paúlu also knows you did it and we haven't found him so far. Until we do you'd better not be on your own too much.' I nodded towards the door. 'Our friend there isn't a great deal of use but even he won't be guarding you when you're out of the force.'

Gleeson rubbed his forehead as if he'd now realised how serious his situation had become. As I stood up to leave, he settled on his pillow and closed his eyes, and when I turned in the doorway to look back, he was staring at the ceiling.

TWENTY-EIGHT

When I arrived in Kenilworth, Sawyer was itching to get on with questioning Alan Johnston.

'We've put him in the cells, sir. Found him at work and he wasn't too happy to be dragged in again — reckoned he'd lose his job this time.'

'I think that's the least of his worries, don't you?'

I'd brought Dyer up to date before I left him and we'd agreed we would probably have enough to formally arrest Alan Johnston on a charge of murder, depending on the outcome of today's interview. It was still largely circumstantial, with no witnesses, though the crucifix appeared to be the final piece of evidence, putting him at the crime scene. A half-decent lawyer could easily argue that Johnston had told his wife he'd lost the trinket and that he was telling the truth but, for now, it was enough for us to keep the groundsman in custody.

Johnston could hardly have been described as well-groomed on the previous occasions we'd met but now he was carrying several days growth of beard and looked like he'd worn the same clothes for a week. He'd been staying on a friend's settee since his wife had thrown him out and the arrangement didn't stretch to laundry and regular baths.

Sawyer and I went through the formalities with him and asked if he had anything to add to his earlier statements. He hadn't.

'Tell us about this cross, Alan, the one your wife gave to you.'

'What's that got to do with anything? It was a Christmas present, that's all.'

I nodded to Sawyer to take over.

'That's nice. Did you hear that, sir? Mrs Johnston bought her husband a present. And you could show it to me if I asked, Alan?'

He shook his head. 'I lost it a couple of weeks after she gave it to me. You should have seen how Stella went on about it. She was furious. Said how she'd scrimped and saved to buy it. Cried for hours and wouldn't speak to me for two days.'

'When did you notice it was missing?'

'Only when Stella pointed it out at breakfast. I'd hardly had the thing off since she gave it to me, only for a wash, like.'

'And you've no idea where it might have gone?'

'Of course not. I looked everywhere I could think of. Down the pub, in my shed at work, all over the house. I even checked round the playing fields and flower beds at school but that was pretty pointless, I'd never remember everywhere I'd been and the ground's so chewed up by football boots at that time of year it would be nigh on impossible to find anything.'

I stepped back in.

'So you can't explain how a crucifix, your crucifix, came to be wrapped round the hands of your girlfriend as she lay rotting underneath the church?'

We still hadn't made public the details of Rose's posing and Johnston looked truly shocked that his present was so closely linked to her death.

'I can't, Mr Given, really I can't.'

I asked a question, though was already certain of the answer.

'Have you ever been down there, Alan, in the crypt?'

Johnston sensed the trap but seemed to realise he'd have nothing to gain by lying.

'I was in there a few times.'

'Why?'

'It was where Rose and I used to go when we wanted ... you know ... to be on our own.'

'Seems a strange place for a bit of romance, Alan — whose idea was that?'

'It was hers. I gave her a tour when I first met her, trying to show off I suppose. Next thing she's asking to go there all the time.'

'And the mattress was already down there?'

'No.' Johnston glanced at the door as if he wanted to make a run for it. 'I dragged it over from the storeroom. There were three or four waiting to be thrown out so I didn't think it would matter if one went missing.'

'Did you have your own key?'

'Where would I get my own key, Mr Given? I always took the one from the office. I'd have a pretty good idea when Miss Clements wouldn't be in so would nip over and lift the key then drop it back later.'

Johnston was answering all our questions in a matter-of-fact way, no cockiness, no challenges to find him out in a lie. It bothered me that I was beginning to believe him.

'When was the last time you were in your little love nest?'

'It was between Christmas and New Year. Rose told me she was expecting and we had a row. I didn't see her again after that.'

Sawyer snorted and came back at him.

'We both know that's not true, is it, Alan? You saw her at least one more time. On the night you killed her. You lured her to the chapel, clouted her with a hammer and then finished her off.'

There was now real panic in Johnston's eyes.

'I didn't kill Rose.' His words barely a whisper. 'It wasn't me.'

We could get nothing else out of him, except his continuing protestations of innocence, so we packed it in for the day. There was no point in charging him from the little extra he'd admitted. If even I was beginning to believe Johnston, we'd have no chance with a jury. I could only hope another period of questioning might break him down after he'd sweated overnight in the cells.

Back at my desk, the message from Harry Wilson couldn't be clearer. 'Raid on Demma tonight. Be at Coventry nick half past six latest.'

I glanced at the clock. It was already quarter to six.

In the corridor I bumped into Sawyer leaving for the night so I told him to change any plans he had and to come with me. To his credit he didn't grumble when I explained where we were going.

'Thanks for coming, James,' Harry boomed, sticking out his hand. 'I take it this is your Constable Sawyer I've heard so much about.' He turned to Sawyer, who was already blushing. 'Inspector Given tells me you're a good man.'

'Thank you, sir.' Sawyer puffed up like a pigeon but the coppers with Wilson smirked. They knew their boss's praise was double edged, he was showing my opinion due respect but Sawyer would also have to earn it in the field. The Coventry inspector only had my word on Sawyer's merits and I knew he still hadn't quite made his mind up about me.

Harry went on to introduce three constables; Clegg, Jameson and Frith. 'Capstick you already know.'

Even though I'd been cleared, I could see the sergeant, like his boss, still wasn't convinced. Harry began the briefing.

'We've had a tip-off that Paúlu Demma and his boys are meeting up tonight at the Swanswell Tavern in Hillfields. It seems they're planning on wrecking a draper's shop run by a Jewish family on Primrose Hill Street. My informant said they were getting together at about eight o'clock so we need to be down there sharpish.'

He gave orders to Clegg and Frith to go to the shop in case we missed the gang, with the rest of us heading to the Swanswell, where we waited in the shadows across the road from the pub.

It was bitterly cold, in the way it can still be even late in March, and I could smell snow in the air. The four of us desperately tried to keep out of the arctic wind, whilst taking turns to keep an eye on the two entrances. It was a large place, recently done up, and occupying a corner position only about two hundred yards from the draper's shop. I knew there was a public park and Swanswell Pool behind the pub and regretted not having the foresight to suggest some coppers be brought along to cover that side.

Every few minutes a customer would go inside, causing Harry and Capstick to confer then nod to me if it was a Coventry villain known to them. All of the ones they indicated went into the same bar. I counted six before two I recognised turned up, the one calling himself "Chamberlain" and Madeley, the man who'd stood up to Paúlu Demma on my behalf, then nearly destroyed my feet.

Demma was the last to arrive. He'd barely passed through the door when Wilson shouted, 'Let's go!' and his sergeant blasted out on his whistle. As we ran across the road Clegg and Frith raced down the hill, responding to Capstick's signal, so at least our numbers would be more or less equal, even if the ones inside were thugs.

We burst through the doors into a tiled hallway. The public bar was on our immediate left and the delightfully named Winter Gardens, further down. Sawyer dived in. He only startled the regulars in the front room so joined the rest of us rushing to the back lounge. Wilson was first inside and stopped in his tracks in the empty room. The only sign that the gang had been there were several hand-painted posters wafting in the icy blast from the double doors which allowed exit to the park. All of the sheets carried the same message — "Go home Jew".

Capstick and two others ran outside onto a paved area edging the lake. The light only bled a few yards from the windows so the three disappeared into the murk after a few steps. I could hear Capstick shouting instructions. Once again it seemed Demma had managed to elude arrest. Like a cat, he courts disaster all the time but keeps acquiring a new life. He was openly recruiting bullies to attack harmless shopkeepers and factory owners, yet still we couldn't catch him. He'd even been brazen enough to abduct me, a police officer, and get away with it. Sometimes I lay awake at night wondering why I'd released him and his brother when I'd had them, stupidly hoping to pick them up on a beefier charge at some point. His escape was confirmed when Harry's men trudged back, unable to find anyone out in the gloom, and I wondered how much effort it would take to find Paúlu Demma again.

Harry and I stayed in the pub whilst everyone else went up to the draper's, just in case the gang decided they'd still go ahead with their night's work. The two of us wanted to have a word with the landlord, Harry deciding to chance his first pint of the night.

The landlord didn't help. As far as he was concerned, the men simply turned up and went into the lounge. He claimed not to know any of them and that the first time he thought anything was amiss was when Sawyer barged through the door into the public bar. He'd not been managing the place for long and seemed genuine, though I've seen enough landlords keep quiet to protect their custom to know I shouldn't necessarily believe him.

Harry and I moved to a table in the corner and I asked if he'd any thoughts on where we might go from here to locate Demma.

'Most of his mates were already on our books, James, so we'll pick them up tomorrow and turn the screw a bit. One of them is bound to crack and tell us where we can find him. Next time we'll make sure he doesn't get away.'

'I'm not so sure, Harry, I've been trying for years and every time I got close the pair just slithered off into the undergrowth. I only hope that Paúlu on his own is not as slippery as his brother.'

The others joined us after half an hour and, two drinks later, when Harry was holding court once again, Sawyer and I left to make our way back to Kenilworth. My younger colleague would have happily stayed to the death, but I couldn't face another night of being the only sober one in ebullient company.

TWENTY-NINE

All hell had broken loose when I walked through the doors of the station at half past seven the next morning. Sergeant Tommy Burns was at the front desk barking down the telephone and there were constables running everywhere, searching every nook and cranny of the building. The night sergeant, Graham Bentham, was sitting in the corner, head in hands, a WPC holding a cup of tea for him. He looked even paler than the cream painted wall he was leaning on.

Burns put down the phone and shouted to me. 'Inspector, I've been calling you for the last twenty minutes. Alan Johnston has escaped.'

I cursed and issued instructions to Burns and the others, trying to lay some order over the chaos, then asked the shaking Bentham what had happened. Johnston had been in the third cell, the only one occupied, and Bentham didn't want a repeat of the Andrew Gibbons tragedy so had looked in on him every half hour through the night. His final round was at quarter to seven, when he shouted for Johnston to wake up. The prisoner hadn't responded, and despite Bentham calling more loudly several times, he continued lying hunched on his bunk. The sergeant, petrified that another prisoner had died, this time on his watch, had unlocked the cell door, stepped inside and locked it behind him. He bent down to shake Johnston's shoulder.

'Quick as a flash he was up on me, sir, must have been planning it all night. Grabbed my arm and threw me to the ground. Next thing I know I'm handcuffed and gagged with one of his socks in my mouth.'

From there it was no problem for Johnston to take Bentham's keys, let himself out of the cell block and disappear through the front door. He was lucky though — five minutes later and the dayshift would have been coming in. One of these eventually arrived to discover the front desk abandoned. He found the sergeant locked in the cell and raised the alarm.

Already I could see the knowing glances and barely disguised sniggers each time a constable walked past Bentham and I had a feeling it would take some time for poor Graham to live this down.

By the time he'd told me his sad story, with apologies for his gullibility at every turn, the search had confirmed that Johnston wasn't hiding in the building. The clock above Tommy Burns' head ticked past eight o'clock as I checked he'd spread the word to men on the beat to keep an eye open for our fugitive. I left him at the front desk and walked through to the grey cell block where Johnston had been kept.

Bentham's keys lay on the corridor floor where the groundsman had dropped them, outside the third cell door. Had the prisoner panicked when he realised he was now in even more trouble than he'd been before? The tubular steel bed had been overturned in the struggle, its palliasse and rough blanket entangled beneath it, and there was nothing else in the cell to tell me more than I already knew.

I was still finding it hard to accept Alan Johnston as a murderer, even though the evidence was stacking up against him. He was either telling the truth the previous night or was one of the most convincing liars I'd ever encountered. And I'd met a lot. So why had he run? Was it the action of a guilty man, or an innocent one?

Ten minutes into my call to Superintendent Dyer I was wishing I'd legged it like Johnston had. I'd spent the first five explaining what had happened and the next five begging for extra bodies to try to recapture the escaped man.

'I don't know what kind of ship you're running over there, Inspector, but it seems like some sad joke. First you lose a suspect by letting him hang in his cell, and then you lose another because your sergeant is too dim-witted to take basic precautions. That's not to mention one of your known enemies being stabbed to death then keeping me in the dark about possible reprisals against one of my officers.'

'That's not fair, sir —'

'Shut up, Given. What's not fair is you're expecting me to pull coppers off other jobs to help clean up your mess. You've not even got a strong case against this Alan Johnston feller. In fact, from what I hear, the pathologist won't actually stand behind a murder finding, will he? So you're just off on your own sweet way again, clutching at straws.'

I couldn't let Dyer get away with that, even if there was half a chance he might be right.

'Now wait a minute, sir, if Rose Spicer wasn't murdered, how would you explain the crack on her head and the way she was found, like a sleeping choirgirl, complete with crucifix? Naismith hasn't ruled out murder, only that he can't prove it. You know how cautious these blokes are — won't admit to anything that wouldn't stand up in court. You're right, though, we don't have a cast iron case against Johnston but he's the best we've got for now and he's run off, attacking one of your police officers on the way. He needs to be brought in, for that alone. We have to question him some more. Now, are you going to make sure that happens or are you going to let him slip away?'

The whole speech came out more strongly than I thought possible and sounded convincing, even to me. Far more convincing, in fact, than I felt.

The boss blustered for a while longer but then came to a conclusion. Despite all his faults, Dyer was an efficient manager and wouldn't shy from making a decision. I didn't always agree with his reasoning or the outcome but at least he had the guts to make one.

'I take it you've warned everyone over your end to look out for Johnston?' he asked.

'Yes, sir.'

'Then I'll put the whole force on alert and we'll have to hope he shows up. I can't spare any more men to help you, so you'll have to make do with what you've got, but I tell you this, Given.' I felt the axe coming down. 'You'd better get on top of this in the next couple of days or you're off it and on to something more productive.'

'But, sir —'

'No buts, Inspector, get it sorted or I'll have your guts for garters.'

I put down the receiver, took a deep breath, counted to ten, and phoned Harry Wilson. His good humour hit me like a sledge hammer.

'Morning, James, how are you this bright day?'

How could he be in such good form after a heavy night's drinking? I wondered if he might still be a little bit drunk. I'd done it for years. Played cards into the small hours, sipping rum after rum, keeping topped up until my luck and money, or that of my adversary, ran out, then falling into bed for a too short sleep. Some mornings I'd appear on deck barely able to stand, wishing I could bluff as effectively with the pack on the table. Most of the time, though, I'd be like Wilson. On the edge.

'I've had better, Harry.'

I told him about Johnson's escape and my subsequent ultimatum from Dyer.

'Well, let me give you some good news. We've picked up three of the boys from last night and Capstick's questioning them as we speak. None of them have said anything yet, but they will. The sergeant's a great one for putting the pressure on.'

Praise indeed from the master. I asked who they were.

'They're all just small-time crooks, nothing major on any of them. Burglary, shoplifting, pub brawls, that kind of thing. Couple of them are heavies, act as muscle to one or two of the big boys from time to time. Something they have in common is they've all got links with Moseley's lot, the British Union of Fascists. It explains why they're running with Demma. We haven't picked up Madeley — couldn't find him. By all accounts he's the brightest of the bunch and most active in the BUF in the city.'

'Do you really think Capstick will come up with anything?'

'Without a doubt. I'd guess the one you know as Chamberlain, Jez Carberry, is likely to crack first. Gerard Joseph Carberry is a weasel, always on the fringes of the real villains, without the guts to do a job of his own. Anyway, I'll let you know how we get on.'

There was a message to contact Walter Naismith waiting when I got back after lunch. I rang him straight away.

'You've not forgotten about us then, Walter?'

He chuckled.

'Certainly not, James. Never. How could you even think such a thing? This body of yours has been keeping me awake at night. Unfortunately, during the day, I've had some slightly fresher ones to look after.'

'So have you found anything?'

'Well, I can't be sure, but there is what could be a puncture mark on her neck.'

'And?'

'I was going with the idea of an air bubble embolism, as we discussed, so I examined the photos of her arms, legs and neck to see if there were any injuries which might have developed one.'

'What about the knock on the head — could that have caused it?'

'I don't think so. The wound wasn't particularly deep and the skin hardly broken. In my opinion it wouldn't force enough air into the blood vessels to cause a problem. No, I can't be certain but if I'm right about this mark then it would suggest someone might have injected air into her jugular vein or carotid artery. If there was enough, Rose could have died of a heart attack or stroke within minutes.'

'A stroke? I thought you said it was a heart attack.'

'I only reported that cardiac arrest was my best guess. In the absence of any other evidence that's all I could conclude and depending on where a bubble was introduced it could affect either her brain or her heart. I'd never have noticed the puncture if I hadn't gone through these photos with a fine-toothed comb because the hole left by a syringe is incredibly small. Though there'd have been some minor bleeding when she was alive there'd be nothing to see after all this time and the general discolouration of her skin makes any bruising impossible to detect.'

'So you're now happy to confirm this was the cause of death?'

'Not so fast, James, all I can say is that it's a distinct possibility. As is poisoning, or natural causes. There's no way I can definitely prove the embolism.'

I had the greatest of respect for Walter but, like all professionals, he was unwilling to publicly commit to a position unless he had one hundred percent proof, whilst I was happy with the odds being only slightly in favour.

'Come on, Walter, stop sitting on the fence and help me out here. What I need at this point are some firm ideas; possibilities to dig into. With a bit of work the proof will come later.'

The line went quiet long enough to make me try jiggling the cradle to check we still had a connection.

'Walter? You still there?'

'Sorry, James, I was just getting my thoughts in order. As you know, I don't think I can completely rule out natural causes, but I now believe there's sufficient doubt and, secondly, I certainly can't opt for the embolism as the definite reason for Rose's death. However, what I will say, on record, is that the mark on her neck is the most likely explanation for why she died. I'm fairly sure that if I take the section of her muscle from around the wound and carefully slice it, I should be able to see whether a needle was introduced and how deep it went in. It won't prove the embolism but it will show that something, be it air or poison, was injected. Is that good enough for you?'

I banged my fist on the desk. Now I had something to get Dyer off my back.

'You're in agreement then, Walter — this was murder?'

'We were more or less there a fortnight ago, James, I simply wasn't prepared to put it in writing. You know I'd trust your judgement in these matters, although you can work on a hunch and I need a little more. Strange method of killing someone though, don't you think?'

'It certainly can't be put down as a crime of passion, can it? Definitely premeditated. Have you ever seen anything like it?'

'Never, James, never. On the other hand, how would we guess unless we were actually looking for it? Could be any number of deaths put down to natural causes over the years because an injection hadn't been spotted.'

Half an hour later, Sawyer dashed into my office.

'We've got him, sir.'

Alan Johnston was sitting, his arms firmly pinioned behind the back of his chair. A red welt across his unshaven cheek suggested the arresting officers hadn't treated him too gently.

He'd been found hiding in the garden shed of a house bordering the school fields. The owner, a retired postman, looked out of his window and noticed the bolt was drawn. He'd been in the shed the previous afternoon and distinctly remembered fastening the bolt when he'd finished, so he called the police. Two constables were sent and they came across Johnston sitting on a wooden box, smoking a cigarette. They said he'd not tried to run away but struggled when they attempted to handcuff him. This was how they explained his bruising.

'Not very clever, Alan. Did you imagine we wouldn't find you? Not easy you know, evading the police. I mean, you'd not gone very far, put on a disguise, or anything. Anyone would think you wanted to be caught.'

Johnston just stared at the tabletop. I heard Sawyer shift in his chair and hoped he wouldn't lose his temper, it would be counterproductive. We might go heavier later but, for now, I wanted to continue the softer approach, gaining Johnston's confidence and gradually coaxing him to admit what he'd done.

'Come on, Alan, why not get it off your chest? We know Rose was threatening to break up your marriage, we know you have no alibi for when she was killed, and we know you owned the crucifix she had wrapped around her hands when she was discovered. This morning you even made a run for it, bashing Sergeant Bentham in the process. What do you think the court will make of all this? I can tell you it will go easier for you, and everyone else, if you confess right now while you have a chance.'

He laughed grimly.

'How will it go easy for me, do you think? They'll string me up whatever happens. That's why I ran away. I've nothing to confess, but you're not about to believe I'm innocent, so I've spent the past few hours in that shed trying to decide what would be the best thing to do. First off I reckoned I could easily get away; I know the fields and lanes round here like the back of my hand and would have no trouble getting away from your blokes. What good would it do though? I'd have no job, no money and always have to be ready to run again. I finally came down on the side of turning myself in and was just about to come into the station when those two coppers knocked on the door.'

Sawyer's words came as a growl from deep inside.

'You're a liar, Johnston. A liar and a cold-blooded murderer. Why would you give yourself up?'

Johnston lifted his head and looked him straight in the eye.

'Because when I was in that shed I remembered something that will prove I'm not guilty.'

THIRTY

Arthur Sprigg's workroom was down a side corridor behind a hall which doubled as the gymnasium. The main school building was deserted this late in the afternoon but Emily Perelle had told me I'd find the caretaker still working. He was tightening a rusty hinge in a vice with one hand and holding an oil-can in the other when I popped my head round his door.

I whistled. 'Wow, you keep a tidy ship here, Mr Sprigg.'

Every manner of tool was hanging from an individual hook, each with its shape outlined in black paint on the wall. Above his bench a series of jam-jars containing screws and nails in varying sizes hung below a wooden shelf, the containers carefully labelled with their contents.

'Aye, I've tried to make it my own, you know. I can't abide things being out of place, must be the engineering brain.'

'You were an engineer? In Coventry?'

'For about twenty years after I did my apprenticeship. I didn't like the factory much though — too regimented. I'd saved a few bob by the time I was forty and when this job came along Peggy and me upped sticks to Kenilworth. Been here over nineteen years now.'

'So you've lived at the school all that time, Mr Sprigg?'

'Oh, no, we could have done but Peggy thought I'd end up being called out at all hours of the day and night if I was too close, so we rent a little place up nearer the town.'

I nodded at the task he was doing. 'Looks like they keep you pretty busy in any case.'

'So many rooms in this place, Inspector, some of them hardly ever used. I keep as many of the doors lubricated as I can but even then I miss the odd one.' To demonstrate, he attempted to fold the hinge but could hardly manage it. 'Then this happens. Anyway, you didn't come all the way round here to listen to my problems — is there something you wanted to ask?'

'Do you remember what you said when I first interviewed you, Mr Sprigg? About you working later than you intended the night your hammer went missing?'

'That's right. I got in trouble from the wife when I got home.'

'So were you late just because you stayed on to fix that screen?'

'Well, yes, I think so.' Sprigg furrowed his brow in thought. 'Hang on! I called in to see young Alan about eight o'clock but I was only there a couple of minutes. He'd lifted a potted plant from the greenhouse for Peggy's birthday and told me to pick it up on my way home. I'd forgotten all about it, especially as the blooms cut no ice with the missus. She was so mad with me for being late she chucked it in the bin.'

'Johnston was at home? Are you sure it was that night, Mr Sprigg?'

'I am now. Definitely. I'd forgotten all about it until you asked me, but I'm certain it was then. As I say, he was giving me something for Peggy's present; I'd hardly have picked it up any other day, would I? She'd have seen it.'

'Was anyone else in the house with him?'

'I don't know, Inspector, I only knocked at the back door then stuck my head in the kitchen. I seemed to have woken up the lad. Looked like he'd nodded off listening to the wireless so I didn't go inside and I hadn't time to chat because I was already late. He gave me the plant and I headed home.'

'And it was about eight o'clock you say?'

'Give or take a minute or two. It's only a short step from Alan's to my house and Peggy had a go at me as soon as I got in about the time, so I couldn't help look at the mantle clock, could I? Ten past eight, it said. Is it important?'

Arthur Sprigg's question had made me smile. The one crucial piece of information which might convict or free his colleague, and he'd asked me if it was important. It's always the detail which we forget because, at the time, it doesn't matter to us. If it were possible to forewarn a person that they would witness a crime and when it would happen, then they'd have no problem committing it all to memory and recounting everything about it. Without that prior notice then black hair becomes brown, a grey jacket changes to navy and a tall woman loses a few inches in height, all designed to increase the burden on the hard-pressed detective.

I telephoned the station from home and told them to release Johnston. If Rose Spicer had met her killer at the time she had in her diary then Alan Johnston couldn't have been the one. It was a fifteen-minute walk from the school to his house. If I added another quarter of an hour, at least, for him to do the deed, arrange the body, and then clean up, it would be half past eight at the earliest before he'd be sitting in his kitchen. Sprigg had also said he thought Johnston was sleeping when he arrived. Even if Sprigg had his times slightly wrong, was it likely that the groundsman could swiftly nod off having just murdered someone?

The only problem now was that I'd lost a suspect and still hadn't a clue who might have murdered Rose Spicer.

I'd barely put the phone down when it rang.

'Jacob?'

'Papa?'

It wasn't Thursday. Ever since mother's fall he'd telephoned every week, at the same time on the same day, regular as clockwork. For him the telephone is still a new invention and he doesn't quite trust it. I imagine he half-believes this is the only time the line between the two of us exists.

'Is something wrong, Papa?'

'No, there's nothing wrong, son, it's just I won't be able to ring you on Thursday this week. And I have some news.'

'About Uncle Gideon?'

'No, not yet. I pray every night and I ask the postman every day to check his bag again but there is never anything. I'm beginning to fear the worst, Jacob.'

'Don't give up hope, they'll turn up. Things are just so difficult on the continent at the moment, he's probably sent letters and they've got lost.'

It seemed a hopelessly weak argument, the sort of desperate consolation we try to give when both parties know that the worst is likely to happen.

'That's probably it, Jacob, the letters have just not made it across the Channel. Anyway, that isn't why I rang.'

'Then what?'

I wasn't remotely prepared for what he said next.

'We're adopting a young girl.'

'What?'

'Well, not adopting, exactly. She's coming to stay for a while. Her name is Meena and she's travelling from Germany. Your Mama and I heard Lord Baldwin's appeal on the wireless for Britain to rescue the children and we've been thinking about it ever since. Special trains have been organised to get thousands of them out and all we have to do is look after her and guarantee a little of our savings.'

I'd heard the same appeal and the ensuing newspaper coverage reported vast amounts of money being raised. Transport was already bringing many hundreds of threatened Jewish children out of that terrible place. The humanity at the heart of the ex-Prime Minister's message, and the public response to it, helped restore my faith in basic decency, which had received a severe bashing during my time on the Coventry cases.

My father went on, almost breathless in his attempt to blurt out the news. 'You don't need your room any longer, Jacob, you're hardly ever at home and when you visit, we can make do.'

'But you and Mama aren't getting any younger, how will you manage?'

My father's frosty reply told me he didn't like to be reminded of the passing years.

'The same way we "manage" with your brother and sister, and Greta is only a year or two younger than Meena. This girl needs our help and if we can give it then we should. I've not been able to stop thinking about Gideon's children and how my brother would be praying someone could offer a home to keep them safe.'

He was right, of course. If we didn't do all we could to protect those in peril how could we expect others to assist our own family when they faced a similar danger. Some of the papers had carried reports of the scenes where parents were giving up their children to be brought to England, and their distress at the sacrifice was heartrending.

'I'm sorry, Papa, you're doing a good thing. If I can help in any way let me know.'

'Just come over when you are able, Jacob. We know you are busy but it would be nice if you could make time to meet our new member of the family. You speak a little German, so that would make the poor girl feel more at home until she finds her feet here.'

We chatted for another few minutes, leaving it that I would try to visit the following week. I could only pray that Rose Spicer's ghost would allow me to keep my promise.

THIRTY-ONE

Emily Perelle swung open the door and parted her lips in a welcoming smile.

'Mr Given, how lovely to see you — won't you come in? May I offer you some tea?'

Even at this time of the morning, on a Saturday when she hadn't to go near a classroom or a parent, her cotton dress swished crisp and starched, her hair had been brushed to a shine and her make-up was immaculately understated. I found myself regretting I wouldn't be in her company for long.

'I'm afraid it's your husband I need to have a word with, Mrs Perelle.'

'Oh.' The brightness went from her eyes. 'I'll just fetch him for you.' She left me on the doorstep whilst she went for the headmaster, all the light in the place leaving with her.

He was less pleased to see me than she'd been. I told him I had a few questions and he ushered me through to his study, which the watery sun hadn't managed to penetrate, leaving it cool and gloomy, a perfect setting for his menagerie of dead things.

Perelle sat at his table and cut off the hissing gas from his Bunsen burner. The concoction in the flask above it ceased it's bubbling.

'That's an hour's work ruined, Inspector, I do hope this is important.'

'I'm not in the habit of wasting my time either, sir, especially at the weekend.' I returned the glare he'd fired in my direction. 'Do you spend all your spare time in this room, Mr Perelle?'

'Mostly. What has that got to do with anything?'

'I was just wondering. Would you have been in here on the night Rose Spicer died?'

'I expect so, I am almost every evening after we've eaten, and I believe my wife has confirmed I was home that night.'

I smiled apologetically. 'Ah, that's right, she did.'

The headmaster dragged a skinned rat, his latest specimen, from the dissecting board on which it was pinned and thrust it into a small canvas sack. 'I'll need to dispose of this soon before it begins to go off, so we mustn't be too long, Inspector. I can't feed it to its fellows because I'd already begun to treat it.'

'Put down all the animals yourself, do you?'

He couldn't fail to notice my grimace.

'Only the frogs and rodents. The reptiles and bigger mammals come from specialist suppliers who preserve them for research.'

'And how do you do it? Injection?'

'Not often. Usually I'd gas them.' Perelle scraped back his chair and started to stand. 'Is that it, Inspector?'

'Just one more question, sir, if I might.' He sank down again. 'What was your relationship with Mrs Spicer?'

'Relationship? What are you talking about, man? The only relationship we had was that she was killed on my school premises. Has someone told you differently?'

'Not at all, Mr Perelle. You do understand I have to ask these questions though, don't you?'

'What I do understand, Inspector, is that you've been digging away now for weeks and seem to be no further forward. I'd think you're becoming quite desperate to find the murderer, so why not try to pin it on me? It would suit you, I imagine.'

'What do you mean by that remark? Why would it suit me?'

Perelle snorted. 'Do you think I haven't noticed the way you look at my wife? If you could put me away it would leave the gate open, wouldn't it?'

My first reaction was to drag him up by his lapels and shake him. To tell him if he wasn't so unpleasant to her I'd have no kind of a chance. Instead, I took as many deep breaths as it needed for my anger to subside, partly because I feared there might be a spark of accuracy in his allegation. The very wish I'd accused Sawyer of harbouring was now sitting on my own front step, waiting to be let in.

'You have it wrong, Mr Perelle,' I tried to sound confident, indignant and friendly even, all at the same time. 'My only interest here is to find the killer of that poor girl. There's information come to light which means we need to ask certain people more questions and I'm afraid you're one of those people. Now, if you'd prefer, I could ask one of my colleagues to take over, though it might mean you'd have to come into the station.'

I left the question hanging. Perelle thought for a moment then shook his head.

'That won't be necessary, Mr Given. I apologise. I've had a lot on my plate recently but I do understand you have your job to do.' Another pause. 'I have to tell you that things haven't been going well between Emily and me over the past year. Entirely my fault I'm sorry to say. I get so wrapped up in my work and forget about her sometimes. You've seen how attractive she is.' I didn't disagree and let him carry on. 'I find it hard to see how any man wouldn't want to take her away from me.'

It felt good to be out in the sunshine for a change. I wasn't sure if it was the pain in my feet now reduced to the occasional twinge, or the light reflecting off the primroses, daffodils and April green shoots, but my mood was definitely lifted. My doctor continued to insist that I take exercise when I could, and this, alongside my own resolve to become fitter, had taken me out for a walk. I'd set off up the hill towards town then I'd turned off across the fields before reaching the Charity School, not wishing to darken my thoughts again. I exchanged a few words with a neighbour plopping bread into the lake for the ducks before I meandered along the path to Bridge Street, finding myself opposite Bill Webb's house. It hadn't been my intention to end up there, though it may have been my fate.

Across the road Rose's father was in the garden, shoulders straining as he dug the winter-heavy clods of soil. After each turn of the spade he paused, then bent and pulled errant weeds from the ground, throwing their corpses into a wheelbarrow. There was rhythm, grace and peaceful reflection in his movements and, though I'm not a gardener, I could see the pleasure he took in performing his labours. I didn't want to intrude on his thoughts and was about to continue my walk when he saw me and raised an arm in greeting, waving me over to his gate.

'Soon be ready to put the spuds in, Mr Given. Hardest job in the garden but the most satisfying when they're lying on a plate, dripping with butter. Can't beat new potatoes just pulled from the ground. You know, some folks have a special day for planting spuds, Good Friday or St George's day, that kind of thing, they reckon it brings them luck, I suppose. Me, I just wait 'til I think the ground's warm enough then get them in. Seems to work alright for me.' He lifted a handful of soil and crumbled it in his hand. 'It's going to be a few weeks yet though, even with this sun.'

We talked for a while about cabbages and carrots, broccoli and beans, topics I knew nothing about other than how they tasted in my Sunday dinner, until he asked me to join him for a cup of tea.

Sitting at his kitchen table, Bill Webb finally broached the subject both of us had done our best to avoid.

'Have you had any success, Inspector?'

'Well, we're following up a number of possibilities but I'm afraid we've no real leads so far. There was so much time passed between Rose's death and her body being found that the trail was very cold even when we started.'

I didn't tell him we'd lost our two main suspects, Gibbons and Johnston, for very different reasons. He'd probably have read about the councillor in the *Courier* or the *Telegraph* but I doubted the news of the groundsman's release would have reached him yet.

'She was a lovely girl, you know, Mr Given. We had our ups and downs, like in most families, but I cared for her and I knew she cared for me. Her work took her away a lot and she couldn't get home much of the time, though that's the way it is these days, isn't it? She wanted more than me and her mother had, quite rightly, and there wasn't anything round here to give her that. She'd only have ended up working in a shop or tied to some labourer and their kids.' Webb squeezed his eyes shut. 'Another way of looking at it though is she might still be alive if she'd married someone like that.'

The poor man was bewildered by what had happened to his daughter.

'Why would anyone want to kill my poor girl? Can you figure it out, Inspector? I know I can't. God knows, she wasn't perfect, but have you any idea what it's like losing your only child?'

Nothing I could say would lessen his grief; it never did in these circumstances. All I could do was to offer my condolences again and plough on. We finished our tea and Rose's father took the empty cups over to the sink. He clattered about in the cupboard underneath before carrying a biscuit tin back to the table. Lifting the lid, he took out around a dozen dog-eared photographs, all except one being of his daughter. The one not showing her was of a younger Bill alongside a pretty young woman, both of them in their Sunday best sitting on a park bench.

'Is this your wife, Mr Webb?'

'Yes, that's my Josie. Our first anniversary it was, the year before Rose was born. We jumped on the bus into Coventry and took a picnic. Ate it in Spencer Park, watching kids on the swings and see-saw. It was a lovely day and we strolled into the town later to look around the shops.'

He continued revealing his photographs, telling the story of each occasion and my heart went out to this man who'd lost both his loved ones in such a short space of time. When he finished I drained my second cup and Webb walked me down the path to his gate. By the time I'd crossed the road and turned back to wave he was already back to his digging, perhaps trying to bury his memories with each turn of the sod.

THIRTY-TWO

In twenty-four hours it would be exactly four weeks since Rose Spicer came into my life and still we had no one in custody. Yet we were so close I could almost taste it. Of the suspects who'd first emerged we were left with only Neilson, Perelle, Joey Atkin and possibly Smith. Only one of these matched the initial in Rose's diary. The medical student ex-boyfriend. He was cocky and showed less respect for the police than was good for him, but we'd nothing to connect him to Rose after she'd left Coventry. Was the diary entry a complete distraction? I'd considered earlier this might be the case and I was coming more and more to that conclusion. After all, we'd lost one suspect with the correct initial and discounted another.

Then again, we'd only taken Alan Johnston out of the frame because he had an alibi for the precise time we thought she'd been killed. What if Rose had met another man friend with the initial "A" at the appointed time and stayed the night with him. Then Johnston's alibi would mean nothing. He could have discovered she was two-timing him and bumped her off next day. That would still be in the right time scale for the state of the body, her father's report of her being missing and for when Stella Johnston said she'd noticed the crucifix was lost.

Bill Webb had asked why anyone would want to kill his daughter and it was a good question. If I had the answer then I'd be several steps closer to her killer.

As important as why she'd been murdered was how it was done. Walter now seemed to think it might be an injection but was torn between an embolism and poison, so who would have the skill to use a syringe with the accuracy required to put a large air bubble into an artery? For that matter, who would be able to use one to deliver poison effectively? If it was a poison, then where might they get one locally that was strong enough to do the job quickly?

I'd put Sawyer onto the job of talking to chemists and farm suppliers around the town but, so far, none of them remembered selling anything remotely suitable to anyone who shouldn't need it. It all seemed so complicated. Why didn't they just bash Rose's brains out with the hammer? Were they afraid it might not work, leaving Rose injured but still able to tell us who'd attacked her, or were they squeamish about the inevitable blood and mess? Could it be someone who still cared for Rose and didn't want to disfigure her pretty face?

No. This had all the hallmarks of an execution. Cold blooded, premeditated and leaving a message. So why use the hammer in the first place? Clearly to knock the girl out cold, but why not just hold her down, she was only a slip of a thing? Was the murderer also small? Unfit? Old? Disabled in some way?

Alan Johnston would have had no problem in physically restraining Rose, he was young and strong from daily manual work. Neilson was the oldest of the bunch and slightly built, an academic rather than an athlete. Would he be able to overpower a fit young woman? Similarly, Perelle was hardly the finest specimen of manhood I'd ever met. He had easy access to the chapel and I'd noticed his room was only a few steps from the back door of the house. He could have easily slipped out, met and killed Rose Spicer in the crypt, then been back at his research in less than half an hour without his wife realising he was gone. He'd made it clear the home laboratory was his sanctuary and Emily Perelle probably wouldn't disturb him without good cause. The headmaster's hobby also provided him with the knowledge of how to administer a lethal injection. Would it give him easy access to sources of poison as well?

Something else that Bill Webb had said had been bothering me all day. After he'd shown me the first four or five photographs he'd laid one on the table of two girls in white dresses, long white socks and veils. He'd told me it was of Rose at her confirmation and I'd asked him who the other girl was.

'Oh, what was that girl's name?' Webb had scratched the back of his head for a second. 'Alice. Her name was Alice. Best friends they were for a while but I hardly saw her after this was taken. It wasn't long afterwards that we moved over to Spain.'

So he'd provided yet another "A" in Rose's life and something was gnawing away inside my head that I'd seen the photograph before. Where?

It was dark when I opened my eyes and for a moment I couldn't work out where I was or what had woken me. It had been a long week so it was hardly surprising I'd dozed off in front of the fire. I glanced at the clock. It was quarter past nine. Then the tap at my door came again, a gentle but insistent rapping on the leaded pane.

Shaking the sleep from my eyes, I rose from my chair and tottered into the hallway, shouting to the caller that I was coming. Then I stopped in my tracks when I saw the silhouette of a veiled girl through the glass. Was I still sleeping? One of those strange dreams where the pictures are so vivid they seem real.

'Let me in, Mr Given, it's only me. Stella Johnston.'

She stood on the doorstep with her coat pulled over her head to protect herself from the pouring rain.

'Come in, come in, Mrs Johnston — why on earth have you come out on a night like this?'

'It only started a few minutes ago when I got to the bottom of the hill. I wanted to come and thank you for letting Alan out and didn't know when I'd catch you at the police station.'

'Really? I thought you two had split up.'

'Well, we have. Sort of.' Her face brightened. 'But I'd have him back in a flash if I thought he'd learnt his lesson. I said some bad things about him to you and I wanted you to know I didn't really mean them. I was just so mad with Alan and would gladly have seen him in prison, even if he hadn't anything to do with murdering that Spicer woman.'

'You lied to me? Why?'

'No, I didn't lie, just polished up the truth a bit.' Stella's smile lifted even further when she looked down at the pool of water dripped from her coat on to my hall tiles. 'Look at me, making a mess of your nice house, Inspector, I should be going and leave you in peace.'

Hailstones rattled against my front door.

'No need to rush, Mrs Johnston, come and sit by the fire for a moment until it eases off.'

I took her through to the kitchen and threw a scoop of coals on to the remaining embers, fanning them until the flame caught. In these few minutes the image at my window and Bill Webb's photograph were beginning to merge, hovering on the edge of showing me where I'd seen them before.

'Are you close to catching who really did it, Inspector?' Stella Johnston's voice shattered my moment of clarity and the rabbit scurried back into its burrow.

'Oh yes, I think we're very close now,' I said, sounding more certain than I felt.

'That's good, I've been so scared in the house all on my own.'

Before I said anything further the telephone rang in my front room.

Leaving my visitor by the fire I dashed through, picked up the receiver and plonked myself in my armchair facing the window.

'Good evening, Inspector, it's Laurence Perelle. Not calling you too late, am I?'

On the windowpane raindrops raced down the glass as if only the winner would make it back home to the sea. I wasn't over keen on being disturbed on a Sunday evening but I told the headmaster it was no problem.

'Is there something I can help you with, Mr Perelle?'

'I'm not going to beat around the bush, Mr Given. You know I wasn't happy with you accusing me of that woman's murder.'

'I wasn't accusing you, I was doing my job, asking questions, but I can't imagine you've rung me to tell me this? If you have, then perhaps you might just leave it until tomorrow when you can make it official and call my boss. Superintendent Dyer is his name and you'll get him at Warwick.'

I was about two seconds away from slamming down the receiver when he came back at me.

'No, that's not what I meant. What I'm saying is that I was so annoyed that I decided I'd try to prove you wrong.'

'And how did you intend doing that?'

'By going through all the schoolbooks I have and finding the handwriting you left with my wife.'

I didn't reply. Was this a breakthrough?

'Mr Given, are you still there? Did you hear what I said?'

'Sorry, Mr Perelle, please go ahead. You found a match?'

'I think there might be three possibles. When you look at it closely the handwriting is quite distinctive, so I could discount most of the books pretty quickly. First of all I kicked out all the ones without that slightly odd letter 's' at the beginning of words. Did you notice it was only at the beginning? When it was used in the middle of a word it was perfectly formed. So that enabled me to get rid of most of the others. As I say, it left me with three with a good enough match and where other bits of style were the same.'

I wanted to scream at him to get on with it.

'So who are they?'

'Oddly enough, Mr Given, one of them was Stella John—'

'Stella Johnston was a pupil at your school?'

'Well, yes.'

'And you didn't think to tell me?'

'I thought you knew, Inspector, she was with us for four years. She only started using Stella in her last year, seemed to think it was more glamorous, asked everybody, including her teachers, to use it. I imagine she'd seen an actress in the pictures and wanted to be like her. Then, of course, she married and her surname changed as well. Her name was Alice Joyner back then.'

I put down the receiver and, eyes closed, rubbed my temples with the tips of my fingers. So Stella Johnston had once been the innocent little girl in Bill Webb's photograph alongside Rose Spicer. I could now see the same photograph standing on the Johnstons' sideboard, with the dead woman cut out of it.

Trembling, I reached out to pick up the telephone to call for some coppers to give me a hand. Stella Johnston was reflected in the window, the light from my desk-lamp sparking off the syringe about to find its way into my neck.

They say everything slows down when you're in life threatening danger but that didn't happen for me. Stella lunged the moment our eyes met in the glass and I ducked to my left, swinging my right arm up to knock hers away. She yelped and the needle skittered across the floorboards. I'm no fighter, my extra pounds of fat make sure of that, but I found strength in my legs I didn't know I had, careering my chair backwards into my attacker. My head hit her straight in the chest and the two of us toppled in the same arc, this now mad woman screeching and digging her nails into my face. I knew I'd have no chance if she managed to grab the syringe when we hit the deck.

The crack as her head bounced off the fire fender told me I wouldn't need to fight any more.

THIRTY-THREE

The trial lasted three weeks, a fortnight less than Stella Johnston had been held on remand, where she'd been examined physically and mentally to confirm her fitness to stand accused. Whilst, in my view, anyone who commits murder is unhinged, either temporarily or permanently, this doesn't conform with legal thinking and all the experts concurred that Stella wasn't insane at the time Rose Spicer died.

The jury heard how she'd attacked me with a syringe containing a solution of aconite in concentration strong enough to kill a horse. A search had revealed a jam jar in a corner of the Johnstons' shed where half a pound of chopped monkshood roots had been soaking for months, or possibly years. The prosecution produced witnesses who explained this would have been the source of the poison. Anyone injected would have been almost immediately paralysed then suffered massive cardiac arrest. The tutor from St John Ambulance confirmed Stella's absence from his meeting on the night of the murder. He also told the court that she would have been proficient in administering an intravenous injection and that needles were relatively easy to obtain, especially by anyone able to demonstrate some medical knowledge.

Sawyer was put on the stand to testify he'd overseen the digging up and sifting of the patch in the front garden which had been cleared. Traces of roots remaining showed that someone, assumed to be Stella, had recently dug up the monkshood in case we came looking. This, and a dog-eared copy of *The Modern Herbal* in amongst her first-aid books, with the entry on aconite underlined in pencil, was conclusive as to the source and method.

We'd discovered after her arrest that Dave Butler had also suffered a heart attack, but we had no other firm evidence to tie her into his death. Personally, I had no doubt she'd used the same concoction to dispose of her first husband, though we were advised by the lawyers not to pursue a prosecution on that one.

The trial was dubbed "the mummy in the crypt" by the newspapers, sensational enough without including a second murder. Instead we'd settled to prosecute Rose Spicer's killing and the attempted murder of a police officer, namely one Inspector James Given. The defence barrister, Mr Ernest Caister QC, tried to have the murder charge thrown out, arguing that everything we had linking Stella and the victim was circumstantial. This was largely true, but her attempt to kill me was beyond doubt and undermined his case.

I found it ironic he might have won that one if Stella hadn't decided, when her husband was released, that it would only be a matter of time before we went after her again. So she came for me first. Her note, intended to implicate Alan Johnston to pay him back for his adultery and to throw me off the scent, was used in evidence and cemented the image of the defendant as a hard, calculating and unemotional killer.

Stella Johnston smirked when the prosecution showed the torn photograph to the jury, alongside Bill Webb's complete copy, and the Crown barrister argued she'd posed Rose in a cruel parody of the missing half, trying to leave a message that her one-time schoolfriend wasn't as pure as the picture suggested.

Throughout the rest of the trial, she sat expressionless until the jury filed in and the guilty verdict was delivered. Then the slightest hint of fear flickered in her eyes. A fear that was warranted a week later when the Honourable Mr Justice Summerfield removed his glasses and donned a black cap to pronounce a sentence of death by hanging.

THIRTY-FOUR

At half past eight on a Thursday evening in May I received a call to get over to Coventry urgently. The sun was sinking behind the castle as I walked to the car, silhouetting the sandstone walls to perfection in its magnificence, although a dark cloud had just appeared on my horizon. Until the telephone rang I'd been in a good humour, and initially hoped it might be Emily calling to say she'd enjoyed herself.

We'd driven out to have tea in a little place in Stratford where we would avoid prying eyes, even though there was nothing we particularly needed to hide. Perelle was aware we'd been meeting socially from time to time and he didn't seem to mind. The couple knew their marriage had been dead for years. Still, people talk and we'd agreed to be as discreet as we could.

Outside of the constraining walls of the school, Emily let her real self blossom. She was charming, witty, well-read and bitingly intelligent, and I loved being in her company. And she wasn't fazed when I'd told her over dessert that I was a Jew. I couldn't see the two of us attending synagogue every weekend but at least it was a start.

The call hadn't been from Emily and had put an end to my agreeable mood with a bang.

Derby Lane hadn't improved in the few months since I was last there and on this visit there were several policemen standing outside Dembowitz's shop. I pushed my way through the small crowd of inquisitive citizens who'd gathered when word of the incident trickled out. Harry Wilson came through the doorway leading Karl Mueller, the factory cleaner I'd interviewed about the earlier attack, by the elbow. The German's hands were cuffed behind his back. Harry agreed to wait for me until I'd taken a look.

Inside, the majority of the watchmaker's stock was strewn across the floor as if a small tornado had swung through and played havoc for a few minutes. Hardly a clock face was intact and thousands of glass slivers shone amongst the golden cogs, wheels, cases and chains littering the room. In one corner lay Paúlu Demma, a pool of blood from one ear staining the glitter. The marble mantle clock which had caused the damage lay beside him. He hadn't been breathing for at least an hour. I was dismayed that these attacks were still occurring, though when I walked outside to see Wilson I was relieved the younger Demma was no longer a threat to society.

'Is the old man, Dembowitz, all right?'

'He's shaken up, James, but not harmed. I've sent him off with one of my blokes to the station, he'll be better off out of here for a while.'

Mueller was standing across the street, flanked by two uniformed bobbies. Harry nodded in his direction.

'At least we've got one of them. Thieves falling out, eh?'

I'd believed Mueller when he'd told me he abhorred what was happening in his homeland and couldn't see how he'd be running with Demma's gang. I told Harry this but he was sceptical, though agreed I could question his prisoner.

'What happened, Mr Mueller?'

He shook his head. 'It is hard to say, Mr Given, it all happened so fast. I didn't intend to hurt him, no matter how bad a man he was.'

'Just take it slowly, one step at a time, we need to know how Demma died in there.'

'I had a feeling in my bones something would happen tonight, so I sent a message to the factory to say I was ill and couldn't work, then I came round here.'

'Were you with the shopkeeper when the men arrived?'

'No, he didn't know I was here. After you came to my home I knew I had to put things right. I called to see Mr Dembowitz and apologised. He is a nice man and didn't deserve the things I said to him before. I came to watch his shop when I was able to get here, to make sure he wasn't attacked again. Tonight three of them came back —' he bunched his fists — 'two others and the one in there.'

Wilson stepped in.

'You're saying you weren't with them, Mueller?'

'Of course I wasn't. Why would I shout for help if I had been with those men? I tried telling your officer before he put these things on me.'

I gave Harry my best "I told you so" look.

'So you're in the street, Mr Mueller, and those three arrive. What did they do?'

'I didn't know for sure that anything was wrong at first, they just looked like customers going inside. Then I heard one of them shouting that he'd told Mr Dembowitz to get out and they'd come back to give him a reminder. The smashing started when I was running in to help him. They'd put the catch on the front door so it took me time to burst through. When I did, two of the men ran off but the other one continued to shake Mr Dembowitz and bang his head against the wall, it was like he'd gone crazy.'

'So you hit him with the clock.'

'I only wanted to make him stop but he wouldn't, he just kept on and on until I hit him again. Then he fell to the ground and didn't move any more.'

Karl Mueller's trial at Birmingham Crown Court attracted almost as much public attention as Stella Johnston's, though of a more uplifting kind. Whilst it lasted, the gallery was packed with row after row of Jewish businessmen, artists, writers and workers of every description from the city, Coventry and beyond, and each time Mueller entered the court they applauded until the usher shouted for silence.

Local and national newspapers were full of letters praising the German factory worker and requesting the Prime Minister to follow his actions in standing up to Fascist aggression or demanding the Home Secretary intervene to quash the charges.

On the second day of evidence I was taking lunch when the Goodman brothers, Levi and Bernard, approached me.

'Do you mind if we have a word, Inspector?'

I invited them to join me and asked if it was something to do with the case.

'Only in a roundabout way,' said Levi Goodman. 'We wanted to thank you for all of your hard work on our behalf, we don't think you are perhaps getting enough credit in the courtroom.'

'I'm only doing my job, gentlemen...'

The younger brother interrupted. 'But it's more than that, isn't it, Mr Given? You understand, because you're one of us. We suspected this when you came to our warehouse, then it only took one or two questions of our friends here in the Birmingham synagogue. Your father is well known and well respected.'

I tried to tell them that my father, my family and my Jewish heritage had no influence on how I'd approached my work in Coventry but the pair only shook their heads.

'We're not asking you to suddenly readopt the shawl and yarmulke, Inspector, just to acknowledge a little bit of what you are. Don't hide your faith, that's all. If you do then men like the Demmas and Adolph Hitler will win in the end.'

Despite my continuing protests, the two brothers stood and shook my hand, Levi Goodman making their parting entreaty. 'Thank you again, Mr Given, and remember what we said.'

Later that afternoon, Dembowitz, looking frail and nervous, gave his testimony in a court quiet as the grave until wild applause erupted when he reached the point where Mueller hit Paúlu Demma with the clock. The judge had to crack his gavel several times to restore order.

When I was called to give evidence about the first attack on the watchmaker's shop I saw my father smiling down from the third row of the gallery. He stood, winked at me and left as I was dismissed.

Next morning the prosecution case fell apart when the officer who'd arrested Mueller, a sergeant from Harry Wilson's team, took the stand and it was revealed that both his notebook and the clock had mysteriously disappeared from the evidence store. The judge pressed him strongly, threatening a charge of contempt of court if he was lying, but the policeman was not to be swayed. He smiled whilst being adamant that the key items had been mislaid and couldn't be found despite the most extensive of searches.

Karl Mueller was released to the most riotous scenes I ever witnessed in a court of law.

Stella Johnston's assignation with the noose had been set for the first week of July, which turned out to be sweltering in glorious sunshine. I've seen one too many hangings and I'm never sure why one killing has to result in another, with victim and offender sharing the final common bond of violent death. But, despite what I might think, we are told that justice has to be done and seen to be done.

Two months earlier the newspapers had gobbled up every sordid detail of her trial; the affairs, the ancient, almost mystical, poison, the attempt on my life and the beautiful young woman at the heart of it all. The headlines were all raked over again in the week before the hanging. As such things do, it dropped further and further down the order each passing day, becoming overshadowed by events in Germany, Russia, Czechoslovakia and Poland. Letters continued drip in to the local and national papers revealing the plight of many thousands now finding themselves in the spotlight of Herr Hitler's hatred.

Being on the inevitable brink of a conflict between Britain and Germany had brought a new perspective into many people's lives. Even the incidents in Coventry had disappeared since the Demma's deaths, as it became clear there'd be bigger battles on the horizon before too many more days had passed. I'd reflected on the Goodman brothers' words many times since Mueller's trial and knew them to be true. I couldn't keep running from my heritage, hoping that if I didn't own up to it then I'd be safe from prejudice and bigotry. The world just isn't like that.

I didn't attend the hanging, despite Dyer's instructions that I should, though I did wait with the crowd guarding Winson Green prison until the official notice of what had taken place in its gallows room that day was pinned outside the gate. In any other setting the sun would have brought a picnic atmosphere to the scene, or made it like a day at the seaside, but this group was sombre and expectant. Beside me stood Bill Webb. We both wanted to be sure Stella Johnston was gone.

EPILOGUE

Inspector Given
c/o The Police Station
Kenilworth
England

26th August 1939

Dear Jacob

I am writing to you because I do not wish to worry your father unduly, I know he has been very concerned about us over recent months. Please let him know that your Aunt Miriam and I are lucky and have found our way to France along with our daughter, Anna. I will tell you that your cousin Lev left us along the way and said he was going back to Germany to prepare for the fight, but please don't mention this to your parents. We have heard the news that Hitler has ordered the invasion of Poland and, in some ways, may God forgive me, I think it is a good thing this has finally happened. Now Britain and others may stand up to stop that evil man, but we are so frightened for Lev, especially now this has happened.

The word from home is that many, many of our friends have been either thrown out of Germany or gathered up and sent to camps in Dachau and Buchenwald, where they are being used for forced labour. We were so lucky to have managed to get away with enough money to survive for a while and at least we should be safe here in Paris.

Please look after your father and mother and pass on my love.

Shalom

Your Uncle Gideon

A NOTE TO THE READER

Dear Reader,

If you've got this far I suspect you've actually finished the book, unless you've inadvertently landed on this page whilst searching for how the story ended. If the former, I hope you enjoyed it, if the latter then you'll perhaps come back later when you have finished.

You'll have gathered that *A Pretty Folly* is the second in a series of Inspector James Given novels and, at the time of writing, there are two more planned. The inspiration for this one came from visiting the National Museum of Ireland displays of bog bodies and the vaults of Dublin's St Michan's Church, where human remains have become mummified due to minerals in the soil. The setting for the novels in 1938/39 means that modern forensic analysis isn't available to our detective and allowed me, as the author, to ask what would happen if a naturally preserved body was found at that time in suspicious circumstances. A number of sensationalist news articles appearing about the potential lethal nature of common garden plants sowed the seed (so to speak) of the murder weapon.

The title of this novel comes from William Shakespeare's *The Merchant of Venice*. A 'folly' can be either a foolish act or an extravagant building out of keeping with its surroundings. So, in the novel, there are a couple of betrayals in matters of the heart, and its centrepiece is the chapel built many years before the school. Tradition says the chapel was built to celebrate the Crusades, when European Christian forces sought to gain control of Middle Eastern sacred sites from Muslims — some would see this as a folly in its own right.

I love to hear from readers, so please contact me through my **Facebook page** or send me a message through **Twitter**. You can also see my latest news on **my website** and sign up for notifications.

Reviews are so important to authors, and if you enjoyed the novel I would be grateful if you could spare a few minutes to post a review on **Amazon** and/or **Goodreads**.

Thanks for reading!

Charlie Garratt

Sapere Books is an exciting new publisher of brilliant fiction and popular history.

To find out more about our latest releases and our monthly bargain books visit our website:
saperebooks.com

Printed in Great Britain
by Amazon